Winter's Age

Last of The Norse

Nicholas Sharp

Prologue

The journey to save a friend is never an easy one. Sometimes a price must be paid. A cold storm now descends as frozen ancients awaken. The gale of Winter is here. This is book two in ***Memories of Crimson Fire***, this is ***Winter's Age.***

Chapter 1: Spells and Schemes

Chase and the others raced toward Norway to track down Loki, while elsewhere at the Black Order base, Leon was in his office doing paperwork at his desk. A knock came at his office door, and Leon waved his hand to open it.

Chelsea entered and took a seat across from Leon.

"Anything new on James, Chase, or Ulf?" Leon asked.

"No, sir, there hasn't been any sign of them since the team encountered them in Greece."

"We knew the risks when we took James in, but for Chase to defy orders and let his emotions get the best of him is inexcusable for a hunter," Leon sighed, opening the reports on James and Chase before handing them to Chelsea. "But what's done is done. They're already marked dead or alive, so it will only be a matter of time. How is the investigation going at the remains of Mount Olympus?"

Chelsea reached into her bag and handed Leon a report. "The investigation is slow, but ongoing, but with coordination from Greece and the European

Union, it is progressing. They're still investigating the magnitude of the earthquake there."

"I see," said Leon, sorting through the troubling findings in the report.

"Our investigators found traces of mystic energy at the site, so that can rule out a natural cause."

"Has anyone else besides those that need to know been informed?"

"No, sir, besides Greece, and both the E.U. and U.N., nobody else knows."

"Good, make sure it stays that way. I also see here there was a body recovered in the rubble."

"Yes, sir. Greece officials have the body and performed their own autopsy."

"Have the investigating team sent out to recover that body," Leon said, handing the report back to Chelsea.

"But, sir, they are still doing their investigation," Chelsea cautioned, knowing the consequences of such an action.

"I don't care. This is a supernatural case. They have no jurisdiction in this matter," Leon commanded.

"Very well, sir."

Leon saw Chelsea's worry but was pleased by her commitment. "Have they discovered the identity of the body?"

"No, sir."

"Make a redacted copy of our report and give it to

the team. That will give the Greek officials something to ferret over. And be sure no one questions anything. All of this must remain a secret."

"Very well, sir. And if there is a disagreement and the officials refuse to hand over the body?"

"There will be no disagreement since they have no authority. But if there is, use your imagination," Leon answered, waving his hand dismissively.

"If still, contact the E.U. and the U.N., they can sort out the mess."

Thoughts raced through Leon's mind as he knew who was responsible for the destruction. "Well, this is just a guess on my part, but we can pretty much determine that those two are behind this."

"The evidence is still scarce, but given their past actions, that conclusion is likely," Chelsea agreed.

"Well, it doesn't hurt to be sure once we conclude our investigation."

"Oh, by the way, sir, there was one more thing."

"What is it?" Leon asked as he looked over other paperwork on his desk.

"At the sight where the body was recovered, vials of a strange substance were also recovered by the Greek officials.

"Have they determined what the substance is yet?" Leon asked, intrigued.

"No, sir."

"I see. Have the team recover those vials as well and send them to the U.S. They have better research facilities, so they will be able to identify what's in those vials. If you don't need anything else, you may go."

Leon thought about what Chelsea had said. Greece should have notified him immediately after the earthquake on Mt. Olympus. That they hadn't surely meant they wanted to maintain control of the investigation and keep it in their jurisdiction. He knew he needed to report the incident to be sure, so the right corrective measures were put into place.

Three days later, Chelsea returned to Leon's office.

"Here are the reports, sir."

"I see the body couldn't be identified but evidently was burned," Leon said, confirming his suspicions and tossing the reports on his desk.

To think that they would actually bring down a god and the ruler of Olympians of all. Oh, but you two don't know the consequences of your actions. Now, the very balance of power will shift, Leon thought as he chuckled in amazement and disappointment.

"Sir, if I may ask, what action must be taken?"

"For now, nothing. We have to wait and see what happens next. But, moving on, have the vials been sent to the U.S. for identification?"

"Yes, sir, they arrived in their labs this morning."

"Alright. I want you to head to the U.S. Keep

your eyes on the progress and see what you can do to expedite it," Leon ordered.

"Sir?" Chelsea asked, confused by Leon's order.

"I need someone I can trust on-site in case those in D.C. try to pull something. Plus, having you there may help establish a coordinated relationship between the Black Order and them," Leon explained, leaning back into his chair.

"I understand, sir, but why do we need to speed it up? Surely they wouldn't dare try anything against us."

"True, but you can never be too careful," Leon assured her. "But, not to worry, this is not a long-term assignment—only long enough to establish a direct form of communication. The United States may have the best research facilities in the world, but they will not expedite their processes for just anyone. Using leverage with someone that used to work with that department will help and is our best option for the moment."

"I see. Your goal is to establish supernatural hunter contracts with the U.S.," Chelsea said as she understood the chairman's plan.

Leon was pleased with Chelsea's quick grasp of the plan.

"Exactly. An opportunity like this is rare and must be exploited. That way, we will be able to expand upon it. We have always tried to establish contracts with the U.S. in the past, but have been refused. Their

Department of Defense has always handled any supernatural threats in the U.S. The DoD has always stood in the way of the Mages Association and other hunter organizations to secure contracts," Leon explained.

"Yes, sir, and with the budget approved by their congress, some of the funding is funneled to a secret federal department that oversees their supernatural activity."

"Yes, Chelsea, that's right. The name of the agency is Defense Against Magic or D.A.M. as it has come to be known. Of course, the general public doesn't know of its existence, but those of us who are aware of it also know their agents leave nothing behind—everything is swept clean."

"You are well informed for someone who never worked for them, sir."

"It pays well to be, and with this new power imbalance among our gods now, we must do what we can to survive. Money is after all, just another tool for that," Leon said smugly. "After the World Wars, the European countries turned their economies and securities over to the European Union. With more threats arising and the revived Roman Empire, Europe has grown soft over the last hundred years. But with the Radix Magic Accords still in place, peace can still be maintained… at least for the supernatural."

"Then your true purpose is to have the

cooperation to hunt those two down isn't it?" Chelsea asked.

"Nothing gets past you, does it?" Leon asked with a smile. "But you're correct. If this partnership is successful and relations can be established, it may lead to something like that for those two traitors along with the little wolf. Now, let me ask you this— knowing everything I have planned, are you willing to accept this assignment?"

"I will follow any order given without question," Chelsea answered, affirming her loyalty. "If it is for the betterment of the Keepers of the Black Order, and if it leads to the capture of those who betrayed their oaths, then I will more than gladly accept this task."

"Good, you leave tonight. A private plane will be waiting for you in Berlin to take you to the U.S. Remember, this is a top-secret assignment. Do not tell anyone what you are doing or where you are going," Leon instructed.

Chelsea took her leave and Leon sat and thought about the changes that would come. He knew everything would be different moving forward, but it didn't matter. He had to tread carefully from there on out.

Chase and the others had arrived in Norway. He landed the airship in a clearing in a frozen forest.

"Why have you stopped here?" Amphion asked as he opened his eyes from his meditation.

"Because I have to cast a camouflage spell on you before we do anything. Your current appearance might scare people," Chase answered.

"Very well," Amphion replied unamused.

"Take this," Chase said, handing Amphion a mystic blue rod from his backpack.

"What is it?"

"It's a Meto Rod—one of my little inventions. As long as you have it in your possession, people will see you as human."

"Very well, I will keep it with me at all times," Amphion said, studying the rod.

"Please do, but now you and Theseus need to dress in modern clothing. I'm pretty sure ancient Greek and Egyptian armor will raise a few eyebrows."

"This generation of humans are sure impressionable. A proper lesson and a tough spine would do them good," Amphion said, looking at his armor, discontent with the idea of removing it.

"It's best you get changed too, Theseus," Chase instructed.

Amphion and Theseus made their way to the back of the ship to change. Neither were happy with the idea of wearing the modern clothing Chase had laid out for them.

"I never got how people today wear clothes such as these. No armor to protect you…one strike, and it's all over," Theseus said to Amphion as they changed.

Chase overheard their conversation and laughed as he set the course to Olso.

"Alright, I'm setting our course. Once we get to Olso, we are going to rest for the night. We should be there in a couple of hours," Chase informed as the airship flew past a winter storm that was closing in.

On the outskirts of Olso, Chase changed course and flew directly into the city instead of the forest he had originally set course for. He had an experiment he wanted to try.

"What's wrong? Why did you change our course?" Ulf asked, walking into the cockpit.

"It's nothing. I wanted to fly the ship over Olso in stealth mode," Chase answered, quelling Ulf's concerns.

"What is the point of being reckless?" Ulf asked, surprised by Chase's brashness.

"Hear me out. If I do this, I can teleport us down in an alley or something, and the ship remains invisible. I can alter its size and put it in my backpack."

"I thought you had to be in physical contact with the object to alter its mass?" Ulf asked, not convinced with Chase's plan.

"Not always. Do you remember, during our visit to Atlantis we came across ancient mystic spells?" Chase said, reaching into his pack and extracting a scroll. "Have you ever wondered how man in ancient times were able to move large stones like those that stood at Stonehenge and other ancient civilizations?"

"I do not study human history, only that of my ancestors. My family has forbidden the study of human history for generations."

"Oh Ya, you told me that once," Chase said as he opened a scroll to show Ulf.

"But this is something important you should listen to."

Ulf sighed, knowing nothing would change Chase's mind, and reluctantly agreed.

"This is the only time I will make an exception," Ulf relented.

"Based on the spell written in this scroll and the history I analyzed on ancient civilizations in the Oracle Library, it was used to alter the mass of objects to make them easier to move. But from what I read in old text, ancient civilizations like the Egyptians and Mayans had their own version of the spell. The spell allowed the caster to alter the size of an object without being in physical contact with it. It can also be used to levitate an object. Ancient practices like this have been lost over the centuries, and I think this is a good way to revive them."

"What is the name of the spell?" Ulf asked, fascinated with what he was hearing.

"It is written in ancient Greek and is called Alterization Mass or αcαλλοίωση μάζα," Chase answered.

Chase put the ship in stealth mode as they got closer to Olso, then headed to the back to give everyone a strangely shaped jewel.

"We'll use the mystica jewel for now. Everyone save yours until you need them," Chase explained.

"Is the jewel for teleportation?" Ulf asked. "I thought you needed to draw the Celtic diagrams in order to do that."

"Normally, yes, but thanks to the scrolls from Atlantis, I found a spell that uses the mystica jewels for teleportation," Chase explained.

"To come up with such a feat is truly remarkable. Most impressive, young warrior, your knowledge may even surpass that of the gods," Theseus said, impressed by Chase.

"I don't deserve the credit. It was Master Shinko who came up with it," Chase said, playing down Theseus' compliment. "Anyway, I put my mystic energy into those jewels. Once I set my mind to the ground below, we will teleport together. So, everybody stay close to me. Arthur, you might want to give me Excalibur, so I can put it away."

"No need," Arthur answered. Pressing the sword to his chest, Arthur made the sword disappear. "Excalibur and I are one in the same. I learned to enchant my sword and always stored it within my body when I was on diplomatic quests."

"You know mystic spells?"

13

"I learned a few from Merlin in my previous life. What you call storage spells were always one of my strong points in magic. One time, I had to hide all of my men's weapons to trick a Saxon army during an invasion of England. Anyway, I will tell you about that another time. Let us focus on the matter at hand for now."

"Ya, you're right. Let's get going," Chase said as he focused on their teleportation destination. "Teleport," he spoke and a blue vortex surrounded them before they appeared on the ground in an alleyway in Olso.

The glow of the stone had diminished as Chase pulled the ancient scroll from his backpack. He pointed his hand up at the airship and spoke the size alteration spell. The airship began to shrink until it was no more than the size of a toy car. "Ελα (Come)," said Chase as he waved his hand, calling the miniature airship to him. "And now you have seen the ancient alteration spell from Atlantis work."

"Amazing, you altered the size and turned it into a small toy," said Theseus, impressed with Chase's knowledge of magic.

"Using magic along with science to alter the mass of an object—I got to say Shinko really knows her stuff."

It makes you wonder what did all her people, the Light Elves really create? With the knowledge in the Oracle Library, she and her people helped shape the ancient world, Chase thought, thanking Shinko's genius.

"Chase, what is wrong? You look like something has enlightened you," Arthur said.

"It is nothing. Anyway, we should head out onto the streets. Ulf, you should turn invisible to avoid any eyes peering at you."

"What is the temperature right now? It feels like it's freezing out here," Arthur said, trying to adjust to the cold.

"It is seventeen degrees. It is going to be cold since it's winter," Chase said, checking the weather on his phone.

Chase looked up at Amphion and was surprised he wasn't shivering. "With normal clothes, you're not freezing at all?"

"I have been in weather much colder than this throughout my life. A winter storm as trivial as this doesn't affect me at all," said Amphion. At the end of the alley, he looked back at Chase. "But more importantly, right now, shouldn't you be tracking Loki using his blood?"

"Oh right," said Chase taking out his scanner.

He configured the sample of Loki's blood and scanned Olso for the trickster but grew frustrated when there were no traces of Loki. "Damn it! He is not here."

"No one here thought we would find him immediately," said Arthur, assuring Chase.

"Like Merlin used to tell me, to achieve anything, you slow down and be patient," Arthur mentored.

"Only mistakes are made for those who lead with haste," Amphion offered.

"I know, I just don't want to drag this out any longer than we have to," Chase exclaimed, knowing they spoke the truth.

"We all understand your reason, Chase Actaeonis, but there are still too many unknowns," warned Amphion advising caution. "Until they are revealed, our path will be shrouded by darkness."

"Can't you scan all of Norway at once for him?" Theseus asked, wondering if they could extend their search.

"I can, but in order for me to get a strong enough signal, we would have to be in the middle of Norway. "It will have to wait until tomorrow. This storm is bearing down and fast on us," Chase said, pulling his jacket tighter around him. "Right now, we should head to the hotel. We can look around Oslo tomorrow to make sure we haven't overlooked anything."

"It seems the son of Odin has returned," said a dark figure looking down upon them, juggling a skull. "Now I think it is time to finish what should have ended long ago. Ragnarök shall finally reach its grand climax." The dark figure laughed maniacally as he disappeared into the blizzard.

"These are cards used to open your rooms. Think of them as a key that unlocks a door. Theseus,

Amphion you have one room together with two separate beds," Chase explained, handing each a card key.

"Arthur, you and I have the other. Ulf, you will be staying in the same room with us."

"Arthur, you want an ale?" said Chase as he grabbed a drink.

"Certainly, a king should never refuse a friend's offer of a drink," Arthur accepted.

Chase handed him an ale as he sat down next to Arthur. "Something about your sword on your mind?" he asked as Arthur stared at the sword. "You can tell me anything that's on your mind. Just like James, I'm your friend, and I'm here for you."

"I'm glad you said that, my friend. It helps ease one's mind when thinking about the past," said Arthur, glad to hear Chase's words.

Placing Excalibur aside, Arthur revealed some of the burdens he bared.

"I was thinking had Excalibur been reforged in my time as king, maybe I would have been able to save England from its destruction."

"Even if it was reforged, I don't think it would have made a difference," said Chase, not wanting Arthur to have doubts.

"What made you draw that conclusion, if I may ask?"

Chase took a sip of ale and placed it on a table. "Because when Cronus showed me the events of

Titanomachy, I was horrified by what I saw." Chase gathered his thoughts, remembering what Cronus had showed them. "After seeing that, I began having doubts. What if things were different, what if the monsters that we see today weren't here? Would the world be a better place? But after I saw James die before my eyes, I started seeing things differently."

Arthur saw the sadness in Chase's eyes and felt the same. "And what do you see now?"

"For the first time in a long time, I saw light," said Chase seeing the image of James appear in his mind. "He showed me that even if we make the same mistakes again and again, we are capable of changing our destiny. To make sure we turn those efforts into something great, something worth remembering. Where all of our efforts, until now, don't turn into nothing."

"I see," said Arthur as he saw the look in Chase's eyes.

Chase tapped Arthur on the shoulder. "You saved England more times than anyone can count. With the sacrifice of your life, you saved many. Don't regret anything. Your legacy has made England a better place where even children look up to you for guidance."

Arthur nodded his head in agreement. "You speak as Merlin used to, and you're right. I shouldn't regret anything I did in my past life. That was the past, and it is a different time now. What truly matters now is what we do," said Arthur, feeling joyful.

"That's right, and what matters right now more than anything is saving James. We have to find Loki and get the Heavenly Life-Lock scroll from him. As his friends, we owe him that," Chase whispered as he thought about James. Arthur remained quiet. "Alright, I am going to take a shower because I've been killing myself these past few weeks.

Arthur nodded his head yes. "You have with all that has happened to you in these last few weeks, and you deserve a rest."

"We all do," said Chase, handing Arthur his ale.

Arthur lifted his ale in celebration. "Even a king."

While Chase was in the shower, Arthur took Excalibur out of its sheath and looked at it.

"This is the first time I have wielded you in so long. I wonder what you will be like now that you have been reforged. Am I still worthy?" Arthur whispered sorrowfully.

He then put Excalibur back in its sheath. "Only time will tell, once a new battle begins."

As the night passed on, Chase struggled to sleep. He stared up the ceiling, thinking about James.

Good night James.

Chapter 2: The Vikings and The Norse Gods

In the morning, everyone met in the hallway and prepared to resume their search for Loki, the God of Mischief.

"It still looks like Loki hasn't stepped a foot in Olso," said Chase checking his scanner. "Oh well, it doesn't hurt to look over things a few times."

"What is our next step in tracking Loki? Do we still go along with our guidance and travel to the center of Norway to get this better signal you have spoken of on your scanner?" inquired Theseus.

"No, not yet. We should look around more. You might be able to find some clues here in Olso to give us a better idea."

"Do you have a place in mind to search?" Arthur asked, wondering where to start.

Chase paused for a moment as he thought. Pulling out his laptop, he looked up information on Viking myth. "Well, being as how Loki is a Norse god, I was thinking about going to a museum to see if there are any artifacts or information on Loki." After searching for a few minutes, Chase said, "There isn't really anything besides the Viking Ship Museum. Oh well, it is better than nothing. We will search there to get an idea. If we don't find anything, then we will move to the center of Norway," said Chase, closing his laptop.

The group set out on foot for the museum with Ulf in his invisible mode.

"Can't you just fly us there on the flying machine you call an airship?" Theseus asked, confused as to why they were walking.

Chase shook his head no at Theseus. "It would draw too much attention even if it was cloaked. And even with all the mystic spells that keep the airship from giving off sound, we have to try and get you old relics used to modern means."

Theseus, Amphion, and Arthur took offense to Chase's words as they remained silent and glared at him. Chase, nervous, smiled at them. "You all know what I mean."

Amphion tried to say something, but Chase stopped him and pointed at Ulf. "Before you ask, Ulf is riding with us, so try not to say anything out loud. We don't want to make people think we are crazy."

"But you just said his name out loud and pointed at him even though he is invisible," said Amphion pointing out his own rule.

A half-hour passed before they arrived at the Viking Ship Museum. Admiring the scenery, Chase stopped them before they went inside. "Alright, before give me your weapons, so I can store them in my backpack."

"Why, can't we bring them inside?" Arthur asked, confused by Chase's request.

"You can't bring weapons into places like this for security reasons."

"Really, back in my time, you didn't worry about such things. Even if an enemy tried to take your life, they would do it on the battlefield."

"It's a different time now—not medieval times," said Chase, sighing at Arthur's reluctance.

"There are different customs and laws you must abide by. Besides, with the weapons and technology the world has now, people can kill you without you even noticing. But to counter this, hunters always use storage spells to store weapons whenever they are in a public place. It was really one of the only things agreed upon with the hunter organizations, the European countries, and the European Union. If there is a supernatural creature inside a public place, we are not allowed to take action unless there are no witnesses," Chase explained.

The group relinquished their weapons to Chase, who spoke the word "store," causing the weapons to disappear into a light. "Alright, let's head inside," said Chase, zipping up his backpack.

Something bothered Arthur about what Chase had said about the hunters. "If I may ask Chase, what did you mean by *few witnesses*?" asked Arthur, wanting to know more about the system the hunter worked in.

"We eliminate them," Chase answered plainly.

Unnerved, Arthur did not speak further as everyone walked through the main lobby.

"And what happens if those few witnesses turn out to be innocent people?" Theseus asked.

"Even if they are innocent, they must die to keep the world safe from the secrets of supernatural. Unfortune as it is, that must be paid. It is one of the absolute rules set forth by the hunter organizations and the European Union."

Feeling Amphion's eyes glare at him, Chase looked at him. "All of you should know, if humanity knew the supernatural, they would try to destroy it. Looking through history, it is one of the only things that is true."

"Yes, I understand all too well. Even when I was free to choose my own path, humans saw me as bringer of death due to my appearance and abilities," said Amphion agreeing with Chase. "But despite all of that, I never once hated them for it. I was just disappointed."

"You are not a monster. I have seen and felt what true monsters are. But more often, humans are the true monsters. Anyway, enough on this subject, let's get to the security check."

"But what if those true monsters stand in your way of getting the scroll—what would you do then?" Amphion asked bluntly.

"If monsters, humans, or even gods stand in my

way, I will kill them all to save my best friend," said Chase, staring back at Amphion coldly.

A man wearing a trench coat walked past the group and smiled as he left the museum. *This just keeps getting better*, he thought.

After getting past security, Chase started to investigate the Viking artifacts. Standing next to him, Arthur looked at one of the displays.

"I know you said we had to put everything away due to security, but why didn't they see anything in your backpack?"

"Because others will only be able to see inside unless I let them. Otherwise, you will only see books in the backpack."

"You put an illusion spell on the bag, did you not?" Arthur asked, laughing at Chase's genius.

"It's an illusion of sorts, but it is more complex than that." Chase unzipped the backpack and showed the inside to Arthur. "Tell me, what do you see?"

"It looks like a vortex going back and forth with a lot of items swirling," said Arthur astonished seeing the swirling whirlwind.

"Then you see what is truly inside. There is a pocket dimension inside this backpack where I store items. Only those I trust, and I can pull out the item they need stored in this backpack. I will give you an example. If you need Excalibur, all you have to do is reach in the backpack, and you will be able to pull it out even without looking. Like I said, people will see what I want them inside," said Chase zipping up the backpack.

"Why am I able to see what is truly inside that bag?" Arthur asked, confused.

"I already told you, James, Ulf, and the others are my friends. I trust you all with my life," said Chase smiling.

I haven't seen people like Chase and James since my time with the Knights of the Round Table. People willing to sacrifice everything they have to protect what matters most. Then, and even now, I will lay down my life for my friends, Arthur thought.

Looking at the Viking ship displays, Chase came across an odd-shaped Viking ship. *That's kind of weird.* Examining closer, Chase noticed a wolf symbol on it and spoke telepathically to Ulf.

"Ulf, are you seeing this?"

"Ya," said Ulf.

Chase looked around the whole ship for any other signs.

"This is the Oseberg Viking ship, one of the most preserved in all the world, "said Chase, revealing the identity of the ship.

Wanting to get a closer look, Ulf jumped on the deck of the ship. "But why a wolf head?"

Chase looked through his texts of Norse myth. "In the Age of Vikings, certain wolves were worshiped as gods. The mightiest of them all was the white wolf Aesir and the black wolf Fenrir."

Ulf ground his canine teeth in anger as he jumped back down silent.

"What is wrong? You went silent," asked Chase sensing something was off with the wolf.

"It is nothing," said Ulf, dismissing Chase's concern.

"Alright, I won't ask if you're uncomfortable talking about it."

Ulf, now calm, nodded his head toward Chase. "Thank you, Chase."

Arthur was looking at a different display and noticed pieces of wood with a serpent carved into it.

"Chase, can you come look at this for a moment?"

"Ya, what's up?"

Chase's eyes lit up with lightning as he closely examined the carved symbol pieces. In pain, Chase grabbed his head as he started seeing images of Thor. *What am I seeing? No, no, why am I seeing this*, Chase thought as the visions became more intense with Thor and the Midgard Serpent during Ragnarök.

The visions rapidly flashed as he saw Thor and the Midgard Serpent dead, his parents dead, and finally James, dead in his arms. *James.* After the moment of seeing the torturous images, Chase's eyes returned to normal. Breaking out in a sweat, he struggled to catch his breath.

"Are you alright?" asked Arthur, worried about Chase.

"What happened?" Chase asked, confused.

"I don't know, one moment you were looking at the wood pieces and then suddenly you grabbed your head. But when you looked at those wooden pieces, your eyes started to glow with lightning in them."

"What?"

"What happened to you, Chase?"

Chase, not wanting to concern the others, dismissed what he saw. "I can't explain it myself. My head just started hurting all of a sudden."

"Maybe we should get you away from this display case. I think those pieces are having some type of effect on you," Arthur said, suspicious about what had happened to Chase.

"Ya, good call."

As they were walking away from the display, Chase wondered about the frightening images he saw. *A fight between Thor and the Midgard Serpent. What was it that I just saw? Was it a message or something sinister?"*

For the next several hours, they looked through the museum for any clues about Loki. Not able to find anything, they met up with the others. "Were you able to find anything?"

Everyone in silence shook their heads no. Chase prepared for their next move.

"I guess we'll move on to the center of Norway to do the wide range scan of the country."

"The Viking did inhabit Scandinavia, which is now Norway, Sweden, and Demark, correct?" Arthur asked.

"Ya, what about it?"

"I was just thinking instead of scanning for Loki's mystic energy in the middle of Norway, how about we scan for him between Norway and Sweden, instead?"

"That could work, but the Vikings were more settled in Norway and Denmark," said Chase, intrigued by Arthur's idea.

"For now, we should focus on the center of Norway first, but if we don't find anything, then we will move on to Sweden and then Denmark if we have to."

"Ok, so what is the center of Norway?" said Arthur, accepting Chase's decision.

Chase checked a digital map of Norway. "It looks to be a place called Holmvassdalen—a nature preserve. We should head out of Oslo first before we fly over Holmvassdalen and do the wide range scan."

"If we do pick up Loki's signature, then I will be able to track him wherever he is."

After leaving Olso, they stopped at the edge of a forest and went into it.

"It is getting dark; we should set up camp for the night," said Chase.

A few hours later, everyone was around the fire, eating. Chase, who was cleaning his weapons, suddenly grabbed his head as it started to ache. His eyes glowed with lightning as he saw images of danger approaching. Concerned, everyone noticed Chase was in pain.

"What is wrong?" said Theseus, worried.

Shaking his head, Chase's eyes turned back to normal as he slowly said, "I don't know."

"Something dark draws near," Amphion warned, opening his eyes as he sensed something ferocious.

Alarmed, everyone stood up and took a defensive stance.

"I am not detecting anything on the scanner," said Chase, scanning the area.

Staring off into the darkness, Amphion noticed movement behind the trees.

"Amphion, what are you sensing? Is it a god?" Chase asked.

"No, it is no god, it something different. Something dangerous, like a rabid animal," said Amphion, summoning his khopesh.

Arthur's eyes tightened, seeing the shadowy figure stalk them. "I see it as well."

Everyone's eyes looked everywhere as they heard brushing sounds throughout the forest. Staring at them viciously, the shadowy creature moved from behind a tree and slowly approached. On guard, they all stared intently at the creature as the shadowy aura around it began to dissipate.

"Wait, I sensed this energy before," said Chase horrified, sensing the familiarity of the dark mystic energy. It can't be you."

"I am only me, no one else, prey," the dark creature snarled.

Staring into the creature's dark grey eyes, Arthur felt the evil within them. The creature stood over seven feet tall and stared savagely at everyone.

"Then what are you?"

The dark creature slammed its hand on the ground creating a hole. "I don't speak to my prey, but since these are your last moments, I'll tell you this before you die. I am a Darkgen," said the dark creature grinning at Arthur.

This creature is a Darkgen, the same as Devoid, Chase thought in shock. *That means he is a Norse monster.*

Angry, Chase demanded answers from the dark creature. "Who are you?"

"What? You don't know? Even your eyes are deceiving you," the dark creature snarled, turning its attention toward Chase. "Tell me, what do your eyes truly see?"

"I remember you, creature," Chase spoke in a deepened tone as his eyes brightened with lightning, recognizing the creature. "I, Thor, recognize your ugly face. You are the monster that slaughtered many innocents in ancient times. I see you, creature, for what you truly are. Grendel."

Chase put his hand over his face as his eyes returned to normal. "Again, that happens."

Shocked by this revelation, Chase confronted Grendel. "How are you still alive? Beowulf killed you long ago."

"And what do you base that on, son of Odin?" said Grendel, mocking Chase.

Arthur pointed at Grendel. "Beowulf tore off your arms during your battle with him. You bled to death in that marsh."

Grendel laughed as he showed Arthur the scars on his arms. "It is true Beowulf tore off my arms, and I did flee into the marsh, but I survived."

"There is no way that you are alive, Beowulf with his sword Nægl, decapitated you. He even killed your mother with it," said Arthur, firm in his belief.

Grendel, angry, slammed its hand on the ground. "Beowulf may have killed my mother, for that I curse him. I wish he was here. That way, I could tear him apart."

Tired of talking, Grendel charged at Chase, trying to grab him with his claws, but Arthur jumped in front of Grendel and blocked his attack with his sword. Arthur struggled against Grendel. As he started to get pushed back, Grendel grabbed the blade, but it burned his hand. He grunted in pain and jumped back.

"What is that sword?" said Grendel grunting in pain.

Arthur wiped Grendel's blood that was dripping from the tip of Excalibur. "This is the holy sword Excalibur, the weapon that purges all evil."

Grendel laughed at Arthur. "I see, so this is Excalibur, the sword that slowly takes the life of its wielder."

"It is true, this sword did at one time take the life of its wielder," said Arthur, speaking in sorrow. Now filled with happiness and courage, Arthur gripped his sword firmly. "But now, because of all my friends, it has been reforged."

In a tense stare down, Arthur pointed his sword at Grendel. "I will finish what Beowulf could not."

As Arthur talked, a light glimmered from Excalibur. "For all the innocents that have been slaughtered by you, I shall now bring justice down upon you," Arthur commanded.

"Justice for humans, you who are nothing more than sacrifices to the Norse gods. You deserve no justice," Grendel scolded, laughing.

Hearing enough of Grendel, Arthur held Excalibur close to him as it began to glow with a white light.

"Everyone deserves justice. In my duty as a king, I had to carry the burden of justice for all of Britain. I carry that justice even now. And by that justice, I will slay you, creature."

Charging at him, Grendel mocked Arthur. "You may think that justice exists, but all you humans will meet the same fate. Just like before during the time of Ragnarök."

As Arthur was about to impale him, Grendel dug his hand into the ground and threw rocks at Arthur. Arthur slashed through the rocks with Excalibur. Dust from the rock got into Arthur's eyes, blinding him.

Seeing his chance to kill Arthur, Grendel smiled as he lunged at Arthur. Arthur heard Grendel lunge at him and stood his ground. With one hand, he slashed his sword forward as the light shot from it. The light of Excalibur slashed through the air and cut deep into Grendel's chest.

The impact from the attack knocked them in different directions. Grendel, who hit a tree, grabbed his chest in pain. He cursed at Arthur as blood dripped from his wound. "You will pay for wounding me, human."

Seeing that he was severely injured from Arthur's attack, Grendel slowly backed away. Dark shadows formed around him as he fled into the forest.

"Let him go," Chase yelled as Theseus and Ulf tried to pursue the ogre.

Chase walked over and helped Arthur to his feet.

"Trying to chase after him in the darkness is a bad idea. It will only get us killed. This is a Darkgen, we are dealing with."

The others stood down and walked back to Chase and Arthur.

"A very wise decision on your part," Amphion said, dispelling his khopesh.

"Staying calm in battle is always the correct course. Fewer people would die if they stayed that way."

Chase took a sip of alcohol as he remembered James. "The only person who makes by emotions alone is James."

"Even you can lose your cool when he is around, huh?" said Arthur.

Chase looked around at them and smiled for a moment. "Ya, for some reason, he has that effect on people. Anyway, we should get out of here. We will go a different route in the forest. Grendel will not dare to attack us again after what he just went through."

After packing up the campsite, they began to hike through the forest. An hour passed before they decided to set up camp again.

"What did that creature say he was again?" Arthur asked, tending the fire.

"A Darkgen," said Chase, throwing more wood on it.

"You seem to know something about them," said Amphion with his eyes closed.

"It's not easy to understand, so listen close," Chase said, taking a deep breath.

Chase stared into the fire as he told his story.

"I will tell you what I know of shadow creatures, known as the Darkgens."

Chapter 3: Running in The North

"As I told you all once before about my past, Devoid, who is the Midgard Serpent or Jörmungandr, killed my parents," Chase began. "With my hatred fueling me, I joined the Black Order in my quest for vengeance. Throughout my years in the order, I trained and studied, preparing for my inevitable confrontation with Devoid. Eventually, I came across a top-secret report about him and what he was. A creature called a Darkgen."

"The Darkgens, what exactly are they?" Amphion asked, curious about them.

"Darkgens are creatures from Norse myth. I don't know how they came about exactly, but there are many of them. For example, the serpent is large enough that it can wrap itself around a mountain. In the moment where I thought I would have my revenge, I failed. and Devoid nearly killed me. A volcano erupted, killing Devoid and my first teacher, Sepher. At the time, I thought that was the end of it, but..."

Chase hesitated as he took a deep breath to push

past his fears.

"…but when I was doing research in the Oracle Library for a way to save James, I also looked further into the subject of Darkgen to learn more about them. I learned something horrifying at that time. I couldn't understand it. But after encountering Grendel earlier, I now understand completely what those texts meant."

"And what was that?" Arthur asked, seeing Chase's reluctance.

"I learned that most of them are the Rökkr of Norse mythology. The creatures of the Norse that broke free and killed the gods of Asgard during Ragnarök."

Everyone around the campfire was stunned into silence as they listened intently.

"The Rökkr are made up of five or more entities, but I don't know the exact number. Here are the ones I know so far," said Chase laying out scrolls on the Rökkr.

The others looked over closely, seeing the dark imagery of the creatures.

"Hel, the Norse Goddess of Hel, who is said to be the most disruptive of the Norse gods. She is not a Darkgen because she is a Goddess. Devoid, or Jörmungandr, the Midgard Serpent. A serpent who killed Thor with its venom, and it is said that when he releases his tail, Ragnarök will begin. Grendel, who you just saw, the ogre that fought the Viking hero Beowulf. Fýri, a ferocious dragon and descendant of the dragon Humbaba and the one who killed the Viking hero Beowulf. This one is the deadliest one of them all," said Chase, gazing at Ulf.

Fenrir, Ulf thought, seething with anger looking at the image of the black wolf.

"Fenrir is a monstrous black wolf that even the Gods feared. It is said that he will keep growing in strength and size and eventually devour the sky.

"The Norse gods tried to bind Fenrir twice, but he always broke free. In desperation, they sought the assistance of Dwarfs, who are excellent forge masters. Dwarfs forged the unbreakable chain of Gleipnir and bound Fenrir with it. But even then, with his ever-growing size and strength, Fenrir eventually broke free for the last time during Ragnarök and killed Odin, the king, and father of the Norse gods."

Seething with rage, Ulf started to growl at the mention of Fenrir. Everyone looked at him and saw his anger.

"Tell me now, Chase, is he still alive?" Ulf asked.

"I can't say for sure, but since we saw Grendel today, it is possible," said Chase, rolling up the scrolls swiftly.

Ulf, convinced Fenrir was alive, nodded his head to Chase. "If he is alive, then I will be the one to kill him."

Arthur looked at Ulf and saw the hatred in his eyes.

"Fenrir is one of my ancestors. He betrayed Aesir

and my family," said Ulf, noticing Arthur's disapproving gaze.

Angry, Ulf looked directly at Chase. "You used to know. Fenrir's betrayal not only lead to the death of Aesir, it set in motion the chains toward Ragnarök."

"Ulf, I understand that you're angry, but remember why we are here," said Chase, trying to calm the wolf. "We are not here to settle your centuries-old grudge against Fenrir. We are here to get the Heavenly Life-Lock scroll to save our friend's life."

"I do know why we are here," said Ulf raising his voice. "But one of the Darkgens have already attacked us. If we do not act, they will again."

"Ulf, I know, and I promise you we will take care of them. But only after we are done here am I willing to help settle your hatred. For now, I need you here with me."

Ulf became calmer as he laid down next to the fire.

"Alright, for James's sake, I will put my hatred aside for now. I just hope you don't wait too long before their darkness spreads."

"We will stop them before that happens."

"It's been a long night; we should get some sleep; we have a lot of work to do tomorrow," said Chase as snow fell.

On their way toward Holmvassdalen, they drew closer to the center of Norway. Chase set the airship on autopilot as he started to clean his rifle to pass the time.

"And what is that you are doing?" Arthur asked, walking in.

"Well, since we have a little spare time, I am taking the opportunity to look at all the parts of the rifle I made."

"What type of rifle is that?" Arthur asked, noticing the strangeness of the weapon.

Chase held up the upper receiver and showed it to Arthur. "It is a rifle that Master Shinko helped me craft."

He dinged the side of the receiver and handed it to Arthur. "The rifle itself is made of Alterian steel, which she said is one of the hardest and rarest metals in the world."

Arthur, intrigued by this, compared it to his sword. "Amazing, I can only imagine if Excalibur was made with steel like this."

Taking the receiver back from Arthur, Chase put the rifle back together. He tested the rifle to make sure everything worked. Satisfied, Chase showed it to Arthur. "This steel is the purest of metals, and it can only be found in Shangri-La."

Showing Arthur the wooden stock of the rifle, Chase revealed the specialness of it. "And the stock of it is made of Elvien wood, which is the strongest wood in the world. It is also only found in Shangri-La."

"Then those trees in the Oracle are?" Arthur asked.

That's right, all of them are Elvien trees. Master Shinko said her people planted them a millennia ago. The trees are the only ones of their kind."

"What is the faint glow I see on it?" asked Arthur seeing a glim light in the wood.

"That is chi energy, which is a type of living chakra found in the Elvien tree. It is energy that helps keep the wood durable and firm."

"And these symbols on the rifle, what do they mean?"

"They are Elvien sigils channeled with my lightning mystic energy and pieces of the Minotaur's horn. The sigils were engraved with volcano mountain ash and silver from the Etherionus. I can tell more about what they mean and do, but I'll give you the short version," said Chase, noticing he was rambling.

"The rifle was made to augment and amplify my lightning."

Chase took out engraved bullets and showed them to Arthur. "And these bullets are also made of Alterian steel. Each is infused with my lightning energy. If I fired these lightning bullets from this rifle, both the piercing power and velocity will be increased. So pretty much I can shoot this at a huge rock, and it will pierce all the way through it."

"I think I understand just a little. What do you call

that rifle?"

"It is called þrumuveður (Thunder Howl)," said Chase, charging his lightning through the rifle, smiling.

"That name sounds like old Norse. What does it mean?" Arthur asked, amazed by the lightning emanating.

"It means Thunder Howl."

"This rifle, when fired, the shot sounds as loud as thunder. Just like the howl and flash of a thunderstorm."

Done tinkering with his rifle, Chase put it back in his backpack and resumed flying.

"Well, that killed a little bit of time."

"But not enough time for you," said Arthur, sensing Chase's eagerness.

"Ya, not enough," Chase whispered.

The hunter tried to concentrate on flying but could not shake his uneasiness about his best friend.

"But the longer we take is a moment too long."

After a few moments, they arrived at the nature preserve. In the sky over Holmvassdalen, Chase touched down the airship in a forest.

"Alright, it doesn't seem like anyone is around, so I am now going to do the long-range scan," said Chase, pulling out his scanner. "The airship's computer will help with the broad range scan."

A three-dimensional map of Norway appeared, scanning all the country for Loki but came back with no results.

"Damn it," Chase yelled, hitting his fist against the wall in frustration.

Blood dripped from Chase's hand as Arthur came over and checked on him.

"Stay calm, my friend. You cannot get frustrated by one setback."

Thinking about James, Chase became more frustrated as he walked past Arthur.

"I know that. I don't see Loki's divine signature anywhere. Where is he?"

"Easy, it just means he is not here."

"But it doesn't make sense. Norway was the main home of the Norse gods. He should be here," said Chase as his eyes turned lightning blue.

Responding to his anger, Chase's lightning aura began to surge from him. "Why? Why isn't he here?"

Chase ripped his scanner from the computer and threw it against the wall.

"You need to get ahold of yourself. You're letting your emotions run rampant," said Arthur, trying to calm Chase.

"How can I remain calm knowing I can't save my best friend?" Chase yelled, pushing him back.

"You don't believe that," said Amphion, appearing before Chase.

"I know you don't."

Seeing the seriousness in Amphion's eyes, Chase composed himself. The lightning dissipated as he walked past Amphion. "You don't know me."

Amphion turned his head as Chase left.

Arthur tried to go after Chase, but Amphion stopped him. "Let him go."

"Why?" Arthur asked, looking at Amphion, worried about Chase.

"This matter he must handle himself," said Amphion.

Arthur tried to argue with him as Amphion picked up Chase's scanner. "But as his friends, we should help him through this."

"No, the best we can do right now is let him be, so he can sort through his thoughts."

Not liking but seeing Amphion's approach, Arthur sat down in his seat. "Fine, I shall do it your way for now."

After he convinced Arthur, Amphion glimpsed at the scanner. His red eyes brighten as he suddenly walked out of the cockpit silent. A blue dot appeared on the scanner.

In the forest near the airship, Chase looked at the night sky, gathering his thoughts. *What should I do? How can I find Loki? Is there anything I can do?* Chase thought, starting to doubt himself. Hearing footsteps behind him, Chase turned his head and saw Amphion. "Not now."

"But I think this might be of interest to you," said Amphion undeterred, showing Chase his scanner.

It can't be," said Chase, seeing the blue dot on the scanner.

Chase took the scanner from Amphion to look at it more closely. "How is that even possible? Why did his divine signature suddenly appear?"

"I do not know, I just saw it on your scanner, so I brought it to you," said Amphion not having an answer for the hunter.

I know for a fact Loki's signature was not there a minute ago, Chase thought unnerved. *Why? Why did his energy signature suddenly appear? This can't be a coincidence. When I looked at that reading earlier, there was nothing on it.*

Chase gazed up Amphion and then back forward. *And going by what Amphion said, the signature of Loki's divine energy only appeared on the scanner but only after I left. He knows,* Chase thought, realizing what was happening.

Chase remembered the man in the trench coat at the museum. *He has been watching us this whole time.*

"What next steps do you want to take?" Amphion asked, seeing Chase in deep thought.

Chase broke his train of thought. "I am sorry, what?"

"I asked what steps do you want to take next?"

"We find him," said Chase without hesitation. "What, he is in Trondheim?" said Chase, seeing Loki's location on the scanner.

"What is wrong? You have the face of someone who has seen a pharaoh for the first time," Amphion asked, seeing Chase's blank expression.

"It's nothing. It's just that Loki is in the same town where the legendary Viking Ragnar Lodbrok ruled during the Viking Age. I see the same Viking king who had the blood of Odin."

He is inviting us, Chase thought, knowing something was not right.

"We need to tread carefully from here on out."

"Is there something to be concerned with?" Amphion asked, unsurprised.

"He knows we are looking for him."

Amphion was silent as he and Chase walked back toward the airship.

"We have our heading."

"You found Loki?" Arthur asked.

"Ya, he is in Trondheim."

"Trondheim, where is that?"

Pulling up the map of Norway, Chase showed Arthur.

"It is a little bit southwest of us. Taking the airship, we should get there in about thirty minutes."

"How were you able to find him?"

"When I ran the scan, nothing appeared. But when I threw the scanner up against the wall and Amphion

46

brought it to me, Loki's signature suddenly appeared."

"It just suddenly appeared. And just as the time you stormed off in anger," said Arthur, suspicious.

Chase lifted the airship into the air as he set a course toward Trondheim. "His energy signature didn't just suddenly appear. He let us see it."

"Why?

"This is Loki, the God of Mischief we're talking about. He sent us an invitation."

As they flew, Chase brought the others in the cockpit. "He knows we are coming. Loki has been watching us from the very beginning."

"If he knows we are coming, then how do we even approach him?" Theseus asked, advising caution.

"I was thinking of going up and talking to him."

"That may be the best option, but I think as a precaution, the others and I should watch you from a distance," said Arthur, thinking nothing would trick the trickster.

"Ya, I think it is our only option at this point."

Once in Trondheim, Chase and the others checked for Loki's signature on the scanner.

"Loki has not moved at all. I wonder why?" said Chase.

Getting closer, Chase was disappointed with where they were. "Really?"

"What is wrong?" Arthur asked, hearing Chase's disappointment.

"He is in a pub," Chase said, pointing up at the sign.

As snow fell, Chase and others got out of the van and stood outside of the pub.

"That's probably why he hasn't moved. He is too busy getting drunk."

Arthur laughed in amusement. "Well, at least he hasn't moved, he may be easier to deal with when he is drunk."

"Alright, you guys know what to do. I go inside first to talk to Loki. And then you guys come in and sit away from us."

Chase walked inside the pub and headed toward a table. He ordered a drink, and he noticed a man wearing a funny feathered hat.

"Is this seat taken?" Chase asked the man.

"It is now," said the man, smiling drinking his ale.

Chase noticed the blue glimmer in the man's eyes as he realized he had found the trickster.

"Loki, I assume."

Loki took off his hat and placed it on the bar. "The one and only. You sure kept me waiting a while," said Loki ordering more ale.

"It was intentional. After all, you do have a reputation," said Chase, justifying his action.

"Indeed I do. As do you. Let me guess, you got struck by your own lightning again. You lost your hammer. No, no, you had it stolen again."

Chase, not amused by Loki's jokes, remained silent.

"What no response, cat got your tongue? Not one for the jokes are you?" Loki sighed in disappointment.

Loki took a drink of his ale and slapped it down on the table. "Well, jokes aside for now. What can the God of Mischief do for you today?" Loki asked.

Chapter 4: Game of Mischief

Loki's behavior was off for the trickster, putting Chase on alert. He knew something was up.

"You know why I have come here?" Chase asked.

"But of course, why else would I have made it so easy for you to find me," Loki said, taking another drink of his ale.

"You were watching me," Chase said, not at all surprised.

"I wouldn't say watched, just a little peek every now and then," Loki joked.

"Aren't you going invite your friends in, or would you rather I did?" Loki asked, baiting Chase.

"You were watching?" Chase asked nervously as it was apparent that Loki had discovered their plan.

Chase nodded his head toward his companions, signaling them to come in. The group sat at a table not far from Loki and Chase. Loki chuckled, snapped his fingers, and a chessboard appeared on the table.

"Before we get to what you want, how about a game of chess?" Loki asked, placing the pieces on the chessboard.

"Alright."

"Tell me, when you look at these pieces in front of you, what do you think they are?" Loki asked.

Chase gazed at the pieces. "Well, with the pieces in front of us and where we are, I say the pieces represent the Norse."

Loki commended Chase on his knowledge. "Very good. What do you think they represent?"

Chase looked at the pieces intensely. "The king is Odin."

Loki then moved to the other pieces one by one. "And the queen?"

"Frigg, Odin's wife."

"And the knights?"

"Thor and Tyr."

"And the rooks?"

"The Vanir, Freyr, and Freyja."

"Now, this might be a difficult one. What about all the pawns?"

Chase looked at the pawns hard. Though distracted by the remarkable intricacy and detail of the pieces, he answered, "Mortals."

"Final answer?" Loki asked.

"Ya," said Chase without hesitation.

Pleased with Chase's answer, Loki snapped his fingers as the pawns disappeared from the board. "Correct. How did you figured it out?"

"If the high pieces represent the Norse gods, it is obvious that humans are the pawns. They were used as sacrifices to open and gain an advance against the Giants."

Smiling, Loki folded his hands on the back of his head. "True, either side, be it be the Jotunn or the Norse gods, they all turn into sacrifices in the end. But you forget something important. They all end up in hell in the end," Loki gleamed as a little flame flickered in his finger.

Not goaded by Loki's taunts, Chase looked at the bishops on the board. "Why are the bishop pieces still on the board?"

Loki picked up his bishop and looked at it. "Because I find the bishop to be the most fascinating of all of the pieces."

He dropped the bishop, but it stopped, suspended in midair. "It is a unique piece. The bishop has no restrictions in the distance it moves on the board, but it can move only diagonally. The most fascinating part about it, no matter what you do, it can always appear behind any of the other pieces, and… it can be the first or last to fall," Loki laughed, dropping the bishop.

"And then you have the biggest problem of them all, once they fall, the pawns can become any other piece," said Chase watching the bishops disappear, and a pawn appear.

The pawn changed into other chess pieces. "A rook, a knight, a bishop, a queen, and sometimes, a king."

"What point are you trying to make?" Chase demanded.

"Patience, my friend. First, let me tell you a story—a story called Ragnarök," said Loki, not giving away his play.

With but a motion of his hand, all the chest pieces appeared on the board again. One by one, Loki tipped them over. "The Vanir, Freyr, and Freyja fall. Then Thor and Tyr fell. And lastly, the all father, Odin."

Chase looked down at the chess board, only two pawn pieces were left standing.

"Until you have the two mortals who survived Ragnarök Ask and Embla."

"Where do you fit into all of this? What piece are you?" Chase asked sarcastically.

"You did say your favorite piece is the bishop. That's right, but I am a trickster, though. I can be any piece or none at all."

"What do you mean?" said Chase, confused.

Loki held out his hand as chess pieces appeared in it. "I can be a pawn, a rook, a bishop, a knight, a queen, or even a king, or no piece at all."

Chase was irritated by Loki's antics but remained calm. "Then you saw the war of Ragnarök as just a game? You're one of the reasons it started in the first place."

"Ragnarök was just the first level. Life itself is the true game," Loki proclaimed, seeing the fury in the hunter's eyes.

Dropping all the pieces, the trickster cleared the chessboard. "As long as it entertains me, it doesn't matter to me how many die."

"Lives are not your toys for your games," said Chase boldly.

"Ah, but they are. They just don't know it. In battle, that is precisely what happens every single day. One moves soldiers to the end of the battlefield, and the opponent moves the same or more to kill them. If you look at war and this chessboard, they are not so different. A game of wits and strategy until one combatant wins or falls. Even you have done this," said Loki, pointing at Chase.

"No, I would never do something like that," said Chase, denying Loki's accusation.

Loki sighed at Chase's denial. "Even you use your friends as pieces even if it's unintentional, but it is only natural."

Taking a deep breath, Chase tried to compose himself. "You may be right, even the ones we call friends. But I am different from you that much I know."

"Now that our chess game is done, how about we get down to business?" Loki said, dropping his façade.

The codex, thought Chase as he watched the trickster place a scroll on the table.

"I know why it is you're here," said Loki, tapping his finger on the scroll. "This is the only thing in this world that can save your best friend's life."

Opening the scroll, Loki tempted Chase with it. "The Heavenly Life-Lock scroll."

Chase tried to grab the scroll, but Loki pulled it away. "Ah, I am sorry; you can't have it just yet. But it can be yours if you can do me a little favor first." Loki squeezed his fingers together. "Just a little."

As Loki looked at the scroll, Chase slowly reached for his pistol under the table.

"Before you do something foolish, you should know I bound this scroll with my life," said Loki, smiling, knowing what Chase intended.

Conjuring a candle, Loki held the scroll over it. "If I die, the scroll burns to ash."

"Alright, what do you want?" Chase asked solemnly, taking his hand off his revolver.

"Something simple, really. Something I think is in your area of expertise," said Loki, snapping his fingers making photos appear on the table.

Chase stared at the photos. "Are those the…"

"Correct—monsters of Norse myth the Rökkr."

"The Rökkr. Why would you want them?"

Loki took a drink of his ale. "Because I am their guardian, but you needn't concern yourself with the details."

"You want them dead?" Chase asked, trying to figure out Loki's motive.

"Oh no, not kill them. I want them brought to me alive. They are important to me, after all." Loki pushed the images closer to Chase. "Hel, Grendel, Fýri, Fenrir, and finally, Jörmungandr."

"I hate to break it to you, but Jörmungandr is dead," said Chase, pushing away the image of the serpent.

"I've heard others say this, but are you sure?" Loki asked gleefully, gesturing his ale.

Chase leaned forward, looking into Loki's eyes. "Ya, I am sure. Jörmungandr was killed by my master months ago in Iceland."

"I am aware, Jörmungandr, or Devoid, as it is so named now, was killed by your master."

"Then why bring it up?"

"Because the Midgard Serpent is alive and well," said Loki, tapping his finger on the image of the Midgard Serpent.

"No, it can't be. He is dead. You're lying," Chase shuddered.

"I may be the trickster, but a liar I am not."

Chase slammed his fist down on the table in anger. "I don't believe you."

"I figured it would come to this," said Loki, shaking his head in disappointment.

"I can tell by your demeanor that you are not going to believe me." Loki waved his hand before Chase's eyes, placing him in a trance. "I am going to show you instead."

Chase grabbed his head as he began seeing disturbing images. "What... what is going on? What are you showing me?" Chase demanded.

"What you choose not to believe," said Loki, amused by Chase's pain.

Chase watched Devoid and Sepher fighting in a painful vision. He yelled out in a panic. "No, no, it can't be."

Waving his hand, Loki stopped the vision. Chase was sweating and in shock. "What was that? What did you just show me?"

"The truth."

"Enough of your riddles give a straight answer," Chase huffed.

Loki shook his head no as he leaned forward. "You saw it yourself, the Jörmungandr is alive, and what's more, your master is alive."

"And how do I know you didn't make all of that stuff I saw up?"

"You don't," said Loki, sitting back in his chair and throwing a badge on the table.

That's... that is Sepher's Black Order badge, Chase thought, recognizing the badge. Chase picked it up and looked at it intently. "Where did you get this?"

"Nowhere special, just down the mountainside."

"Hvannadalshnúkur in Iceland? But that place erupted and covered all the surrounding area in lava and ash."

"No, I didn't say Hvannadalshnúkur. The place I found it was right here in Norway."

Chase's eyes widen as he thought, *It can't be.* Not sure what to believe, Chase threw the badge back on the table.

"Do you believe me now?"

"No, I don't, but…" said Chase, nodding his head.

"But what? Tell me, I am all ears?"

Chase looked at Sepher's badge and then directly at Loki. "But I will see for myself, and if the serpent is still alive, it won't be for much longer."

"Do we have an agreement?" Loki asked joyously.

"You heard me. I said I would do it. Do you want it writing?" Chase barked.

"No," said Loki, snapping his fingers, making words appeared in the air. "By you saying yes, you have already agreed to the contract."

A paper appeared on the table. Loki handed it to Chase. "Now, let me tell you about the terms of the contract."

"You didn't say anything about requirements," said Chase in anger.

"It is because you didn't ask beforehand, and besides, I leave the petty details till the end," Loki said, shrugging his shoulders.

"You lied."

"Technically, I didn't lie to you. I just withheld it," Loki said, playing with a deck of cards. "I am the trickster, after all. It's what I do."

"Fine."

Loki put the cards away and moved the paper closer to Chase. "All of it is necessary. Your teammates and you are to hunt Rökkr individually."

"What?" Chase said in disbelief.

Loki conjured images of Chase's friends. "The one you call Amphion, he will hunt the grey ogre, Grendel. The one you call Theseus will hunt the goddess, Hel. The one you call Arthur will hunt the Norse ice dragon, Fýri. The wolf Ulf will hunt the black wolf, Fenrir. And lastly, you will hunt Jörmungandr, the Midgard Serpent," said Loki. "You all cannot hunt at the same time; you must hunt them in order starting with Amphion, then Theseus, then Arthur, then Ulf, and finally, you. You cannot assist or have assistance from anyone, and you must complete all these tasks within three days' time."

Chase remained silent as he looked at the others.

"You either accept these terms or not. You still can back out since I'm a nice gentleman. But know if you do, the contract will be null and void, and I will burn the scroll," Loki warned. "And if you fail to complete the contract within the three-day time frame, then I will also burn the scroll."

Amphion nodded his head yes toward Chase. Chase closed his eyes as he thought about James, determined to save him.

"It will get done," said Chase staring ferociously at Loki.

"Then it now begins," said Loki, snapping his fingers, and the sound of a ringing bell was heard.

"What was the dinging sound?" said Chase looking around the room, confused.

"It is just a little something I do when I'm happy. Now, it is time for me to tell you my part of the contract." Loki pressed items toward Chase. "These will help you find the Rökkr. A wart off the back of Grendel. A piece off the crown of the Goddess Hel. A scale of the ice dragon Fýri. A claw of the beast wolf Fenrir. And finally, for you, a poison fang from the Midgard Serpent, Jörmungandr," said Loki, poking fun at Chase. "You can use the items at your leisure, but bring me the Rökkr alive."

"You'll have your monsters," Chase rebuffed, grabbing the items.

As Chase was about to leave, Loki grabbed his hand, stopping him. "Just one more thing."

Chase stared back silently at the trickster. "If you let your personal vendetta against Jörmungandr get the best of you, your best friend James will be cursed forever," whispered Loki, letting go of Chase's hand. An hourglass appeared on the table. "You might want to get started because your time starts now," said

Loki, smiling as he flipped the hourglass over. Loki handed Chase a card. "My card."

"What is this for?" said Chase looking at the joker card, confused. When Chase looked up again, Loki had vanished. He watched the sand falling in the hourglass and knew he needed to hurry.

"Are you ok?" Amphion asked, noticing Chase's discomfort.

"We need to go. There is no time to lose," Chase said, hurrying from the pub.

Back on the airship, Chase nervously prepared to go over everything that happened. "I got to tell you what Loki told me."

"There is no need," said Amphion, stopping Chase. "Ulf and I overheard everything, including the terms of the contract. So, save your words and tell us what needs to be done."

Oh Ya, I forgot you and Ulf are animals. Of course, you have sensitive hearing, Chase thought.

Chase scanned Grendel's wart to pick up his energy signal then searched all of Norway. He was able to pinpoint the ogre's location. "We only have three days in total to hunt the Rökkr. As you heard, we can only catch them, not kill them. No help, only hunt alone. I wanted to test this first, but we don't have enough time," said Chase configuring a mystica jewel to the scanner.

"We will have to do fieldwork instead. I configured the jewel so it can teleport to anywhere throughout Norway. But the jewel can only go to one location and back. After that, they will not work again. I found Grendel. He is nearby in the Trolltunga Mountains. You're up first, Amphion. I set the timer to eight hours," said Chase, handing the scanner and mystica jewel to Amphion. "You must find and capture Grendel in that time."

"I will not fail."

"I know you won't. I put the coordinates in the scanner, so it will get you where you need to go. Remember, we are counting on you."

"I will see that it's done," said Amphion as the blue vortex enveloped him.

"Are you sure it is a good idea to teleport in public like that? People might have seen," said Arthur.

"If people did, their memories are already wiped." Shocked, Arthur remained silent as Chase walked into the cockpit.

We don't have time to worry about such things. No matter how high the price is, I am ready to pay it.

Elsewhere, outside the Trolltunga Mountains, Amphion emerged from the blue vortex. Tracking through a blizzard, he followed Grendel's mystic signature leading him to the north, near Lake Ringedalsvatnet. "The creature is near."

After a few hours, Amphion reached the top of the Trolltunga Mountains. With his glowing red eyes, he looked down from the mountain, and he saw Lake Ringedalsvatnet off in the distance. *It seems Grendel is in the middle of the lake.*

Descending, Amphion finally reached the edge of the frozen lake. He looked through the blinding snow and saw a shadowy figure walking toward him. Amphion waited patiently as he heard the cracking of ice with each step the figure took. Now able to see the figure, Amphion saw that it was Grendel.

Grendel stopped a few feet away from Amphion. "Why have you tracked me, demigod dog?" Grendel snarled, stopping at the lake's edge.

"I am here to fight you," said Amphion, summoning his khopeshes.

Grendel smiled as he elongated his claws. "If you came here to die, then I will be happy to rip you to shreds."

Amphion raised his khopeshes and clicked them together. "I will take that low intellectual response as a yes."

A dark aura formed around Amphion, and he enacted his prism. "Sphere of the Alati."

The blizzard suddenly stopped as an invisible sphere appeared all around Lake Ringedalsvatnet.

"What is going on? What have you have done?" Grendel asked in anger and confusion.

"I placed an invisible barrier around us. Neither you nor I will be able to escape from it."

"You dog, this was your plan from the beginning."

"You are a coward just as you were from the legends," said Amphion, mocking the ogre. "Running from the hero Beowulf, instead of dying with honor. A coward and a monster like you does not deserve mercy, so I enacted this barrier to prevent you from escaping as you did before."

Grendel grew angrier and charged Amphion, trying to claw at him but slipped, cracking the ice.

"You are not very careful, are you?" said Amphion, chuckling at Grendel's clumsiness.

"The one who survives in the end is the victor," said Grendel, standing up, smirking. "I survived while Beowulf failed and died. And now you, demigod, dare to challenge me?" Grendel laughed maniacally. "Very well, I Grendel, the grey ogre, will make this frozen lake your grave."

Amphion did not respond to Grendel's threat as the dark aura around him dissipated. Walking slowly toward Grendel, Amphion prepared to do battle. Amphion then brandished his khopesh at Grendel. "Enough of your stupid threats."

"I will rip you apart until there is nothing of you left," Grendel snarled in anger.

Charging at Amphion, the ogre's claw clashed against Amphion's khopesh, and the battle between monster and demigod began.

Chapter 5: Spira of the Jackal

Several minutes passed, and Amphion nor Grendel was able to get the advantage over the other. Amphion grew frustrated at the stalemate and jumped back a safe distance.

"It seems you are holding back," said Amphion, bleeding and catching his breath.

"As are you. You are not putting your full might into your swords," Grendel grinned, also bleeding.

"If either one of us uses our full strength, we will split the ice apart and fall in."

This is frustrating. If this keeps going like this, I will not make it back before the time limit is up, Amphion thought, gazing at his wounded shoulder as he studied the ice on the lake. He knew the ice would crack as Grendel had said but felt he had little choice.

"I will have to increase my speed," said Amphion, removing the weights on his legs.

"You're full of surprises," Grendel laughed, seeing Amphion throw the weights into the water. You are definitely a true warrior. I can't wait to feel your blood on my hands."

With my khopesh, I'm more suited to fighting with my speed anyway, thought Amphion, readying himself.

Grendel rushed at Amphion with speed as the ice broke underneath him.

Not wanting to take an attack from Grendel standing, Amphion rushed at him. The moment they were about to clash, Grendel broke through the ice and dove into the water. Clearing the water from his eyes, Amphion looked around for Grendel.

Where did he go? Amphion thought, stepping lightly on the ice.

Hearing the cracks of ice underneath, Amphion looked down. Before he could react, claws pierced through the ice and into his foot. Amphion saw Grendel staring up at him through the ice.

"Your blood. I must spill more of your blood," said Grendel, relishing in Amphion's pain.

Amphion tried to move, but Grendel grabbed his foot through the ice. "You will not escape."

Before Grendel's claw attacked again, Amphion pierced his khopesh through the ice severing several of its claws

"Ahh," Grendel grunted in pain, retreating into the darkness of the water.

Amphion, now free from Grendel's grasp, jumped back to a safe distance. He set his Kopeshes down and examined his wounded hand. It appeared that Grendel had severed tendons in his fingers, and he wouldn't be able to use his left hand. In silent frustration, Amphion waved his hand and the khopesh disappeared.

Blood dripped from Amphion's wound, and he knew he would not be able to sustain the battle. He was surprised that Grendel could survive in the freezing water. This put him at a great disadvantage.

Hearing cracking, Amphion looked and saw the ice begin to split. *And as I foresaw, the ice will not hold out for too much longer either. I have to finish this fight soon.* Realizing his situation, Amphion gripped his khopesh tightly. *I have no choice; I have to use that technique. But I need to lure that creature above the ice in order for it to work,* Amphion thought, waiting for the ogre's attack.

You will pay for wounding me," said Grendel, growling in pain underneath the ice.

Swimming toward him, Grendel stopped as he noticed the deep cut in Amphion's hand. He was pleased with what he saw.

Amphion heard the water move and jumped back as Grendel's claw struck through the ice, missing him by inches.

"You are my prey," Grendel said.

After the failed attack, Grendel swam around and broke through all the ice on the lake. Noticing the ice give way, Amphion retreated. With all the ice broken, he balanced on a single piece of ice on the lake.

"Now to end you," said Grendel delighted.

Amphion did not react as his khopesh disappeared from his hand. He closed his eyes and placed his hands together in prayer.

"Eye of Ra," Amphion whispered as a miniature sun appeared in his hand. "Ascend."

The miniature sun rose toward the sky. Grendel jumped from the water behind Amphion and tried to impale him.

"Enlighten," said Amphion, waving his fingers in a hand sign.

"My eyes," Grendel yelled as the miniature sun brightened, blinding him.

Grabbing his eyes, Grendel fell back into the water and started to thrash. "My eyes, my eyes, I can't see."

Amphion grabbed Grendel by the arm and threw him high into the air. Getting his footing on the ice, Amphion kicked Grendel in the stomach. Grendel splashed into the water and back on the shore of the lake.

"Ah," Grendel grunted in pain, struggling to stand.

Amphion emerged from the water as he summoned a spear. "Spira."

He threw the spear at Grendel and impaled his shoulder. In tremendous pain, Grendel looked at Amphion, enraged.

"Unforgivable. Unforgivable. You wretched dog, I will kill you for that."

Amphion ran at him and drove the spear deeper into Grendel's shoulder. With the spear, Amphion forced Grendel backward and pinned him to the ground.

"Be silent," Amphion commanded, staring down at Grendel with his glowing red eyes.

He punched Grendel in the face, knocking him out, pulled his spear from the shoulder, then cleaned the blood from it. "And another thing, I am not a dog. I am a jackal."

At the water's edge, he dispelled the spear and looked up at the miniature sun. The miniature sun flew down and hovered in his hand.

"Thank you for guiding me," said Amphion, praising the Egyptian god, Ra.

The miniature sun disappeared as Amphion was satisfied with the battle. "In the name of the Sun God, I dedicate this battle to you."

Amphion finished his prayer to Ra and returned to the still unconscious Grendel and hoisted to his shoulder. He had time to spare.

"Dispel," said Amphion dispelling the barrier over the lake.

The blizzard raged once again as Amphion took out the mystica jewel. The jewel glowed with a blue light as Amphion looked into it.

"Teleport," said Amphion, disappearing into the blue vortex.

Back at the airship in a forest just outside of Trondheim, everyone waited patiently for Amphion's return.

"Amphion should not be taking this long," said Theseus, staring outside at the snow. How much time has passed since he left?"

"Five hours and five minutes," said Chase, looking at his timer.

"And how much time do we have left on the contract?"

"Forty-two hours and forty-five minutes."

"Are you concerned he will not be able to handle this task?" Arthur asked.

"Of course not. He is a strong warrior and demigod," said Theseus.

"I don't like these games that trickster has put us through. It goes against everything I was taught in Athens. And most of all, having to bring back such savage creatures as the Midgard Serpent and Grendel alive. They have been a plague to the world for centuries and should be killed with haste," said Theseus, expressing his contempt.

"We have no choice. Those are the terms of the contract we made with Loki," said Chase. "We have to hunt individually and bring them all back alive within two days. I don't like it any more than either of you, but we must do it in order to get the scroll from Loki."

"And how do you know Loki will keep his end of the bargain?" Theseus retorted.

"I don't, but I can only hope that he will. After all, even Loki has his pride as a god. He laid out all of the guidelines for the contract and signed it just like I did."

"He could still be holding some details back," said Arthur, reminding Chase. "He may have the pride of a god, but that pride comes from being the trickster. Don't look for him to fulfill his side of the bargain, Chase."

"I know, but we can't just kill Loki," said Chase, gripping his fists tightly.

"He tied the scroll to his life, and according to the details of the contract, if he dies before it's complete, the scroll will burn to ashes."

"Then we have no choice," Arthur agreed.

"He has almost every eventuality covered where it would turn in his favor. We have no choice for now but to stick to the rules and hunt the rest of the Rökkr," Chase reaffirmed.

As they spoke, Grendel was thrown in a heap at their feet.

"We are now one step closer," said Amphion, dusting the snow off him. He sat with a sapphire healing stone and began to treat his wounds.

"You really did a number on him," said Chase, looking down at Grendel.

"I have no obligation to hold back against that evil," said Amphion ruthlessly. "But the creature is fortunate. If it wasn't for the contract you made, I would have killed it without mercy."

"Well, as long as you brought him back alive, that is all that matters," said Chase nervously, not wanting to provoke Amphion.

"Do as you will. His fate is no longer any concern to me."

"Is that the Alterization Mass scroll?" Arthur asked, seeing Chase pull out a scroll.

"No, this one is a bit different. This scroll contains a spell called Living Mass; it allows the caster to alter living mass. Living Mass," said Chase placing his hand on Grendel.

Grendel shrunk down to the size of a toy as Chase put him in a jar. "The spell can alter the mass of anything living. The living object can be shrunk or enlarged depending on the caster's intentions."

"Fascinating. It is similar to what Merlin once tried to teach, but I could never master," said Arthur, excited.

"We can admire Chase's spell casting later," said Theseus, trying to keep them on task.

"Right now, I am up next to hunt, and I am hunting the Goddess Hel."

Chase looked at Theseus and handed him the scanner. "I know. When we were all talking, I put the piece of Hel's crown into the scanner and tracked her location in Norway."

"You were able to do that even when you were shrinking Grendel?"

"It is one of the advantages of being me," said Chase, smiling.

Wondering about Hel's location, Theseus looked at the map on the scanner. "Where in Norway is she?"

Chase pointed on the map to her location. "She seems to be at… no, wait… but that's the…"

"That's what?"

"She's at Gaustatoppen where the Yggdrasil tree once stood."

"You mean the Norse tree of the Nine Worlds?" asked Arthur.

"The same tree which is also called the tree of life. Actually, when I looked at the texts in the Oracle Library on that subject, I found that there are multiple trees of life throughout the world. Those trees were called Ethernia in the Elvien language, which translates to life bringers in English. The other trees and plants throughout the entire world are the roots of the Ethernia."

"I remember," said Arthur, recalling his tutelage under Merlin. "During my apprenticeship with Merlin, I remember him speaking about the tree of life. But I never imagined that there was more than one or that they were of such importance."

"Those trees are one of the very reasons that the sasquatches, or Earth Guardians, keep humans away from the deep forest at all cost," said Chase, pointing out the need for their secrecy.

"The trees of life are ones that give life to this very Earth. Because of that, knowledge of their existence needs to be kept secret from humans."

Chase closed his eyes as he thought about the time Timber showed him one of the trees of life. "Timber showed me one of those trees."

"You mean the huge tree in the forest of the Oracle?" Arthur asked.

"Yes, that tree is called Elvien," Chase answered, opening his eyes.

"I promised Timber to keep all this secret, so I ask all of you to do the same. If such knowledge gets out, people will seek to find these trees and abuse their power."

"There is no need to ask us to keep its existence a secret," Amphion scuffed. "That decision was made the moment you told us. If it is to protect their existence, I would gladly give my life for them."

"We will as well," Theseus vowed.

"Thank you, guys," said Chase, bowing his head.

Chase handed a mystica jewel to him as Theseus prepared to leave to begin his hunt. "I already configured the scanner to the Gaustatoppen Mountain, but I was only able to translocate it at its base."

"Why? You were able to get Amphion close to Grendel."

"I don't know why, but there is interference around the top of the mountain. You will have no choice; you will have to climb to the top."

"As a warrior, I learned nothing is ever tranquil," said Theseus, understanding. "It matters not, though. I used to climb the mountains in Greece all the time."

"Since you are going up against a goddess, you are going to need more time on this one. Twelve hours is the max you can do. Once the time limit is up, the jewel will automatically teleport you back here," Chase explained. "But if you happen to defeat and capture her before the time limit ends, then just look at the jewel and say teleport," said Chase with humor. "When the blue vortex appears around you, you will teleport back here."

"I understand," said Theseus, walking out in the snow. As he looked back at everyone, the blue vortex surrounded him.

Amphion nodded his head in approval.

"Teleport," said Theseus as he disappeared into the vortex to face Hel.

After a few moments, Theseus arrived at the base of the Gaustatoppen Mountain. Looking out to the north, he saw storm clouds on the horizon.

Judging by the distance and the pace of the storm, it will reach this place in about half an hour, Theseus thought, preparing for the storm's arrival. *I have to make haste if I am to endure it.*

Beginning his ascent, Theseus climbed to the top of the Gaustatoppen Mountain. As the hours passed, the full force of the storm settled in.

Tracking through the blizzard, he felt an ominous presence the higher he climbed. *"I am sensing a feeling of a gluttonous hunger.*

At the top of the mountain, a woman slept. She opened her eyes, sensing Theseus getting closer to her. "Someone has entered the Heaven of the Gods. Only ones whose hearts are noble may enter this domain," said the woman looking down at the blizzard below. "But no matter who it is, it is my sworn duty to protect this realm."

The woman walked back toward the tree as she moved past skeletons of fallen warriors. "Every one of these warriors has either fallen to their own sword or to their own greed during Ragnarök. They ran at the sight of the ones we faced in the final battle. In my eyes, they are nothing more than a disappointment," said the woman, sitting under the tree waiting for Theseus. "I hope this warrior's heart is more valiant than theirs."

An hour passed. Theseus reached the top of the Gaustatoppen Mountain.

"There is a barrier here," said Theseus, sensing it. "Is that to keep something contained or to prevent something from coming in?"

Suddenly, a hand reached through the barrier and pulled Theseus in. "A little bit of both."

Theseus was thrown against the tree with such force, a couple of leaves fell. He stood up immediately and noticed the tree of life, Yggdrasil.

"This is the legendary Norse tree, Yggdrasil," said Theseus, mesmerized by its beauty seeing the blossoms and colorful leaves. The one tree from Norse legend that stretched over the nine worlds and into the heavens. Seeing it with my own eyes it looks just like it was described in the fairy tale."

"Indeed, it does, and I am one of its protectors," said the woman, appearing before Theseus dressed in Norse armor.

Theseus looked at the woman and noticed her armor as her flowing black hair blew in the wind. "You must be Hel, Goddess of the Norse underworld."

Hel tasted the blood she'd drawn from Theseus.

"What is going on? I can't move," said Theseus.

"You won't be able to move, old warrior, for I have bound you," said the woman. "When I tasted your blood, you became immobile. But enough with formalities. I am the Goddess Hel, but I go by Hela, and as for as the Norse underworld, I am not the ruler of because there is no Hel."

"What? In every scripture of Norse legend, there is always mention of the underworld realm Hel and that you were its ruler," said Theseus.

"Mankind always gets the verses wrong. There has never been anything accurate written about me because of my ferocity on the battlefield," said Hela, dusting off her armor. "There is no underworld, and even if there was such a realm, I would have no interest in ruling it."

Theseus looked into Hela's eyes and saw she wasn't lying. "Then what are you the goddess of, if I may ask?"

Hela pointed off in the distance. "I am a goddess of this land that you stand on. What the Vikings called Asgard."

"Asgard, the home of the Norse gods?" Theseus asked, surprised.

"Indeed," Hela answered, amused. "Now, a question for you. What is a Greek demigod doing so far north from his home?"

"How can you tell I am a demigod and that I am from Greece?"

"It is in your blood, old warrior. I know the taste of Greek God blood. So, answer my question. What are you doing here?"

"I am here for you," said Theseus, not holding back the truth.

Hela sensing her own divine energy come from Theseus, looked at his clothes. "You tracked me by my divine energy."

"How can you tell?"

"I can sense my own energy on you," said Hela brandishing a Valkyrie sword. "Tell me, why did you come all this way from your home to meet me?"

Chapter 6: Goddess of The Valkyries

"I would like to avoid fighting you if I could," said Theseus nervously. "But I am bound by my Athenian code of honor, so I will not lie."

"Go on," Hela requested.

"One of my friends, James, has been cursed by the entity known as Death. In order to break that curse, we need a certain scroll that is currently in the possession of the God of Mischief, Loki."

"Loki again," Hela whispered in anger, hearing that name. "Let me guess, Loki has sent you here to collect me in exchange for that scroll."

"I expected as much from the Goddess of the Valkyries. Nothing gets past you. But it isn't just you Loki wants, Goddess Hela. Loki also wants four other beings of the Níu Heimar (Nine Worlds). "Fenrir the Black Wolf, Grendel the Ogre, Jörmungandr the Midgard Serpent, and Fýri the Ice Dragon. After we capture these beings alive, we are to bring them to Loki in exchange for the scroll."

That little trickster seeks the power of the Rökkr, Hela thought, troubled by Loki's intentions.

"I ask you Goddess Hela, will you come back with me? I know this is a selfish request, but as a warrior, please believe me," Theseus requested, speaking with sincerity.

Hearing enough, Hela waved her hand and released Theseus from his paralysis. "Honesty and honor are very rare traits to find in a man. And you are a handsome as well," said Hela, brushing Theseus' face gently. "I wonder, will you be able to satisfy me?"

"This is serious. I wouldn't be here if it wasn't," said Theseus, grabbing Hela's hand.

Hela looked into Theseus' eyes and saw the anger. "Such fury, such determination, it makes you all the more appealing."

Theseus let go of her hand as he reaffirmed his request. "Will you help me or not?"

Hela walked around the Yggdrasil tree as she mulled over the request.

"I would really like to avoid fighting you at all costs," said Theseus, following her.

"You are even careful with your words, and it also shows your intelligence," said Hela, impressed with Theseus' cautious nature. "Another compelling trait about you, warrior."

I can't repeat myself, or she might get angry, Theseus thought, being careful. *I have no choice. I have to use physical force.*"

82

Theseus ran to Hela and grabbed her by the shoulders. Hela took delight in this as she smiled.

"I will ask for the third and final time. Will you help me in this endeavor?"

Hela swatted his hands away and levitated Theseus into the air before slamming him against the tree, pinning him.

"I have seen the worst in men: their fear, their betrayal, their hatred, their deception. But when I look into your eyes, no others have had such an appeal as you," Hela said, leaning closer to Theseus.

Enticed with what she'd seen of Theseus, Hela kissed him passionately. Releasing him, she walked to the mountain's edge. "You have satisfied me a little, so I may consider helping you. But only if you can fully satisfy me," said Hela, looking back at him, smiling.

These warriors, they are Viking, Theseus thought, gazing down at the skeletons, disturbed.

Hela noticed Theseus gazing at the fallen warriors and chuckled. "It is not what you think. All these skeletons you see are of warriors of who fled during Ragnarök."

"And how did they die?" asked Theseus.

"I killed them," Hela answered casually. "The Norse Gods have no use for warriors who are cowards."

"And how do you want me to prove that I am not a coward?" Theseus asked, walking toward Hela.

"You are the first man to ask me that," Hela said, surprised, taking off her armor.

Theseus, embarrassed, felt an attraction to her as he gazed at her beauty. A bright yellow aura appeared around Hela, blinding Theseus. When the light dimmed, Theseus opened his eyes and saw Hela donned in Asgardian armor.

"Regardless of if it's a man or woman, the one thing that appeals to me the most is a show of strength," said Hela, challenging Theseus.

So, it has come to this, Theseus thought, not surprised by her challenge.

"Very well, I will show you my strength," said Theseus as a green aura enveloped him.

Donning Athenian Armor, Theseus drew his sword. "The power that defeated the Minotaur."

"Ah, so that is the legendary Athenian armor Μινώταυρος made from one of the horns of the Minotaur," said Hela, fixated on the armor.

Hela summoned a black sword, revealing it to Theseus. "This is the legendary goddess sword of the Norse Valkyries, Aklauss. It has been passed down to me by Frigg."

"That is the sword of the first Valkyrie," said Theseus, seeing its dark aura.

"Your knowledge impresses me to no end. I hope your strength is as impressive.

Hela swung her sword forward, but Theseus saw nothing. Silent, Hela pointed to clouds off in the distance. Looking on, Theseus saw the clouds split in half.

"This sword can strike as far as the land of Asgard. It is the reason why all Valkyries can appear and strike in any part of the Nine Worlds."

Theseus thought about Hela's words and knew that she could attack him from anywhere. He gripped his sword tightly. *But I can tell when she swung that sword, she must physically see what she wants to cut.*

Without warning, Hela swung her sword forward. Theseus blocked her attack. A gust blew violently around him, impressing her.

"Oh, you realized how my attacks work."

Theseus slashed his sword through, breaking apart the gust. "It was when you first swung your sword. When you swung at the clouds in the distance, they didn't immediately split apart. The air current created by the swing of your sword takes a few moments to slash what you see, depending on the distance. But that also means you can only cut what you see within your line of physical sight."

"Impressive, no one has ever deduced my power before," said Hela, offering her praise. "With that, you have truly piqued my interest." Hela smiled at Theseus. "But don't think that is the limit of my power."

Wanting to show Theseus more of her power, Hela slashed her sword at him. A violent gust of wind shot through the air toward Theseus.

"That attack will not work on me again," said Theseus, splitting the gust.

Hela, unmoved by Theseus's confidence, pointed at his leg. "Are you sure about that?"

Theseus looked down at his leg and saw a deep cut suddenly appear. Feeling the pain, he dropped to one knee. *What is going on? I was sure that I blocked her attack.* Placing his hand on the wound, Theseus tried to cover the bleeding. *Her attack cut deep but not to the tendon.* Theseus struggled to stand. *But still, what was that? Did she swing her sword twice? No, she couldn't have, I was watching, and I know for a fact that she only swung once*, Theseus thought, gazing at the Valkyrie's sword. *Whatever that attack was, I need to figure it out, or I am going to end up dead before too long."*

"You asked me before what Goddess I am, and I told you, I was the goddess," Hela said, pleased to see Theseus stand.

"What about it?"

"I am not just the Goddess of Asgard. I am also the Goddess of the Valkyries."

"I thought Frigg was the first Valkyrie?" Theseus asked, surprised. "Isn't that sword proof that she was the Goddess of the Valkyries?"

Hela held up one finger. "Both of your questions are correct; my mother Frigg was the first Valkyrie and also the goddess of them all. But by right, as her successor, she passed the Valkyrie sword Aklauss to me. I also inherited all of her titles and responsibilities that came with both the Valkyries and Asgard. That is why I am called the Inheritor of Valkyries and Goddess of them. "Now enough of this, I never did like talking for too long," said Hela, pointing her sword at Theseus. "But since you have so many enticing traits, I will not hold it against you."

"Very well, Valkyrie Goddess, I will not keep you waiting any longer."

Hela smiled as she charged at Theseus. He blocked the sword pushing her back. "Apologetic and appeasing, two more traits enticing in a man. I think I will give you an award."

Not able to push back against Theseus, Hela jumped back. She slashed her sword through the air and a gust of wind at Theseus. Theseus again cut through the gust but was cut on the shoulder.

It happened again, Theseus thought, grabbing his shoulder in pain.

Swinging her sword again, something caught Theseus' attention. Theseus blocked the attack but got cut on the arm. *Wait, that's it. When she swung her sword, there was a slight flick of her wrist.*

"What is this? Are you resigning to your fate?"

"No, I'm not. I was thinking I want to test something."

Hela raised her sword. "Whatever it may be, it will not work."

Theseus closed his eyes when she swung her sword at him. Theseus blocked her attack but wasn't cut.

"What is going on?" Hela asked, surprised. "Why didn't my attack cut you?"

"I figured out your attack," said Theseus, lowering his sword. "When you swing your sword, it may appear you are swinging once, but you are swinging twice. It was your wrist. When you first swing your sword, I can see the attack coming. But you twitch your wrist slightly, and then in less than a blink of an eye, the second swing comes."

"You figured that all out by only seeing it a few times," said Hela, impressed. "Your intelligence for taking the time and figuring out my power is brilliantly seductive. But you still haven't demonstrated your physical strength to me."

Theseus looked down at the deep cut on his arm. *I can barely use my arm. I need to end this now.*

"Your strength as Goddess of the Valkyries is truly unmatched."

Theseus put his sword back in its sheath as he took a battle stance. "Very well, I will show you my true strength."

Hela took a defensive stance. "Come, let us end this."

Planting his feet deep into the ground, Theseus charged at her with great force and speed. Hela guarded herself with her sword as Theseus pulled out his and struck against hers. A shockwave erupted from their clash, shaking the earth and dividing the clouds. In a split second, Theseus spun around, creating a vacuum of wind between them.

"Άνω Αιγαίο (Upper Aegean)," said Theseus, slashing sword upward.

The slash knocked Hela back violently as her sword fell from her hand.

Theseus wrapped his hand around her back, saving her from falling. With a swing of his sword, he disbursed the wind. "Well, that was a close one."

"You saved me," Hela said.

"Well, you did say you wanted to see my strength, but I still need you with me. Are you now satisfied with my strength?" Theseus asked, sheathing his sword.

Hela, pleased by Theseus' show of strength, wrapped her hands around him. "Yes, more than even I could handle."

"Does that mean I pass?"

"Not yet, let's see how you handle me first, but first, let us get you cleaned up," said Hela, rubbing Theseus' face.

Theseus swept Hela off her feet as he carried her to the Yggdrasil tree. "Hopefully, this demigod can satisfy the goddess of all Valkyries."

Many hours passed as Theseus spent the night with Hela. He woke in a daze and realized his time was nearly up. "That much time has passed."

Hela walked over to him. "I see you have awakened, old warrior."

"I am pressed for time, so I will only ask you this once," said Theseus, getting up. "Have I fully satisfied you for you to come with me?"

Hela pulled Theseus closed to her, kissing him. "That and then some."

Theseus was relieved. "What will you do when you are with Loki?"

Hela snapped her fingers, dispelling her armor. "Do not worry about that. Loki has sought my power for the longest time. The contract you have with him works in my favor, for it gives me a chance to avenge the Norse Pantheon for his betrayal."

"I am for your plan, but you must wait until the contract with him is complete," said Theseus, letting her know his concern. "The scroll we seek is the key to saving my friend's life. He has tied the scroll to his life. If you were to kill him before the contract ends, the scroll will burn and be reduced to nothing but ashes."

"I see, so if anything were to happen to him during this timeframe, the scroll you seek will be destroyed," said Hela, seeing Theseus' reasoning.

"Yes. We have tried to come up with different solutions, but Loki has foreseen nearly all possible outcomes."

Hela caressed Theseus' cheek gently as she walked past him toward the Yggdrasil tree. "Well, there is me that he won't account for. But I will wait until the contract ends, and if he double-crosses you, I will take the scroll myself and hand it to you."

"You would do that? Me, a person you just met."

Hela stopped at the mountain's edge, looked back at Theseus, and smiled. "Old warrior, I am a Goddess. I can do anything I want. You have shown me your strength and valor. All the right traits that I love in a man and more. The least I can do is reward you for your effort."

"But what about the Yggdrasil tree?" Theseus asked, looking up at the life tree.

Hela looked up and watched the leaves change colors like a rainbow. "That is not a problem. I was only visiting here. But I guess I should place a guard here, just in case of intruders." Hela whistled, and a large grey wolf appeared before them.

"Garm, my dear, I need you to watch over this place for a little while," said Hela, petting the wolf.

Garm jumped up, barking up in excitement. Jumping up on top of a tall branch, he began his watch over the domain.

"Is this Garm, one of Odin's guardian wolves?" Theseus asked, astonished seeing one of the legendary wolves.

"The wolves of Odin have watched over this land for thousands of years," said Hela. "Since their wolf ancestors left them here to learn. But we really don't have time to talk about them, do we?"

"You're right, we don't," said Theseus, pulling out his mystica jewel.

"What is that?" Hela asked, curious about the jewel.

"This is the jewel I used to teleport here. I am supposed to use it to teleport back. Stand close to me because I am now going to start."

The blue vortex developed around them as they disappeared. "Teleport."

"He barely has any time left," said Chase, noticing Theseus' time was almost up.

Amphion opened his eyes, looking at Chase. "How long do we have left?"

"Thirty-one hours and fifty-five minutes."

"Then we best move to the hunt," said Theseus outside.

Seeing Theseus, Chase rushed over and opened the back of the airship for him. "Where is Hel?"

Hela appeared behind Chase.

"Right behind you."

Chase reached for his pistol, but Theseus stopped him. "Easy Chase. She is here to help us."

"Are you sure? She is one of the Rökkr," Chase said, letting go of his pistol.

"I was able to talk to her and convince her to help."

"What did you have to do to convince her to help? Does she know of everything?"

"Yes, she knows. She has her own vendetta against Loki. And before you speak, she knows about the scroll and that it is tied to Loki's life."

Hela walked into the airship and stood in front of the others. "I will not kill Loki until your contract with him ends. If he tries to betray you after you complete the contract, if I get the chance, I will take this scroll from him and hand it over to you personally."

"I did not account for any of this," said Chase, surprised by Hela's assistance.

Theseus tapped Chase on the shoulder. "Ya, and neither did Loki. The last thing he would suspect is one of the Rökkr aiming for his life. He will think we incapacitated all of them when we hand them over to him."

"That is true, but I don't think things will go that smoothly. It is always good to have a backup plan if things go south."

As Theseus walked inside to rest, Chase whispered to him. "Wait, you didn't tell me how you managed to convince Hel."

Theseus remained silent as Hela overheard Chase. "First off, it's Hela, and second, let's just say he showed me how strong he was."

He didn't do what I think he did, did he? Chase thought, confused.

Chase looked at Theseus and saw his embarrassed look. *He did. He laid with her. I can't be thinking about this right row.*

Chase took the scanner from Theseus and placed the scale of Fýri into it.

"Alright, just a little more, and I got it," said Chase, pinpointing the ice dragon's location.

"You found Fýri's location?" Arthur asked, looking at the map.

"Ya, he is in the Glittertind Mountains, which, if I remember correctly, is the second highest mountain in Norway."

Arthur hit his fist against his hand in excitement. "Excellent, Merlin always had me fight dragons in my youth. I have an abundance of experience fighting them."

"Ya, I bet you do, King," Chase said, laughing as he handed him the scanner.

"Alright, the scanner is configured with the jewel, so you will now be able to teleport to Glittertind Mountains. All you have to do when you get there is follow Fýri's mystic signature, and it will lead you straight to him."

"Alright, leave it to me."

"I set the timer to twelve hours. Once you capture him, teleport back here using the mystica jewel. If you fail to capture him within the twelve-hour time frame, the jewel will teleport you back here." Chase hit Arthur against his chest. "Alright, Your Majesty, bring us back a dragon."

Standing outside in the falling snow, Arthur looked back at Chase. "Have no worry, my friend. I will find this dragon and defeat it."

"I know, I was just making sure you know," said Chase, smiling at Arthur.

The blue vortex surrounded Arthur as he smiled back.

"Be careful, this dragon isn't any dragon. Fýri is a dragon of ice, one more powerful than any other dragon that breathes fire."

Arthur nodded his head yes and disappeared into the vortex.

Chapter 7: The Dragon of Ice

A few minutes passed. Arthur appeared on a ledge of the Glittertind Mountains. The blizzard had caused the ledge to be icy, causing Arthur to lose his balance and tumble down the side. Arthur grabbed out for anything he could find to stop his fall. The drop was sheer and ended in rocks.

"That was close," said Arthur, grabbing the ledge, looking at the drop below. Arthur was grateful that Chase had provided him with the best winter and mountaineering gear. It was the highest peak in Norway and certainly a treacherous climb in good weather, much less a blizzard.

Arthur held the scanner up to the mountain as it tracked Fýri's mystic energy. He was able to track the energy coming from a peak not too far off. He guessed it would be another two hours before he arrived. Arthur adjusted his jacket and picked up his pace, fearing the blizzard would worsen.

Fýri opened his pale blue eyes after centuries of sleep when he sensed another presence in his domain.

It was strong and more powerful than any he'd sensed in centuries. Not since the Age of Dragons.

Fýri snarled in annoyance at the intrusion. "Whatever reason this presence has come here for, I will freeze them where they stand," said Fýri, breathing its icy breath.

Feeling relief Fýri laid back down and fell asleep on vast piles of gold, thinking that perhaps the intrusion would be entertaining—he hadn't been challenged in centuries.

After a couple of hours, Arthur reached the peak of Glittertind Mountain. He explored the area, looking for the ice dragon but was unable to find him. Arthur was annoyed at the limited visibility but also wondered if the scanner had led him to the correct location.

A loud roar suddenly shook the mountain. Arthur lost his footing and fell in the snow. The beast had roared and caused an avalanche.

Before he could react, the avalanche hit Arthur at full force. Tumbling through the snow down the mountain, he went over a cliff and fell several feet in a pile of snow on the mountain's side. Arthur was able to dig himself out of the snow but grew scared when he looked up and saw another wall of snow falling toward him. He was buried again but was able to dig himself out.

"Ah, I almost suffocated. Where am I now?" Arthur asked out loud, trying to get his bearings. He looked up and saw that he'd been pushed down the mountain a few feet.

Another roar sounded as another avalanche came down. Sighing, Arthur braced himself for another wall of snow. When it didn't come, Arthur opened his eyes and saw an avalanche had not been generated by the last roar.

Arthur brushed the snow off and noticed a cave that he hadn't seen before. It had probably been buried beneath the snow. Arthur pointed the scanner at the entrance of the cave and saw Fýri's energy signal—the dragon was in the cave. The signature hadn't been coming from the top of the mountain after all.

Arthur moved cautiously inside the cave as there was ice everywhere making the footing slippery. Merlin had always cautioned Arthur to be careful around ice. *Come to think of it, why did Merlin always say that?* Arthur wondered.

He continued walking into the cave, and even though he stepped carefully, Arthur lost his footing and slid some distance down an icy path, slamming hard onto a huge pile of gold.

Arthur stood, amazed by all the gold he saw. "By Merlin's beard, even when I was King of Britain, never have I seen such a treasury."

"Take one step forward, and I will freeze you where you stand," said Fýri, his voice echoing through the cavern.

"Who is there? Is it you they call Fýri?" Arthur demanded, now on his guard.

"You know who I am?"

Arthur noticed a large white tail by his feet. "Of course. You are the legendary ice dragon of the Norse, whose wealth in gold is vast."

Fýri impressed, raised from a pile of gold. He lowered his head toward Arthur and looked at him with his pale blue eyes. "Don't think all that praise will stop me from killing you."

"I don't expect it too," said Arthur, not fearing the dragon. "You are definitely as the legend describes. The dragon whose scales are as white as the snow itself."

Fýri dismissed Arthur's praise. Arthur felt the chill of the dragon's breath—so cold, it formed ice.

"Tell me why you have come here," Fýri commanded. "Did you come to steal my gold? Or have you come to slay me?"

Arthur remained calm. "Neither one."

Fýri was surprised by Arthur's answer.

"I speak honestly when I say this. I am here to hopefully convince you to come with me to help a friend."

Fýri remained silent, listening to Arthur's heartbeat. *He is not lying*, he thought before speaking. "Very well, I will listen to what you have to say."

"Do you know the Norse God, Loki?"

"I know the God of Mischief, Loki," said Fýri, answering in an angry tone. "The one who sods mistrust and deceit. The one who led the Norse Gods to their demise."

"You see, the Norse God of Mischief, Loki, has something that will help save my friend, but in order to get that, I was tasked with capturing you and turn you over to him alive."

Unnerved by Arthur's words, Fýri circled its head around him. "And what is it that you seek from Loki?"

"It is called the Heavenly Life-Lock scroll. It has the power to save my best friend's life," Arthur answered honestly.

"And do you think that if you turn me over to him that Loki will just give you this scroll?"

"I don't know if he will honor his part of the deal or not. After all, he is the least trustworthy of all the Norse Gods. I made a promise to help save my friend's life." Arthur walked toward Fýri and looked him in the eye. "I intend to keep it."

Looking into Arthur's eyes, Fýri felt the gravity of Arthur's words. *There is sincerity in his eyes. To think a human in this age would be capable of that.*

"That is why I make this request to you. Will you help me in this matter?"

Fýri whipped its tail into the pile of gold, spreading it everywhere. "And what makes you think I will help you?"

"What do you want? What will it take to convince you?" Arthur asked without fear.

Fýri looked away from Arthur, thinking about Loki. "I don't really care for Loki. In fact, I would prefer it if he was dead."

"That is our intention once our contract with the trickster is done. The Valkyrie Goddess herself will see to that, for she has a grudge against the God of Mischief."

"Hela the Goddess of the Valkyries," Fýri whispered under its breath.

"I may consider honoring your request on one condition."

"And what would that be?" Arthur asked, slowly reaching for his sword.

Fýri chuckled at Arthur. "For a sincere human, you sure think like all the others—thinking that all dragons are nothing but bringers of chaos and destruction. That is the same mistake Beowulf made when he came to slay me. But since I have awakened from centuries of sleep, I would like to hear a tale from a lost hero. A tale of your life story from your beginning to end. After I hear it, then will I make my decision."

Arthur was nervous by the dragon's response. "A decision?"

Fýri slowly breathed ice. "Yes, a decision to honor your request or freeze you where you stand. So, decide now—leave and be spared or stay and take that chance."

Arthur stood his ground. "I have come all this way just to see you, I am not leaving now. I made a promise, and I will see it through."

Then you have made your choice," said Fýri, impressed with Arthur's courage.

Fýri blew its icy breath encasing Arthur in ice up to his neck. "I will leave your head out for you to breathe, but if your story bores me in the slightest, I will freeze you solid, and you will become nothing more than an ice statue for me to break."

"Well, since my life depends on your mood, I will be sure not to bore you," said Arthur, smiling confidently. "But I must warn you, my story is not an easy one to tell."

Fýri laid down in front of Arthur. "I will listen from beginning to end, it matters not to me how you tell it."

"Alright then, now where should I start?"

Arthur then closed his eyes, remembering his destiny.

"It started when my master Merlin and I were training in the countryside of Camelot. It was at that time he revealed to me that I had been chosen by destiny. Chosen by the Sisters of Fates, to remove the holy sword Excalibur from the rock and to save Britain by becoming king."

Arthur told his life story to the ice dragon over the next eight hours, from its blessed beginnings all the way to its tragic end.

"I have told you my whole life story from my beginnings, all the way to my resurrection now. Now, what is your decision?" Arthur requested, opening his eyes.

Fýri chuckled. "An interesting, heroic, and tragic tale. One very worthy of praise by the Gods for its self-sacrifice. Before I make my decision, I have one final question. If you take this scroll to save your friend's life, what would you do then? What would you do with your second life?"

"I haven't thought about it much. But since my friends struggle and suffer from the actions of others, they still smile and stay together despite all of that. I'm inclined to stay with them. It reminds me of when I was with my mentor Merlin and my friends of the Knights of the Round Table. How despite all odds, despite all tragedy we faced in our lives, we will be gathered around to drink ale at the table. When I was king, I realized this sword is not what defines me and my legacy. It is the actions I take and my friends who define who I am. What I seek from my second life is to help them in any way I can. That is my answer to you," said Arthur proudly.

"Now tell me, dragon of ice, what is your answer?"

Fýri opened his eyes as a blizzard appeared, blinding Arthur. After a few moments, a sword cut through the ice around Arthur, freeing him.

"Who are you?" Arthur asked, seeing a man wearing a wolf pelt.

"We have made my decision," said the man, staring at Arthur with his pale blue eyes. "I have decided to help you not with just this task with Loki, but to help you look over your friends to make sure you and they stay true to themselves."

"Then you are the ice dragon, Fýri. I didn't know you could change into a human."

"Originally, I was human a long time ago when I faced the dragon here."

"Wait, does that mean you are?"

"Correct, I am Beowulf."

"How are you still alive? I thought the ice dragon killed you."

"In a sense, it did, but when I fought the dragon, as both of us were dying from our battle, our bodies somehow fused. His conscious with mine."

Wanting to calm Arthur's fears, Beowulf placed his hand over his heart. "I am both Beowulf, the Viking hero, and the ice dragon Fýri. With your help and mine, we can help those boys forge it. This is the promise I make to you, Arthur, my new friend."

"I am glad, my new friend, may we help them have a bright future," said Arthur, shaking hands with Beowulf.

Arthur looked at all the gold around them. "By the way, why all the gold?

"That was the same question I had for the ice dragon when I faced it," said Beowulf, chuckling. "He never gave me an answer. But after we merged, I found out the reason."

"What was it?"

Smiling, Beowulf did not answer Arthur as he stood in front of all the gold. "What would you have me do with all this gold? It would be a waste if it stayed here."

"Well, we could use it on our journey, and as you said, it would be a waste to leave it here."

"You mentioned you came to Norway with your friends. Where are they now?"

"They are waiting for me just outside Trondheim."

Beowulf snapped his fingers, and suddenly, all the gold disappeared.

"What did you do?" Arthur asked, surprised.

"I teleported it to your friends," said Beowulf, smiling.

Laughing, Arthur placed his hand on Beowulf's shoulder. "Once we get done with this journey, you and I have to drink some ale to consummate our new friendship."

"I would like that."

Back at the airship, Chase was looking over his weapons. "This stuff always gets dirty."

Chase looked up when he heard a strange sound and saw a shadow form above him. "What is that? Oh no," said Chase as a pile of gold buried him.

"Chase, are you alright?" Theseus asked, rushing over.

"Ya, I am fine," Chase said, digging himself out of the gold. "What?"

"Where did all of this gold come from?"

"Well, I didn't expect gold dropping on my head, but we could definitely use it," said Chase, laughing.

Back at Glittertind Mountain, Arthur and Beowulf walked to the cave entrance. The blizzard was still strong. "Well, I see, the storm has not broken yet. Aren't you cold?" Arthur asked, seeing Beowulf walking outside.

"To us Vikings, weather like this is normal."

Arthur chuckled and walked out into the storm and stood next to Beowulf. "Well, we're all heroes in the end regardless of what region we herald from."

"Indeed."

"Teleport," Arthur spoke.

Arthur and Beowulf disappeared into the blue vortex, teleporting back to the others.

Chapter 8: The Black Wolf

"I'm back," Arthur announced as he and Beowulf appeared.

"Where is the ice dragon, Fýri?" Chase said as he rushed over to greet Arthur.

"This man right here shares a body with Fýri," Arthur explained, pointing at Beowulf.

"Wait, what?" said Chase, dumbfounded.

Sharing the same bodies should be impossible, but there have been some rare cases where two bodies joined together and became one, Chase thought, looking at Beowulf. A *man and a dragon sharing the same body should be impossible because their anatomies are completely different. According to legend, it's only happened once.*

Arthur tried to explain, but Chase didn't want to hear. "Don't explain. I'll hear everything you have to say when we have time."

"Since you're standing right here next to my friend, I take it you are here of your own free will."

"I am, Arthur has explained everything, and I am here to offer my assistance in any way I can," said Beowulf, easing Chase's mind.

"Then welcome aboard, I am Chase,"

"Thank you. I am Beowulf."

"Wait, Beowulf, the Viking hero?"

"The same. I see my legacy has survived through the ages for you to know about me." Noticing Chase had doubts, Beowulf continued. "I can tell you have doubts. I can't say that I blame you. After all, the stories did say I perished. But I assure you, I am Beowulf."

Beowulf walked outside, conjured a blue aura, and transformed into Fýri. "I did not perish that day— I survived."

"I see your mind and body fused with Fýri."

"Yes. Do you still have doubts about me?" Beowulf asked, transforming back into human form.

"No, once you transformed into a dragon, I was convinced."

Pulling out a book from his backpack, Chase showed it to Beowulf. "And, because of this. This book here tells your true story."

"I didn't realize my story was written."

"The known written history about you does mention you did battle with Grendel and his mother," said Chase, showing Beowulf the passages. Even your battle with the ice dragon, but most written texts say you perished in that battle. This one alone has the true written accounts of those events—including your merge with Fýri."

"Then why did you doubt me before I transformed?"

"I used to believe everything I read. That was until I witnessed true history itself. So, when I saw you change into your dragon form, I knew then what was written into this book was true."

"Since we are talking about Beowulf, Chase, did you receive all that gold I sent?" Arthur asked, interrupting them.

"Wait, that was you? You sent all that gold that fell on me?" Chase asked angrily.

"Actually, that was him," Arthur said, pointing to Beowulf. "He was the one who teleported it."

"All of that gold fell on top of me. My head is still thumping because of that."

Beowulf chuckled in amusement. "I can tell why you two are friends."

"Anyway, how did you teleport that gold?" Chase asked, letting go of Arthur.

"It is one of the ice dragons' abilities. He can teleport any item within his sight, to anyone or anyplace," Beowulf explained.

"Really?"

Then with his ability, he could teleport the Heavenly Life-Lock scroll out of Loki's hand if he sees it, Chase thought, realizing the usefulness of Beowulf's ability.

"Do you know everything, including our deal with Loki?"

"Yes, but not all the details."

"Then let me ask you this. If you saw a scroll in Loki's hands, would you be able to teleport it?"

"Yes, as long as the dragon or I see it and as long as I know the person who is receiving it. I can teleport it anywhere."

So that's why that gold fell on me. "The reason the gold appeared to me is that you knew my name."

"That is why all the gold from the ice cave appeared before you."

Chase's stopwatch started sounding. Looking, Chase noticed the set time was up. "It has been ten hours."

"Then it is my turn now," said Ulf, jumping out into the snow.

My turn to hunt, Ulf thought, thinking about Fenrir. *To hunt the black wolf Fenrir.*

He's still thinking about that. I hope his rage won't cloud his judgment, Chase thought.

"We only have twenty-four hours left."

Chase configured the scanner to track Fenrir's mystic energy. "Alright, I have his location. Fenrir is in the Torghatten Mountains, which is on the Northern Isles of Norway."

Chase strapped the scanner to Ulf's leg. "Remember, don't let your personal feelings get the best of you. Do this for James's sake."

110

"I know," Ulf whispered.

The jewel is configured with the scanner so that you can teleport to Torghatten Mountain. I know how you feel. I feel the same way about Devoid still being alive. I promise you, you and I will settle our grudges against them one day."

Seeing the conviction in Chase's eyes, Ulf nodded his yes. "For James then."

"For James," said Chase.

Ulf tapped his paw, and the mystica jewel glowed bright. "Teleport."

The blue vortex surrounded him; Ulf teleported away.

Don't let this encounter change you. Remember who you are and stay true to that. If you can do that, then you will be able to overcome any darkness that stands in your way. Even the one of the black wolf, Chase thought, looking at the night sky.

Seeing what transpired between them, Beowulf stared at Chase. *They must be Norse descendants from what I sensed from them.*

Arthur placed his hand on Beowulf. "Do not worry, my friend, the wolf and he will be fine."

"I know, but when I looked at them both, I see something about those two felt familiar," said Beowulf walking inside with Arthur.

"Familiar, how?"

"Like people I once knew from my past."

Ulf appeared on the shore close to Torghatten Mountain.

"You have come, descendant Aesir," said Ulf angrily, sensing Fenrir's presence. Turning around, Ulf saw a large black wolf sitting on a rock on the shore. "Fenrir."

"Huh, a growl of a little pup," said Fenrir sarcastically as the tide crashed against the shore.

Ulf rushed at Fenrir, but the black wolf jumped out of the way as the other smashed through the rock. "Too little power."

Ulf tried to attack Fenrir again, but Fenrir appeared in front of him. Fenrir bit down on Ulf's neck, throwing him to the ground, and then pressed his large paw against Ulf's neck, pinning him.

"What is the matter, little pup, done already?"

Ulf, in pain from the bite, looked up at Fenrir. "Tell me why. Why did you betray Aesir?"

"Even if I were to explain it to you, I doubt you would understand," said Fenrir, closing his eyes.

"Why?"

Clamping his jaws on Ulf, Fenrir threw him into a boulder. Ulf struggled to stand.

"I'm not done," Ulf said.

Fenrir scoffed in disappointment at Ulf. "If you are the reincarnation of Aesir, then show it to me."

"Not yet."

Growing impatient with Ulf not showing his strength, Fenrir charged at him. As Fenrir drew close,

Ulf waited for his moment to attack. Suddenly, Ulf scratched Fenrir across his snout.

"Not enough," said Fenrir, rubbing the blood off his snout.

In retaliation, Fenrir bit down on Ulf's neck and dragged Ulf along the rocky ground. Ulf struggled to free himself as Fenrir's fangs gashed into his neck. Ulf bit into Fenrir, freeing himself, and then retreated a safe distance.

Impressed by Ulf's ferociousness, Fenrir looked at him as blood dripped from his mouth. "I will acknowledge this, little pup, you do have some bite behind your fangs."

Ulf, feeling weak, charged an aura around him. "I haven't begun to get started yet."

"Then show me your true strength, little pup. Your strength as Aesir," Fenrir barked.

Ulf and Fenrir charged at each other, beginning their long battle. After a couple of hours, Ulf, unable to overcome Fenrir, collapsed from exhaustion.

Fenrir, wounded and gashed, stood tall over him. "You are still not there yet; you still lack Aesir's strength." Ulf barely moved. "If you will not show me your true power, then I will have to tear you apart until you do."

A black aura started around Fenrir as he started to get bigger. "I will now show you true fear."

His appearance became more monstrous. "This is my true form as I once devoured this whole sky during Ragnarök." Fenrir bit down on Ulf and flung him around, ripping into him. "It seems this is the end for you. How disappointing," said Fenrir, seeing Ulf not moving. Fenrir pressed his paw on Ulf's neck, preparing to kill him. "For your effort, I will at least give you a merciful end."

Ulf looked up at the night sky as he started to lose consciousness. *Is this how it ends? Will I really be killed by my most hated enemy?* Ulf ground his teeth in defiance. *No, I refuse to die here. I don't care about my hatred anymore. Please, grant me the power to stop Fenrir. Not for myself, but to help save my friend, James,* Ulf thought, asking for help.

Opening his eyes, Ulf saw a silhouette of a white wolf stand in front of him. "You have the power of me within you. You always have. Remember who you are." The white wolf turned walked away. "Remember who you are, and stay true to that. Now awaken, awaken and show him your true self," said the white wolf, dashing into the sky, disappearing.

Suddenly, Fenrir felt a quake come from Ulf. Seeing a white aura glimmer from Ulf, Fenrir was blown away. Fenrir regained his balance and looked on as Ulf changed and grew bigger. "That is the true power I sought." Ulf opened his white eyes and stared at Fenrir.

"Now show me true power. Your power as Aesir," Ulf heard the voice of the white wolf.

Thank you, ancestor, for your words, Ulf thought.

"I now remember who I am. I am the descendant of the white wolf," Ulf proclaimed.

Ulf's fur turned completely white as he howled. The wind howled, and the water vibrated from Ulf's howl.

Fenrir excited, prepared himself. "It doesn't matter what you have become. Your power will still not surpass me, little pup."

Ulf stopped howling and took a step forward. "Time to find out."

Ulf and Fenrir charged at each other as their battle resumed. After several hours, they reached a stalemate. Heavily wounded and exhausted, both of them collapsed.

"You ask me why," Fenrir faintly whispered. Why did I betray Aesir?" Ulf struggled to lift his head. "I will now tell you the reason. For centuries I was bound by Norse Gods because they feared my power. Aesir was the only one not afraid of me, and he was the only one who understood me."

"Then why did you betray him?" Ulf demanded.

"Aesir and I were one in the same at one time."

"What? There has never been mention by my ancestors that you were once a part of Aesir. The only thing my grandfather Night told me was that you were the one who betrayed him and that you were the reason he was dead with Thor during Ragnarök."

Fenrir chuckled. "That betrayal that you talk about, it was the separation of our original self. The whole of Aesir."

"I am the dark part of him that was split from him."

"Then who split you in two?"

"It was Odin. At one time, we were loved by all of Asgard," Fenrir revealed. "Over time, as Ragnarök fast approached, Odin, in fear of our power, split us apart. But it was that fear that set the chain of events of Ragnarök in motion. Aesir became the destined companion of Thor, who stood with him during his final battle. Odin realizing, he made a mistake, bound me in Asgard for centuries. I broke free from my bonds several times, and in revenge for my imprisonment, I slew and devoured Odin. In my anger, I continued to grow and devour the sky for days. When I learned how to control my size, I went looking for Aesir. But by the time I found him, he was already dead—killed by the Serpent of Midgard who killed Thor."

"If this is true, why are you here now? If you were once one in the same wolf, why fight me at all?"

Fenrir, bleeding from his wounds, stood up. Staggering, and picked Ulf up. "Because you are his reincarnation and to bring out your true potential as Aesir."

"You seek to become whole again?" Ulf asked, looking into his eyes.

Fenrir shook his head yes. "I have waited for so long for you to return."

"I can't merge with you—at least not yet."

"Loki?"

"Yes."

"But I promise you once is this all over, we will be whole again."

Fenrir smiled as he lost consciousness. "Thank you."

Ulf pulled out his mystica jewel just before losing consciousness too. "Teleport."

Enveloped by the blue vortex, they disappeared. Emerging from the vortex, Ulf, with Fenrir on his back, staggered toward the airship. Chase, hearing Ulf's howl, rushed to greet him, catching him before he fell.

"He is with us," Ulf whispered as he lost consciousness.

It seems you are lighter now, Chase thought, bringing him up.

Walking over to them, Arthur picked up Fenrir. "The black wolf, Fenrir."

Gazing over at the black wolf, Chase's eyes turned lightning blue as he had a vision of what happened between them. *I understand.* Welcome home, old friend.

Chase's eyes turned back to normal as he and Arthur walked into the airship. "Fenrir is going to help us too."

"Splendid. The more, the better," Arthur said, laying Fenrir down next to Ulf.

Seeing the severity of Ulf's and Fenrir's wounds, Chase looked toward Amphion. "Amphion, can you heal them?"

"I will do what I can," said Amphion, kneeling to evaluate their wounds.

Chase handed Amphion some healing sapphire stones. "Use these, they may not do much, but they will help treat the injuries."

Amphion nodded his head and started treating Ulf and Fenrir.

"Now then," Chase began.

"Now all that is left is to capture the Midgard Serpent," said Theseus.

"Ya."

"I will leave you to your thoughts then. Take as much time as you need to prepare."

Only thirteen hours left until this all ends, Chase thought as he looked at the timer.

Loki sat, drinking mead in a pub in Trondheim, watching the sand in the hourglass fall to the bottom. "Only thirteen hours to go, and then the real fun begins. They have already captured four of the Rökkr. So, at the pace that they are going, I say they are making good time. Wouldn't you agree?" Loki asked, staring at the dark side of the room.

A hooded figure emerged from the darkness. "Yes, all we need now is to push Actaeonis over the edge. Once Actaeonis is broken, and his despair is unleashed, lure him to the Ice Wall," said the hooded figure, glancing back at Loki by the door.

"Then what do you want me to do with Jörmungandr after he is back in my possession?"

"Use him however you see fit. Just make sure the power of Thor within Actaeonis is awakened. With that power, he will then lift Thor's hammer of, and the frozen seal will finally be broken. Make sure you follow our plan accordingly. There will be no forgiveness for failure," the hooded figured warned coldly.

"I'll be sure to," Loki said, taking a sip of his mead. "The expression on his face when I take his only hope to save his friend will be all the more fun. And through that despair, will give him all the motivation he needs."

Turning his attention back to the hourglass, Loki smiled. "This is beginning to be interesting."

Waving his hand, a reflection appeared. Loki looked through it and saw Devoid standing on a mountain as snow fell. Swirling his mead, Loki took a drink. "But the game is just getting started."

Loki disappeared, leaving a joker card on the table. A hand reappeared and grabbed the card. "Forgot my card."

Chapter 9: Fall of The Black Order

Chase prepared for his turn to hunt. Thinking about his family, Chase remembered the darkest day of his life—the night his parents were killed in front of him by Devoid. Recalling his time training with Sepher and their final moment together on Hvannadalshnúku,

Chase went outside into the cold night. *Now let's get this over with.*

Placing the fang of Jörmungandr into the scanner, Chase configured it to Devoid's mystic signature as it tracked all of Norway. "Found you. Fannaråki Mountain," Chase whispered, looking at the map.

Arthur walked outside and handed Chase a mystica jewel. "This is the last one, and then it is over."

"Ya, one more, and we can finally get the Life-Lock scroll."

"Are you sure you're up for this?"

"Ya, I've taken all the time I need to prepare."

"Alright then, we leave the rest to you. Go and complete your hunt," Arthur said, slapping Chase on the shoulder.

Stepping back, Chase disappeared into the blue vortex.

On top of Fannaråki Mountain, Devoid looked at the wilderness below. "This time, you will not escape," said Devoid, smirking, sensing Chase draw near.

A black aura formed around as he changed into the Midgard Serpent. Wrapping his serpent body around the mountain, Devoid breathed his poison in the sky. "This time, I shall give you true despair."

Chase emerged from the vortex at the shore of a lake. "You're there," Chase said, climbing up the ledge as the blizzard bore down on him.

Chase struggled to see his timer. "There is no time to lose. I have to finish this before it is too late."

Feeling a presence watching him, Chase looked up at the clouds above him. "Loki, I know you are watching, so let me tell you this. I will not play your game, but I will see this through and uphold my side of the deal. And when this is over, you will die."

James, just wait a little longer. I promised I'd be there when you woke up. And that is a promise I am going to keep, Chase thought.

Leon walked down the hall at the Black Order base, looking at the paperwork in his hand.

"Normally, people knock before they enter my office," said Leon, seeing a man in a black suit and sunglasses sitting in his chair.

"I would under normal circumstances, but this is not one of them," said the man in black, getting up to approach Leon.

Leon smirked, sitting down in his chair. "Alright. What can I do for the executioner of the mages today?"

The man pulled out paperwork, tossed it on the desk. "I will get straight to the business then. I'm here on the request of the E.U., and it has come to their attention that two of your operatives are now rogue. With the Radix Magic Accords that was agreed upon between the E.U. and the Mages Association, this is unacceptable."

"Yes, but we have already taken the steps in handling the matter," said Leon, trying to dismiss the concerns. "They have been marked for death, and once they are caught, they will be executed for violating the accords."

The man started to sort through the paperwork. "And yet they are still alive. For months they have alluded capture. If those two are allowed to live, it sets a dangerous precedent for mages and hunters that they don't have to follow the rules that have been in place since the end of World War II."

"Yes, and we will handle them once they are in our custody," Leon assured.

The man in black adjusted his sunglasses. "That is the problem—you will not have any involvement in this matter. The E.U, and Mages Association have appointed me to handle this personally."

Before Leon could respond, the man in black pointed to the paperwork. "The incident in Iceland that involved Akatsuki and Actaeonis, over 102,000 lives lost. Another incident they were involved in, the earthquake in Greece, over 3,000 lives lost."

"Well, it is like the contracts, situations come about where events like that are unavoidable," Leon justified.

The man in black chuckled. "That is nothing but a poor excuse from a leader who can't control his men. It is also inscribed on those contracts for hunters to minimize the damage caused by the supernatural as much as possible. Their recklessness and your carelessness are the cause of these disasters, and that is unacceptable."

Leon leaned back in his chair. "Then what do suggest we do?"

"You will do nothing," said the man in black, dismissing him. "In light of these recent catastrophes and the Black Order's careless actions, the European Union has decided unanimously to withhold and cancel all further contracts with the Black Order."

"The Black Order has dedicated years to protecting the secrets of the supernatural and hunting threats in it," said Leon, getting up from his chair. "We have maintained our pledges to protect Europe, you have no right."

Remaining calm, the man in black looked up at Leon. "And you have failed to uphold those pledges, as you have failed to reign in Akatsuki and Actaeonis." As of this moment, as decreed by the first vampire Primogenitor, the Black Order is to be erased," the man in black decreed, staring blankly at Leon.

Standing up, the man in black took off his sunglasses as he walked toward him. "You were warned not to stand in our way, and now you will pay the price."

"You are… you are Jonathan Cain of the fourth blood," Leon said, recognizing the man in black.

Cain folded his sunglasses and put them away. "I prefer to be called Cain, but whatever suits you is fine."

Without warning, Cain grabbed Leon by the throat, lifting and pressing him against the wall.

Leon struggled to breathe as Cain squeezed his throat. "Primogenitors usually don't take an active role in the lives of humanity. But with the resurfacing of the old Gods, and now the demise of most of the Olympians, we decided to make a special exception."

"What do you vampires want?" Leon asked, gasping.

"Two things. One all information regarding James Akatsuki. And two, the utter dismantling and destruction of the Black Order."

"And if I refuse?"

Cain, losing his patience, threw Leon back into his chair. "Then you die here." Cain grabbed Leon by his face. "I am willing to let you walk out of this building alive. All you have to do is give me what I ask about James Akatsuki."

"Go find him, yourself," Leon said defiantly.

Cain sighed in disappointment. "Wrong answer." Cain grabbed Leon by throat and squeezed harder.

"You will never win. The Keepers will always rise again."

"No, they fall here and now," said Cain, snapping Leon's neck, killing him.

Throwing Leon's dead body into his chair, Cain dusted himself off. "I never did have the patience for this sort of job."

"Adrian you may start the cleanse," Cain said into his phone.

"I am already ahead of you brother, my familiars and I are finishing up now," Adrian said, speaking on the other end. "Hold on one minute." Adrian snapped his fingers as one of his dark familiars attacked and ferociously killed a man who was running. "Now you were saying?"

Cain sighed, watching Adrian on monitors. "Again, how many times do I have to tell you to wait until I give you the order?"

Adrian shrugged his shoulders. "Why? We were going to kill them anyway."

"That is not the point, Adrian. The master holds us to a higher standard than humans. If you can't follow orders, then the master will have you terminated."

"Well, I am sorry, bro. I just wanted to speed things up since we are on a time constraint."

Cain sighed again. "Since you're my brother, I will overlook your mistake."

"And let me guess, lunch again in exchange?" Adrian said, interrupting Cain.

"No, dinner this time, an expensive one," Cain said, hanging up the phone.

"Family, another thing I never really had the patience for. If it wasn't for him being my brother, I would have killed him long ago for his stupidity." Putting on his sunglasses, Cain looked over at Leon's body. "Now to clean up the mess."

Cain ignited the whole base as he left to meet Adrian outside. "This is the end of the Black Order."

Cain and Adrian watched the base burn. "Hey bro, did you finish the deal?"

Cain punched him in the stomach. "How many times do I have to tell you? Call me Cain."

"Alright, alright," said Adrian gasping.

Cain adjusted his black gloves. "Did you kill everyone?"

"Ya, I did, but there was no sign of that Chelsea woman in any part of the building."

"She wasn't here after all. She must be on a different assignment somewhere."

Pulling out the paperwork from Leon's office, Cain looked it over. "According to this paperwork, she is in Washington D.C."

"Washington D.C.? What is an operative of the Black Order doing in the United States? They have nothing to do with any of the hunter organizations of Europe."

"Maybe Leon was hoping to strike some sort of deal with their government," said Cain, putting the paperwork away.

"What type of deal?"

"The chairman was not surprised by our arrival; he knew we would be coming for him. But yet he did not try to flee. And the question is why."

"Maybe he knew he couldn't escape."

"Maybe, or it is something else entirely."

"What do you mean?"

"Whatever the case, as long as she remains in the United States, we cannot touch her."

"But, what if word of this gets to her? What if she stays in the United States? After all, she does have citizenship there."

"Shut up; you are giving me a headache with your stupid questions," said Cain as he started the car. "If she stays there, then there is nothing to worry about. As long as she is in the United States, she cannot do anything."

"What do you mean?"

"Have you forgotten again? The United States has its own defense against the supernatural, the Defense Against Magic. As long as they are watching her, she cannot even breathe."

Driving away, Adrian expressed his doubt. "I hope you're right."

Cain, annoyed by Adrian's doubt, grabbed him and hit him against the dashboard.

"What did you do that for, bro?" Adrian asked, grabbing his head.

Cain scuffed at Adrian's question. "That was for doubting me. And this." Cain grabbed Adrian again and slammed his head into the dashboard once more.

"Alright, alright, I am sorry, Cain."

Satisfied, Cain focused on driving. "Alright then, let's get going. You still owe me that dinner."

The Keepers of the Black Order came to a bloody end, and their base burnt to ashes.

In Washington D.C., Chelsea sat at her desk in the hotel room doing paperwork.

"Was everything successful?" Chelsea asked, feeling a cold chill behind her.

A man appeared behind her. "Yes, everything went as I had foreseen. Now with the destruction of the Black Order and you becoming a high figure in this government in D.A.M, you can now move freely."

Chelsea moved closer to the man. "I hope it was worth all the sacrifice. After all, if any of this gets tied back to you..."

The man dismissed Chelsea's concern. "It matters not since I have much pull in the United States government. I am a senator, after all," said the man holding Chelsea's chin.

"Don't forget about the deal you made with me," Chelsea said, removing his hand.

"You will have what you seek as long as you play the part. Only then will power be yours."

"I will be sure to," Chelsea said with a smile.

Looking back at Chelsea, the man revealed his ominous eyes. "Be sure of it."

The man left, leaving Chelsea as she resumed her work. "It just needs a woman's touch."

After a couple of hours, Chase reached the peak of Fannaråki Mountain.

"I know you are here, Devoid. I can sense your evil presence all over the place," said Chase.

"You come as the last incarnation of Thor," Devoid echoed as darkness appeared behind Chase.

Chase, unfazed, turned and saw Devoid emerge from it, staring into its green eyes. "It is true—you are still alive."

"Did you think I would have been killed so easily? That your weak master would be able to slay me, the Midgard Serpent?" Devoid said with an evil smirk.

Chase, hearing enough, fired a round from his pistol past Devoid's head. "How did you survive?"

"I survived, nothing else, nothing more."

"Was it Loki?"

Devoid remained silent and appeared behind Chase as its hand glowed green.

"I am not going to fall for that again," said Chase, charging a lightning aura around him, stopping Devoid's attack.

Seeing Chase had awoken to his true power, Devoid smiled. "I see you finally tapped into your true power. The power of the thunder god."

"And this power will be what defeats you," said Chase, pulling out his rifle.

"We shall see."

Chase fired two shots at Devoid with lightning surging through them.

He charged his lightning element into those bullets, Devoid thought, summoning his serpent tail to deflect the bullets. *But they will still not pierce through my armored skin.*

Chase snapped his fingers as the bullets split in half, ricocheting off each other. "Lightning Bullet Split."

More lightning surging throughout them, the bullet fragments flew at Devoid.

There is not enough time to react. Devoid hardened his skin. The bullets pierced shallowly into its skin. Devoid looked down at the bullet fragments. "Even with your lightning, you couldn't pierce through my armored skin."

"Don't be so sure," said Chase, pointing at him.

"Lightning Shock." Chase snapped his fingers, and the surging bullet fragments sent shocks through the serpent.

"You little wretch," Devoid yelled, dropping to its knees in pain. Devoid was immobilized by Chase's lightning.

"You killed my father and my mother. You even tried to kill my mentor," Chase said as he slowly walked over to Devoid.

"Tried," Devoid laughed demonically.

Chase, in silent anger, looked down at Devoid. "You are going to tell me something. Where is my master?"

"He is dead, his body burnt to ashes when he fell in that volcano."

Chase shot a lightning bullet in Devoid's shoulder, who roared in pain. "No, Sepher survived that fall. He continued to pursue you all the way here in Norway. Answer me, where is he?" Chase demanded.

Devoid, enraged at being wounded, charged his dark aura, forcing the lightning from his body. It tried to attack Chase, but a hook blade stabbed through his back.

"Sepher," said Chase, seeing him knock out Devoid.

"Hey kid, long time no see," said Sepher, pulling his blade out of Devoid's back.

Chase was in disbelief. "It really is you."

"Of course, it's me, nobody else can be. Anyway, how many times do I got to tell you, never let your guard down?"

Chase's lightning aura dissipated. "Master Sepher, you are alive."

"Ya, just barely, I almost got burnt to a crisp," Sepher said, lighting a cigarette. "You need to capture this one, right?" Sepher asked, picking up Devoid and putting it on Chase's shoulder.

Chase was uneasy. "Yes, but how did you…"

Sepher cut him off. "My instincts, and I saw you fight him; you could have killed him if you wanted to. But since you didn't, I figure you had your reasons."

Chase felt the shift of the wind a realized a blizzard was upon them. *Another storm.*

"Anyway, you should get out of here before the blizzard hits."

Struggling to see Sepher, Chase took a couple of steps, but he was gone. "Master Sepher? Master Sepher, where did you go?" Chase yelled.

Chase listened closely, but there was no reply. For several minutes, Chase looked but couldn't find Sepher. *He vanished without a trace. Was that really Master Sepher or was it an illusion of some kind?* Chase thought, looking over the ledge.

Pressed for time, Chase pulled out his mystica jewel. *No, it definitely was him. Devoid's wounds wouldn't be there if he was an illusion. And the words he spoke, Master Sepher used to tell me them all the time when we were on missions.*

"Where did you go, Sepher?"

Why did Sepher disappear? Was Devoid lying? No, now is not the time for doubt. I need to focus on completing this contract first.

Staring into the jewel, the blue vortex surrounded Chase. *But he really is alive.*

"Teleport," said Chase, disappearing into the vortex.

"Foolish to the end," said Sepher, watching Chase teleport.

"Everything is now set in motion."

Standing on the edge, Sepher looked up at the sky and smiled wickedly. "That look in your eyes, the joy and happiness that you felt when you saw your precious master alive was trilling. Enjoy them for now. Because when I take it away from you, the true despair will begin," said Sepher as his eyes turned pitch black.

Sepher raised his hands as he morphed into Devoid. "Once we have our fated battle, Ragnarök will begin anew. And with it, your death will be all the more satisfying."

Chapter 10: The Trickster

After a few minutes, swirls of wind appeared outside the airship. Chase emerged and yelled to the others.

"Hey, I'm back."

"You're back," Arthur said, hearing Chase outside.

Chase tossed Devoid down on the floor as he sat to get warm.

"That is Devoid, the creature that killed your parents?" said Arthur, staring at the creature.

"Ya, to tell you the truth, it is taking everything I have not to kill him."

Chase used the Living Mass spell and shrank Devoid. "Living Mass."

"I made a promise and a deal, so I will not let my emotions get the best of me."

"What do we do now?" Arthur asked.

Chase walked into the cockpit with Arthur and pulled up the three-dimensional map of Norway. "Now we find Loki again."

"Do you think he is at that pub?"

"No, I don't think Loki will be back there again. He is the God of Mischief; he will take any chance he gets to mess with us."

"Ah, I'm hurt, do you think I would do something like that," Loki huffed, appearing behind them.

"What?" Chase said, stunned as he and Arthur looked back.

"Well, knowing me, I probably would."

Chase turned back and saw Loki on a screenless monitor waving at him. "Hey there, champ, I see your little reunion with the Midgard Serpent went well."

"Enough these games, Loki," said Chase, tired of Loki.

"Ah, but the games are so much fun."

"We aren't here to entertain you."

Loki was disappointed with Chase's attitude. "Party pooper, you take the fun out of everything, but oh well."

"Where are you, trickster? We were just about to look for you," Arthur demanded.

"Oh, I know, I know. I just thought that I would pop in and say hey and maybe... change our agreement a little," Loki said, appearing next to them again.

Arthur tried to grab Loki, but he disappeared and appeared back on the screenless monitor.

"You fiend."

Loki smiled at Arthur's rage. "Oh, calm yourself, little king. You're not even part of the deal anymore."

"What do you want?" Chase demanded.

"Good, it seems I have your attention now," said Loki. "Here are my conditions to you."

Loki started to teleport around the cockpit and toy with Chase.

"Chase, you will come alone and deliver the Rökkr to me," said Loki, appearing back on the screenless monitor.

"That wasn't in the guidelines in the contract or the agreement," Chase yelled.

Loki smiled at Chase's resentment. "They are now."

"We had a deal, Loki. You are bound to the same rules as the others. As a God, you have to honor it."

"And I intend to. If I started breaking my contracts now, I literally couldn't live with myself," Loki said.

"But you forgot descendant of Thor. I hold all the cards. I am the one who makes the rules."

"You can't do that."

Loki snapped his fingers, and the contract appeared in his hand. "Of course, I can. I just added it to the contract when you weren't looking. Oops, you weren't supposed to hear that part," Loki joked.

Chase slammed his hands on the controls. "You bastard."

Loki ticked his finger at Chase. "Ah uh, no cursing now. You have one hour to bring them to me. If you don't, this scroll you see here..." Loki conjured a fire before himself, "...will burn, and you will lose your only hope to save your friend from his eternal torment. Tick tock, times a wasting," said Loki, disappearing.

Chase slammed his fist on the controls in frustration. "Damn it. He is playing us again."

"Chase, I know how you feel, but you can't be thinking about that right now. You are pressed for time. You only have one hour."

"I know," said Chase, pulling up the three-dimensional map of Norway, tracking Loki.

After they tracked Loki, Chase and Arthur walked to the back the ship to report the change of events to the crew.

"Don't bother—we heard everything," said Amphion. "Only you can go. Loki has changed the conditions of the contract."

"I know. I'm just tired of Loki changing the rules."

"As long as he holds the contract, you have no choice but to play his game. But that doesn't mean you can't beat him at it," Amphion said, looking back at Chase.

Chase, assured by Amphion's word, silently nodded his head.

After a couple of minutes, Arthur, Theseus, and Amphion, with Ulf on his shoulder, got off the airship as Chase started it up. "I am sorry."

"You have nothing to apologize for," said Arthur dismissing his apology. "Now go. You have no time to waste."

Chase closed the back of the ship. "I will be back for all of you in a little bit."

Arthur waved at him. "We will be waiting. Be careful in dealing with that trickster."

Lifting into the air, Chase turned to Beowulf and Hela. "I am sorry, Loki has changed the rules of the game."

"Do not concern yourself, young warrior. If anything goes wrong, we will take care of everything," said Hela confidently.

Chase looked down in regret. "I'm sorry for this."

Charging his lightning in his hand, Chase shocked Hela and Beowulf, knocking them out. "Not when it comes to my best friend's life."

I am not going to fail now, not when I'm this close, Chase thought, setting a course for Olso.

Walking down a dark street in Olso, Chase tracked Loki to a pub. "Another pub, this is getting old."

Walking inside, Loki clapped his hands as the lights dimmed and confetti fell everywhere. "But something that is old is the best, and we all know I am."

"Let's just get this over with," said Chase, sitting across from the trickster.

Chase set jars with the Rökkr in them on the bar.

"I'm impressed you managed to complete the task," said Loki, dinging the hourglass. "And with twenty minutes to spare." The hourglass and confetti disappeared when Loki snapped his fingers.

"Enough, just give me the scroll so I can go. I don't have time for this or your jokes."

Loki pulled out cards and started dealing them. "Ah, that's the thing though, you do. For you have all the time in the world as long as I hold all the cards."

Chase charged lightning in his hand. "No, I don't."

Seeing the lightning in Chase's hand, Loki pulled out the scroll. "Un ah, you need to calm those nerves of yours, or this scroll will go poof."

Chase calmed himself and dispelled his lightning.

Reaching behind the bar, Loki pulled out drinking horns. "Now then, can I offer you a drink? Maybe a mead?"

"No thanks," said Chase, pushing Loki's hand away.

"Oh well, more for me," Loki said, drinking the horns full of mead.

"I'm definitely feeling that one. I think I need to sober up a little."

Chase rolled his eyes. "You done?"

"Indeed," Loki said, tossing the horns aside.

Loki pointed to the jars. "Now alter those in the jar back to their original size. I want to make sure they are intact."

Opening all the jars, Chase placed all the Rökkr on the floor. "Living Mass."

All the Rökkr changed back to their original size. "There, verify them yourself."

Seeing that they were intact, Loki nodded his head yes. "I can see it was a great challenge for you and your comrades to capture all of them alive."

"Very well done," Loki said, smiling.

"Good, I completed my part of the bargain," said Chase, ready to leave. "Now honor yours and hand me the Life-Lock scroll."

"I will."

Loki snapped his fingers as the Life-Lock scroll appeared in his hand. He held the scroll to Chase.

Chase reached to take the scroll, but his hand passed right through.

"But not yet."

Furious, Chase attempted to shoot Loki but missed as the trickster teleported back to a safe distance.

"I've had enough of your trickery. I have done everything you asked. I have followed all of the conditions of the contract."

"I know, but you missed the last part," said Loki lighting his finger on fire, writing out the guidelines in the air. "Confront your fate and break the seal."

Loki showed the life-lock scroll to Chase. "Only then will you get your precious scroll."

Chase fired multiple shots, but Loki teleported all over the room, dodging them.

"What fate? What seal?"

"You'll see," said Loki, appearing next to the door, smiling.

Rushing at him, Chase tried to stop Loki, but he left through the exit door. "I'll be in touch."

Chase rushed outside, looking in the dark, but Loki disappeared into the night. In a silent rage, Chase ripped the door of the pub off its hinges and threw it down the street. Crying, Chase looked up at the night sky as snow began to fall. "Ahh."

Silently walking back into the pub, Chase looked at the ground and noticed the Rökkr were gone.

"Damn it," Chase yelled, exploding into a rage.

Shockwaves of lightning surged through the whole pub, breaking the glass and blowing out the windows. Chase dropped to his knees. "James, I am sorry. I am so sorry."

Loki watched Chase from the top of an ice mountain.

"Good, he is starting to despair," said Loki, smiling. Waving his hand, Loki dispelled his magic. "All he needs now is one more push." Loki looked behind him. "You know what to do. Kill his friends and make sure you show him their dead bodies."

Five dark shadows took off into the sky, going in one direction. "You shall know terrible pain, Chase Actaeonis. Remember it and that of Thor."

Flying back from Olso, Chase felt dread. *I have failed James.* Thinking about Loki's last words to him, Chase became more determined. *If I have to wait, then so be it, but I will not stop. Not until I get that scroll and save James's life. I just hope the others can forgive me for what I've done,"* Chase thought.

In the forest near Trondheim at their campsite, Amphion continued to heal Ulf as he made steady progress. *I never felt anything like this.*

"How is he?" Arthur asked, walking into the tent.

Amphion wrapped Ulf's wounds with bandages. "He has escaped death; all he needs now is rest. I have done what I could within my abilities. It is up to him now whether he will regain consciousness or not," said Amphion, standing up.

Looking down at Ulf, Amphion's eyes tightened as something bothered him.

Arthur noticed Amphion's silence. "I can tell something is bothering you."

"I don't believe it is anything to be concerned with but..." Amphion said, seeing Ulf's mystic energy with his glowing red eyes, "Ulf's mystic energy is undergoing a metamorphosis."

"A metamorphosis?"

"Each living creature has different mystic energy, both mortal and divine. And, depending on the element they wield, the energies will be different colors." Amphion walked past Arthur. "Ulf's mystic energy is changing."

"What does that mean?" Arthur asked calmly. "What is causing this change?"

"I do not have that answer," said Amphion, stopping at the entrance. "But I will tell you what I believe. Ulf's mystic energy is evolving. Evolving into something divine."

"Is it something bad?" Arthur asked, staring back at Ulf.

"No, I didn't sense anything malevolent, but it feels ominous. I can see his mystic color steadily change."

"Then what color is his mystic energy turning into?

"Pure white. White as the white fur of the god of all wolves, Aesir."

Aesir, I heard that name once before, Arthur thought, crossing his arms.

"There is nothing to be concerned with. I will continue to watch him until he wakes up. Now, get some rest, you have not had any sleep in the past few days."

Arthur yawned. "Good idea, a nap is just what I need."

Walking toward his tent, Arthur waved at Amphion. "Let me know if you need anything. And make sure you get some sleep too. I know for a fact you have been up for a couple of days as well."

Letting go of the tent entrance, Amphion gazed back at Ulf. *That white aura I see his mystic energy change into. Is it of the God of wolves?*

Heading toward his tent, Arthur noticed Theseus sitting next to the campfire, staring into it. "You stare into the fire too long, and you will burn your eyes out, my friend."

"I was just thinking about each of the three Rökkr that decided to help us," said Theseus, looking at Arthur sitting down.

"Hela, Beowulf, and Fenrir."

"Yes, what about them?"

"It is just that I look at history now—even you and I are living history. I look at it now and see that texts of certain individuals and certain events are badly misinterpreted."

"Yes, I agree. History, even ones of heroes and significant events, have become distorted."

"When did you first discover the wrong telling?"

"I think I've always known," said Arthur, taking a moment to answer.

"I simply didn't want to believe it. But I still hold faith that, despite the inaccuracies in our legends, people can still look and learn from them. Still, the flaws in history cannot be overlooked. Beowulf was written to have killed Grendel, who once terrorized all of Norway, but he lived and continued to terrorize it. He himself was written to have fought and died against the ice dragon, but yet he is alive."

Thinking of Hela, Theseus nodded in agreement. "Yes, it was the same when I faced Hela. Norse legends told she was the Norse Goddess of Hel, but yet she isn't. Instead, there is no Norse Hel, and she is, in fact, goddess of all Valkyries."

Arthur put his hands together. "It makes one question everything they learned. History is always written by the victors, and through that, history is like you said, greatly misinterpreted. A few true phenomena are told correctly in the beginning, but with the passing of time, even they are distorted or even erased."

"Yes, it is one of the many faults of being human. We are afraid of what we don't understand, so we tell a lie to give us comfort. And what we do understand if the truth is terrifying enough, it is sought out and destroyed."

"It can even make you question your own legacy and how it is told," said Theseus, thinking back of Athens and his battle against the Minotaur.

"I disagree," said Arthur vehemently. "You should never question your own legacy."

"You have never questioned your legacy before?"

Arthur folded his arms across his chest. "I cannot say that I have not, but I never once regretted it."

"As long as people can learn from my mistakes, and take just a tiny piece of my example, then I am satisfied with that." Arthur pointed at Theseus and himself. "And because of you and me, we are alive to tell our legacies. Not many heroes who have lived for centuries can say they had the chance to do that," said Arthur jokingly.

Theseus chuckled. "True enough."

Sharing this joyful moment, Arthur stared into the fire. "And besides, I am happy that all my struggles and efforts in life were not in vain. Britain still exists and prospers to this day. Just like you should be happy Athens and all of Greece still exist. That in itself is proof of your legacy and the mark you left on the world."

"Yes, you are right. Athens and Greece, it is all still there."

Arthur stood up. "Now then, I believe we should get some rest. After all, we still have a lot more we have to do."

"Then I wish you a good night," Theseus said, waving. "One day I would like to hear about your legend from you."

"Alright, my friend, but I must warn, it is a long tale. I would like to hear your legend as well."

"Then I must warn you, it is a long one as well."

Arthur chuckled. "I will look forward to it."

Sensing something ominous, Arthur and Theseus lost their smiles. The wind blew around them, and two shadowy figures appeared. Arthur and Theseus vigilantly stared as they felt their murderous intent. Knowing the danger, they raced back to their tents to grab their weapons, but the dark figures cut them off. Without warning, the dark figures attacked them. Theseus and Arthur fought them unarmed but were injured.

"What are these creatures?" Arthur asked, stepping back close to the campfire with Theseus.

"I do not know, but the murderous intent I am sensing from them is truly frightening."

"All the more reason, we need to retrieve our weapons to fight them."

"I smell blood," said Amphion, standing up in his tent.

Rushing outside, he saw the dark figures step slowly toward Arthur and Theseus.

Overhearing their complaints, Amphion waved, levitating their swords from their tents. Amphion swiftly flew the swords to their owners. Theseus and Arthur caught them.

"How did you?"

"You requested your swords, so I sent them to you," said Amphion, summoning his khopesh.

Happy, Arthur drew Excalibur from its sheath as Theseus drew his. "Thank you, my friend, Amphion. Now that we have our weapons, we can fight properly."

Not knowing the reason why the dark figures attacked them, wielding their legendary weapons, the heroes prepared themselves for the dangerous battle against the mysterious foes.

Preparing to attack the figures, Arthur noticed another dark figure appear. "Amphion behind you."

Amphion tried to move but was pierced through his shoulder.

Arthur tried to rush over to help, but the dark figure before him blocked his way. "Darn it, who in the devil are you? Why are you attacking us?"

The dark figure remained silent, brandished its beastly claws, and charged.

"No answer, huh? Then taste my sword. Maybe that will loosen your tongue."

As the dark figure pushed the sword deeper into his shoulder, Amphion gripped the blade, stopping it. Pushing through the pain, Amphion hit the dark figure in the face, knocking it back. "Your sword means nothing to me," Amphion declared, pulling out the bloody sword, throwing it at its feet.

The dark figure picked up its sword.

Amphion smirked. "Impressive. You show great skill, but that skill will not help you against me," Amphion said, brandishing his khopesh.

Amphion saw Arthur and Theseus struggle against the dark figures. *We are at a severe disadvantage here. With Ulf still unconscious, we need to move this battle away somehow.*

Amphion's red eyes glowed. "Do you two still have your mystica jewels?"

"Yes, but Chase said there is only enough energy left in all of them for one more teleportation," Theseus yelled back.

"Wait, are you wanting us to teleport away to fight them," Arthur asked, blocking an attack.

"We cannot teleport all together, we do it separately. That way, we will have greater odds of defeating these creatures of darkness."

"But we can't leave Ulf behind. He is still unconscious."

"Do not worry, my friend, we are not teleporting to get away, we are teleporting to fight."

Seizing the moment, the heroes pushed the dark figures back. Standing together, they prepared to enact their plan.

"As I said before, the jewels only have enough energy left for one more teleport. And, without a destination, they can teleport us anywhere in Norway."

"I am well aware," said Amphion, gripping his khopesh tightly. "But we have no choice. To protect Ulf, we have to activate it."

"Alright, I'm just making sure you understand the risks."

"Do not worry. I am sure Chase will find us later, for tracking mystic energy is his specialty," said Arthur smiling.

Theseus smiled back. "Yes, I know. He is the only one who could find us once we become lost."

Amphion yelled at them as he pushed back one of the dark figures. "Enough of your talk. The more time that passes, is more time that we are at a disadvantage. We need to act now and divide them."

"Alright, we follow your lead," said Theseus.

"It is good to fight alongside friends once again. Now, it is time to divide the enemy and conquer them."

The dark figures took defensive stances as the heroes changed directions and charged them. Caught off guard, Arthur, Amphion, and Theseus moved behind them, wrapping their arms around their necks constricting them.

"By Merlin's beard, the strength of these beasts is truly great," said Arthur struggling to hold the dark figure.

"Indeed, I never fought against one so strong since the Minotaur."

Amphion red eyes glowed bright, tightened his grip around his mystica jewel. "Save the admiration of their strength for later. we have to move now."

Each one pulled out a mystica jewel and they disappeared into the blue vortex, its light shooting up into the sky, scattering them throughout Norway to battle in places unknown.

Chapter 11: Lost in The Land of Midnight

Theseus and the dark figure crashed down from the sky over the water and landed on top of an ice barge. Theseus, not able to get his balance, began to roll down the side of it.

The shadowy figure also on the side, jumped onto the flat surface of the ice barge as the shadow engulfing him dissipated. Falling off the side of the ice barge, Theseus stabbed his sword into the ice, preventing him from sinking into the frigid water below.

"Beowulf?" said Theseus, seeing him as the dark shadows dissipated.

Feeling his sword starting to come loose from the ice, Theseus looked down and saw the waves crash against the barge below.

"If I did not act, I would have plunged into those fridge waters," said Theseus, staring at the waves below.

As strong winds blew, Theseus punched his fist into the ice to hold himself.

Why? Theseus thought as he stared up at Beowulf. *Why would Beowulf attack us? Was Hela amongst them? She had to have been. I remember one of those dark figures having a female physic.* Theseus thought back and remembered Beowulf and the other dark figures cloaked in shadow. *Could those shadows around them be the reason why they attack us? Chase, what in the name of the gods happened between you and Loki?* Theseus thought, worried about the others.

Wanting answers, Theseus climbed back up. He looked over at Beowulf, who was standing on the ledge. "Why did you attack us? What happened between Chase and Loki?" Theseus yelled as the wind and waves raged.

Beowulf remaining silent, turned around, and stared at Theseus with his dark eyes.

Looking into Beowulf's dark eyes, Theseus was unsettled. *This sinister presence I'm sensing from him. Could it be possessing him?*

Pushing Beowulf back, the ice underneath them began to crack and collapse. "Tell me, what has Loki done? What has happened to you?" Theseus demanded. Beowulf remained silent, and Theseus prepared himself. "Very well then."

He used his strength to thrust Beowulf back. "I will do what I must."

"I shall break this malevolent darkness that has hold of you and make you come back to your senses," Theseus vowed.

The unstable ice barge rocked back and forth before finally breaking up in the water. Theseus struggled against Beowulf, trying to keep his balance. *I never imagined he would be this strong.*

Pushed toward the edge, Theseus looked down at the icy water below. *If I don't do something, he will knock me over the edge into the water. I have no choice; I have to charge at him head on and get him away from the middle,* Theseus thought, seeing the ice give way.

Theseus tried to move around Beowulf but was stabbed in the shoulder. Bleeding, Theseus pushed through the pain tackling Beowulf.

Theseus got back up, pointed the tip of his sword downward. Beowulf tried to stop him but failed.

"Hope you can swim," said Theseus, piercing through the ice.

The ice barge completely collapsed from the sheer force of his power as they both fell into the freezing water below.

Theseus rose above the surface, seeing standing ice off in the distance swam to it. "That was a close one," he said, getting up on the ice, shivering from the cold.

Trying to get warm, Theseus looked into the water and was shocked as he heard a loud roar. The ice dragon, Fýri, broke up through the water, soaring into the sky.

This is not good. That is the ice dragon Fýri, Theseus thought, seeing the ice dragon disrupting the clouds.

Theseus knowing he was in danger, ran as Fýri turned his darkened gaze at him.

The ice dragon flew above him and fired its ice breath. Theseus easily slid out of way of its path.

"That ice breath freezes everything instantly," Theseus said, seeing the breath frost the surface. "If I get hit by that, I will definitely be killed." Running, Theseus looked for solid ground.

Fýri flew back around to attack him, blowing its icy breath again. Theseus saw a wooden Viking ship stuck in the ice off in the distance. He managed to get to the ship and jump into it just as the icy breath froze its side.

"This is an ancient Viking ship," said Theseus, recognizing it.

Fýri was flying back around to attack. Theseus picked up a spear and a wooden shield from the deck. "This will have to do."

As Fýri flew closer, Theseus put the shield up and threw the spear at Fýri but it started to freeze. Planting his feet, Theseus jumped high into the air, fracturing the wooden ship. Theseus grabbed the spear and got onto the dragon's back. He flung the spear, piercing the ice dragon's eye. Roaring in pain,

Fýri dove downward, crashing into the remains of the wooden ship.

"No, you don't," said Theseus, seeing Fýri slowly move on the ice.

Running at Fýri, Theseus jumped on its back.

Fýri ascended into the sky, roaring. Theseus held on tightly as Fýri soared off in the distance over the tundra.

I must attack now, before I lose my grip, Theseus thought, struggling to climb the dragon against the wind.

Fýri looked back, and saw Theseus draw his sword. Fýri flew straight up to shake him off, but Theseus held on fiercely. Unable to shake Theseus, the ice dragon fired its ice breath. Theseus wielded the wooden shield and blocked the ice breath, but his hand froze still holding tightly to the shield. He used his sword to shattered the shield. Pieces of the shield and his hand fell away, and he grabbed his arm in pain.

"That was for my hand, dragon," Theseus yelled, thrusting his sword deep into the neck of the dragon.

Fýri roared in agony and fired its ice breath wildly. Theseus slashed repeatedly into Fýri's wings. Fýri let out one last pained roar and disappeared into the clouds. The pain overcame the dragon and lost consciousness, falling from the night sky, crashing violently into the trees. Theseus was thrown from the dragon's back and crashed hard into the tundra.

Theseus was unable to move from the pain but chuckled. *I can't move. It feels like every bone in my body is broken.* Theseus gazed over at the unconscious dragon. *That is the first and last time I'm flying on a dragon. I just hope the others are alright,* Theseus thought, losing consciousness staring into the night sky.

Elsewhere in Norway, running in a frozen taiga forest, injured Arthur got behind a tree. Trying to catch his breath, Arthur peered around the tree and saw Grendel ripping down branches, looking for him. *Never did I imagine that dark figure was Grendel. His power is much greater than before.*

Grendel looked at all the trees with his dark eyes. Turning his gaze away, the ogre walked away. Arthur, relieved, tried to rest for the moment, but a claw ripped through the tree into his shoulder. Arthur agonized in pain. Freeing himself from Grendel's grasp, Arthur retreated to a safe distance. Arthur watched Grendel in disbelief as he ripped through the tree making it collapse.

Arthur's blood dripped from his claw; Grendel licked the blood off it. "You fiend."

Arthur, barely able to move his arm, meagerly lifted Excalibur. He blocked Grendel's attack, but the force from it knocked him back hard into a tree. Coughing up blood, Arthur looked up at Grendel standing over him.

"I will see that justice is done for all that you have killed, monster," said Arthur defiantly.

Grendel remained silent as he lunged down at Arthur with his claws to kill him. Arthur desperately held his sword. It illuminated, blinding Grendel. Arthur saw his chance to escape and ran. Moments later, Grendel's vision returned, and he looked around for Arthur but didn't see him. Grendel saw a trail of blood leading away. He silently tracked Arthur with the intent to kill him.

Deeper in the taiga, Arthur painfully staggered to a river. Looking back at his blood trail, Arthur started to fade. *It will be before too long. I must...*

Before Arthur could finished thinking, he passed out and fell into the raging river. Grendel arrived at the edge of the river and saw blood in the water. Further up the river, Arthur still unconscious, carried by the stream, was rescued by a large, white-furred figure.

Pulling Arthur from the raging current, the white figure laid him on the snow. *His wounds are moderate, but what is a human doing out this far in the wilderness?*

Looking down at Excalibur, the white figure immediately recognized it. *I see.*

The white figure's eyes glowed white, read Arthur's thoughts. *You are him.*

Placing Arthur on his shoulder, the white figure carried him into the frozen taiga on the path toward a mountain. "Have no worry, little one, you are not destined to die here."

Elsewhere, on a snowy mountain, Amphion fought the dark female figure. Pushed back toward the ledge of the mountain, Amphion looked down at the frozen depth below.

She has pushed me against the ledge, Amphion thought, seeing that he was trapped. *Whoever she is, she has tremendous strength.*

She lunged with her sword, but Amphion blocked the attack with his khopesh but was forced over the edge from the sheer power. Amphion grabbed the dark figure's arm as he fell and pulled her down with him. They plunged down the mountain as they fought. The clash of their swords echoed in the distance. Crashing into the snow below, they were caught in an avalanche. Amphion grabbed a tree branch and held on until the avalanche was over.

I may have broken my ribs from the impact of that fall, Amphion thought, grabbing his side. He tried to lift his arm but couldn't. *And it seems my left arm is broken as well.*

Pushing through the pain, Amphion staggered downward. Walking to the remains of the avalanche, Amphion found Hela, who was unconscious.

It was the Valkyrie Goddess who attacked me, Amphion thought seeing the darkness leave her. *Why would she attack us?* Amphion closed his eyes. *This must be Loki's doing.* Sensing the faint dark aura, Amphion opened his eyes. *This is magic I am sensing. It is wicked in nature.*

"Now, I release you from the darkness that binds you," said Amphion, using his sun, dispelling the dark magic.

Pulling the rest of it from her, Amphion dispersed into nothing. With the dark magic no longer controlling her, Amphion placed her on his shoulder. *What happened that lead to this? Chase, what happened between you and Loki?*

Not wanting to dwell on these thoughts, Amphion continued downward. *I hope the others were successful in the battles. I pray to Ra that they're safe.*

Taking a few steps, Amphion stopped as he saw many mountain peaks in the distance. He closed his eyes and pressed forward, trekking through the blizzard.

Back at the campsite, Ulf finally woke up. "Huh? What happened here?" Ulf said to himself, seeing the campsite torn apart.

He tried to find the others but couldn't find a trace of them. "Amphion, Theseus, Arthur, where are you?"

"They are all gone," Fenrir said, appearing before Ulf.

"Fenrir, what are you doing here? Aren't you supposed to be with Chase?"

"I was."

"What do you mean?"

Destroying the remaining darkness around him, Fenrir stared intently at Ulf. "The one you call Chase; Loki betrayed him."

"What happened? Is Chase alright?" Ulf asked, concerned.

"I do not know, but I suspect he is on his way here."

"Then what about the others? What happened here?"

"I am in the dark when it comes to them."

Fenrir looked around the destroyed campsite. "This place was torn apart and this dark magic I am sensing—they were most likely attacked by the Rökkr."

"Attacked?"

"Yes."

Ulf tried to search for the others, but Fenrir jumped in front of him. "Your search would do you no good. They are not here."

Ulf didn't believe Fenrir and closed his eyes, trying to sense his friends. He could only sense the remnants of their mystic energy.

"You're right. Why did the Rökkr attack my friends?" Ulf asked angrily.

"I don't reason why they attacked your friends, but I do know this—Loki sent them."

"Hela was known throughout Asgard for her hatred of Loki. She would never help the likes of the trickster." Fenrir stopped and looked back at Ulf. "I suspect he is controlling him with his trickster magic. I know what you're thinking, for we are the same. So, I will tell you this now. Aimlessly roaming around without knowing anything will accomplish nothing. The best thing you can do right now is wait for your friend Chase."

"Ya, you are right," Ulf begrudgingly agreed.

"Now, for the main reason I am here. Have you felt the change within you?"

"What do you mean?"

Fenrir pointed his paw at Ulf. "Feel your mystic energy."

Ulf, still confused, charged his mystic aura. "Ya, it does feel different. What does it mean?"

"It means you have fully awakened. That white aura around you is the aura of Aesir."

"What?".

Standing in front of Ulf, Fenrir charged his black aura.

"What are you doing?" Ulf asked.

"Now we can finally become one again," said Fenrir as he started to fade away.

Before fading, Fenrir walked directly into Ulf. "Aesir will be reborn anew."

Both auras turned bright white, and shot up into the sky, enveloping Ulf as he howled.

"Aesir will return," said Ulf as his voice echoed.

Back on the airship, Chase, almost to the campsite, saw the white light aura. "What is that light? This mystic energy that I am sensing is coming from that light. It is Ulf's, but I hardly recognize it."

Landing near the light, the white aura dimmed. Chase walked through the remains of the campsite. *What on earth happened here?*

Sensing Ulf's mystic energy close by, Chase walked toward it. He saw Ulf with white fur and a bright shining white aura.

"Ulf. Ulf, is that you?"

Ulf opened his eyes and looked at Chase. "I am what you see before you, nothing more."

"Why is your fur white?"

"I have gone back to my original self."

"Your original self?"

"Originally, Aesir and Fenrir were one in the same wolf. One half who became the white wolf Aesir, the companion of Thor. The other half, the black wolf Fenrir, was destined to kill Odin and devour the sky during Ragnarök. I, being Aesir's reincarnation and descendant, fused with Fenrir to become what Aesir once was. The spirit of the wolf and the god of all wolves."

"Then are you a god?"

"No, I am still mortal. I just have divine energy now," Ulf answered.

Chase walked over to Ulf and touched his white fur.

Ulf annoyed, hit Chase with his paw. "I am still me; nothing has changed."

"I know that. I was just making sure. You didn't have to go and hit me."

Ulf held out his paw to silence Chase. "But there is something you need to know. Fenrir was under the control of Loki."

Loki again, Chase thought.

"How?"

"He's bound just like the others by Loki's dark magic."

"Others?"

"Beowulf, Hela, and Grendel, they are now controlled by Loki. And they were sent here to attack us."

Chase tightened his fist. *It is all my fault. I knew Loki was a snake, and I still let him bite me.*

He is blaming himself, Ulf thought.

"Fenrir was sent here to attack me, but he managed to free himself from Loki's dark magic."

Does that mean the other Rökkrs are under Loki's control? Chase wondered.

"Wait, how do you know all of this?" Chase asked, recalling Loki's warning.

"When Fenrir became a part of me, all his power and knowledge became a part of me as well."

166

"I understand now what you mean by that, but what happened to others?"

"As I said, the Rökkr attacked the others. But I do not know where they went."

Then where have they gone?

"What are thinking?" Ulf asked, seeing Chase in deep thought.

"I was thinking if you were still unconscious when the Rökkr attacked, Amphion and the others would not want to put you in danger."

"I was unconscious for a long time, and when I awoke, they were already gone."

"Ya, that's the thing. If I know them as well I as I think I do, they might have used the mystica jewels to teleport individually to different locations."

"Why different locations?"

"Think about it, Amphion, Arthur, and Theseus are warriors. Even though they have fought together before, they would probably want to fight their opponents individually."

"That is possible, but..."

"I know it is not a guarantee either. But it's the thing we have to go on to find them."

"I didn't put more mystic energy in those jewels, so if they teleported, it was only good for one more charge. Those jewels were only configured to teleport throughout Norway."

"If they didn't set a destination, they could be anywhere," Ulf said.

"Yes, anywhere in Norway."

"Wouldn't it be faster to teleport to them?"

"It would, but I don't have any more mystica jewels, so we have no choice but to fly to them," said Chase, starting up the airship. "It doesn't matter where we start as long as we find them."

Pinpointing Theseus' mystic energy, Chase pulled up his location on the three-dimensional map of Norway. "Alright I got Theseus' location. He is on the islands just west of the town of Fenes in Northern Norway."

"Hold on guys, we are on the way," Chase whispered.

All that has happened is my fault. If I would have listened to the others, none of this would have happened. Chase, frustrated with himself, gripped the controls hard. *I am so sorry.*

Chase, you cannot blame yourself for what has happened, Ulf thought, sensing Chase's guilt. *We all took a vow to save James, so no one will hold anything against you.*

Chapter 12: The Freezing Mountains

After several hours, Chase and Ulf arrived at Theseus' location.

"Whichever one of them was fighting Theseus, must have had one fierce battle," said Chase, looking down at the destruction caused by Theseus's and the ice dragon's fierce battle.

"Ya, a true battle between two legends," said Ulf.

Chase saw Theseus's mystic was close and touched down the airship. "The scanner says we are getting closer to Theseus' mystic energy, so he must be near."

Ulf saw Theseus and Beowulf off in the distance. "I see them. They are just off to the north."

"Ya, I see them now. You got sharp eyes as always, Ulf."

Chase landed the airship in the tundra. "Hopefully, they are alive."

Tracking through the deep snow, Chase looked at the scattered trees. "Be careful, this snow is really deep. Try not to rush through it, or you will tire yourself out."

"I am aware of that."

Stopping, Chase noticed a trail of blood in the snow.

"This is Beowulf's blood," said Ulf, recognizing the scent.

Chase, more concerned now, moved faster. "Then we must hurry."

"Even though you told me to track slowly through the snow, you are the one who is now tracking fast."

But with this sense of urgency that you feel, I cannot fault you, Ulf thought, running behind him. *Just do not let the guilt weigh you down. It will only cause you to make mistakes.*

Following the trail of blood, Chase found Beowulf lying in the snow. He knelt, pulled out the Sapphire Healing Stone, and started to treat Beowulf's wound.

"How are his wounds?"

"The wound is deep. From what I see, it looks like his neck was pierced by a sword. He is still breathing. All I can do right now is stop the bleeding to prevent him from dying. But we have got to get him out here and inside where he is not exposed to the elements."

"Can you check on Theseus and see how his wounds are?" Chase asked, seeing Theseus laying not too far.

"Of course."

"He is unconscious, his right hand is gone, and frostbite is starting to set in," Ulf reported.

"Alright."

Chase managed to stop the bleeding from Beowulf's neck and rushed to examine Theseus. "He has many broken bones, but despite that, it doesn't look like his life is any danger. It is best we get them inside, so we can treat their wounds better," said Chase, carefully picking Theseus up. "Can you carry Beowulf? I was able to stop the bleeding, so none of his blood will get on your fur if that is what you're worried about."

"I wasn't worried," Ulf said, smirking as the white aura appeared around him.

Ulf's eyes turned bright blue as he grew larger. "Direwolf."

Looking back at Chase, Ulf noticed his stunned silence. "This is the true form of Aesir before he was split by the All Father Odin into Aesir and Fenrir. This form is called Direwolf."

"Ya, I can tell, you have very large fangs now," Chase joked, watching Ulf put Beowulf on his back.

"Despite all your seriousness, you will still have time to make jokes," Ulf said.

Back on the ship, Chase treated their wounds. "I will do what I can, but I will not be able to heal them. Only Amphion has the ability to do that. I'm sure he will do what he can for them with his mystic energy. I will do more studying in healing alchemy when we get back to Shangri-La."

With as many broken bones and internal bleeding as they have, it is like they fell from the sky, Chase thought. *I don't even know if I will be able to stabilize their condition. We have Amphion—only he will be able to save them now.*

Chase, I have known you for a long time, I'm always able to tell when you are lying, Ulf thought, closing his eyes before walking into the cockpit. *Because you were never any good at it.*

"Alright, I've done what I can. It will be up to Amphion now," Chase said a couple of hours later, stepping into the cockpit.

"I saw you managed to close Theseus's wound. Is there anything that can be done to restore his hand?"

"Not at the moment. Something like that is beyond the mystic or medical healing I know. The level of alchemy and mystic energy required to regenerate a whole hand or any other missing body part are at a level that only Master Shinko or Timber have. And even if I did, I don't have the right magical ingredients for the Immortalem regeneratione (Immortal Rebirth) potion to regenerate his missing hand."

"Only Master Shinko or Timber would be able to restore Theseus's hand? Then we need find Amphion to heal Theseus."

"The computer is already tracking Amphion's mystic energy, so we will be at his location before too long," said Chase, pointing to the location on the map. "Besides, Theseus will still not be in any shape to fight for a while."

"Then what about his mystic energy, is it stable?"

"Yes, it is for now. Mystic energy is the magical energy that flows through the body of mortals and all living creatures. Only the body can replenish mystic energy, but only if it has proper time to recover. That is why we need Amphion to heal Theseus' internal injuries because it is hampering the recovery of his mystic energy. If the body doesn't heal, then the mystic energy will not flow and replenish. That is why it is imperative we find him right away." Chase put the airship into full drive. "Let's just hope Amphion is not injured."

"Try not to overthink it," said Ulf, warning him against such thoughts. Ulf remembered his battle with Amphion. "After all, he is a demigod and a strong warrior."

"Ya, he is stubborn with honor and pride. That is the reason why he won't lose even if it's against a God. I've pinpointed his location to the Jiehkkevárri Mountains. There is large blizzard all around the mountains, so we will have to be careful when we flying into it. Taking that into consideration, we should arrive there in about half of an hour," Chase said.

A blizzard like that will not even phase him, Ulf thought, smirking at the thought of Amphion being in it.

In the Jiehkkevárri Mountains, Amphion sensed Ulf. Bearing into the winter storm, Amphion continued to track through the snow.

This blizzard is relentless, I can barely see what is in front of me, Amphion thought, trying to find shelter. He clutched his hand and noticed the frostbite. *I need to get to shelter and soon. Even though I do not feel the cold, it can still kill me.*

After several more miles through the mountains, Amphion came across a cave. Summoning a torch in, Amphion started a fire. He heard movement and saw Hela start to move. She opened her eyes and saw Amphion tending the fire. "You have awakened. I am glad to see that."

"Where am I?" Hela asked in a daze.

"I have no knowledge of where we are. But maybe you can answer a question of mine. Do you remember anything that happened?"

Hela remained silent as her thoughts were clouded.

"I see," said Amphion seeing that she didn't remember.

"Why am I bound?" Hela asked.

"You are bound because I haven't determined whether you are a threat or not."

Hela tightened her eyes at Amphion's remark. Sensing the power of the bounds binding her, Hela realized she could not break free. "And what makes you see me as a threat?"

"A spell was cast upon you with dark magic. While under the control of the dark magic, you attacked my friends and me." Summoning more wood, Amphion tossed it into the fire. "I suspect Loki was responsible for this."

Hela, furious that Loki was controlling her, tried to keep her composure. "The last thing I remember is, I was on that airship with the one you call Chase, and before I knew what had happened, I lost consciousness."

"I suspected that Chase would do something like that, desperation even gets the better of the strong," said Amphion unsurprised. "Especially when it is to save a friend's life." Walking toward the cave entrance, Amphion observed the raging blizzard. "But that is not of concern. Right now, we have no choice but to wait until this storm passes."

"I can do something about that," said Hela, sitting up.

"You can break this storm?"

"I can, but not while I'm bound. You will have to trust me. You are stronger than me and can kill me at any moment. All I ask is that you release me from these bounds, so I can get us out of this blizzard."

"Very well," said Amphion, closing eyes waving his hand, releasing Hela.

Hela walked out into the blizzard. "I will disperse the clouds."

Amphion remained still, thinking, *Now allow me to observe why you are called the Goddess of the Valkyries.*

Holding out her sword, Hela swung in many different directions, sending shockwaves into the sky. The blizzard stopped as the storm clouds broke apart.

"Impressive, I can see now why you called the Goddess of the Valkyries," Amphion said, observing the now clear sky. "But know this, even after what you have just done, you have not earned my trust. If I sense that you are even the slightest threat, I will kill you without mercy," Amphion whispered.

Hela sheathed her sword, and gazed at Amphion's back. "I will be sure to remember that."

Trekking down the mountain, Amphion and Hela waited for the others to find them. A short while later, waiting at the base of the mountain, Hela was upset. "How did I end up here in the frozen mountains of Jiehkkevárri?"

"You and other dark entities attacked us at our campsite. During your ambush Arthur, Theseus, and I separated you and then teleported to different locations."

"I will make sure he suffers greatly for this," said Hela, clutching her fist in anger. "To force me, the Valkyrie Goddess, the warrior woman of the Norse, to do such dishonorable actions is unforgivable."

It shouldn't be much longer now, Amphion thought, ignoring Hela.

"Wouldn't you be able to teleport us back?"

"Unfortunately, no. We do not have the necessary energy to teleport to a specific destination," Amphion explained. "The jewel held only enough mystic energy to teleport once. We have no choice but to find a path that will guide us out of the mountains."

"Or if your friends find us first."

Amphion closed his eyes and faintly sensed Chase's and Ulf's mystic energy. "Then we will wait until they arrive."

"That was strange. I've never seen a storm break apart like that. Come to think about it, there was a shockwave that caused some turbulence the moment it dispersed," Chase said.

Hela is close by," said Ulf, picking up her scent.

"What?"

Suddenly the airship rocked violently. "Hold on."

Seeing Hela fly past the airship at great speed, Chase regained control. "That was Hela."

"Yes, it was. I would never mistake a scent."

Ignoring Hela, Chase focused on Amphion. "I don't know where she is flying off too, but right now we need to find Amphion."

"We already found him," said Ulf, pointing at the windshield.

Looking out, Chase saw Amphion standing on the nose of the airship. Engaging the autopilot, Chase opened the back of the airship.

"Are you alright?" Chase asked, when Amphion jumped in.

"As best as I can be, given the circumstances."

Noticing Theseus on the floor unconscious, Amphion walked toward him. Amphion knelt and looked over him and saw Theseus's hand was missing. "How long as he been like this?"

"I do not know for how long, but he is in really bad shape."

Amphion's eyes glowed bright and he saw all the broken bones inside of Theseus' body.

"Can you heal his broken bones?"

"I will do what I can, but it will take time."

Charging his aura, Amphion placed his hands on Theseus's chest and started to heal him.

"I will leave it to you then," said Chase, walking back into the cockpit relieved.

Sitting down in the pilot's seat, Chase shifted his attention to finding Arthur. Chase pulled up the three-dimensional holographic map of Norway and configured the scanner to Arthur's mystic energy. "Alright, I got his location."

"And where in Norway is that?" Ulf asked, recognizing the location.

Chase eyes glimmered with lightning. "He is at the top of the Gaustatoppen Mountain, where

Yggdrasill, the mystical tree from Norse legend, lays."

Chapter 13: Earth Guardian of Asgard

Arthur awoke in a daze under Yggdrasil tree at the top of Gaustatoppen Mountain. He looked around and was mesmerized by the beauty of the tree. "I haven't seen anything this beautiful since traveling to the Isle of Avalon. Have I died again?" Arthur whispered.

"No, you are still very much alive," a voice answered him.

Arthur looked up at the large tree and saw a white-furred figure standing on a branch. It jumped down toward him.

"I found you unconscious and injured, so I brought you here to the Yggdrasil on the Gaustatoppen Mountain to heal your wounds. I can see by your expression that this is not the first time you have encountered one of my kind," said the white-furred figure.

"Yes, I have met many other Earth Guardians throughout my life, even one quite recently as a matter of fact."

"I expected you to say something like that. After all, you were chosen by the Celtics, the Fairies of Avalon, and even the Earth Guardian of Scotloch to be the one true king of England."

"You know of me, great Guardian?"

"I do. No one, not even amongst the Earth Guardians, does not know of you and your nobility. But while you were resting, I did read your thoughts to confirm who I thought you were."

"I see that explains very much. Then can I ask of you your name, Earth Guardian?"

"I am Kindle, the Earth Guardian of Asgard and protector of this land," he answered.

Kindle pointed up at the Yggdrasil tree. "And this tree you see before you is the Yggdrasil. One of the life trees that gives life to this very Earth."

"The Yggdrasil tree that, the same one from Norse Mythology?" asked Arthur.

"Yes, the same one that stretches through the nine realms and into the heavens," Kindle answered.

Lifting his hand, Kindle showed Arthur all the clouds and mountains around them. Looking closely, Arthur saw a ruined castle city appear on top the clouds.

"This place, it is Asgard," said Arthur.

"What you see before you, are all that remains of Asgard home of the Norse Gods," said Kindle gazing upon the ruins in the distance.

"How was this place destroyed, even Merlin did not know its location?

Kindle chuckled. "You already know the answer to that question."

"Ragnarök," Arthur whispered.

"That was the destined end of the Norse Gods," Kindle confirmed. "Asgard itself was destroyed during the battle with the fire giant, Surtr."

"I thought it was Loki that lead to the end of Norse Gods with his children."

"In a way, he did. But he was just one of many reasons why the prophesized end came to pass."

Feeling regret about humanity, Kindle waved his hand as Asgard became camouflaged behind the clouds. "Humans have always been a disappointment to my kind. Not just because of their destructive nature, but also their interpretation of the truth."

Arthur remained silent, knowing Kindle spoke the truth.

"You don't dismiss my arguments. A true sign of a wise king," said Kindle, commending Arthur. "One who listens to reason and does not look away from the truth. I see now why you were chosen. I thank you for your sincerity, for listening to me, but that is all I can give you, for your enemy draws near," Kindle warned.

Arthur closed his eyes and sensed Grendel's mystic energy not too far away. "I must make haste then and meet him for battle."

Arthur stood up for a moment but collapsed in pain.

"You are still too injured to confront your enemy," Kindle cautioned.

"Then what must I do? As you said, the ogre draws closer," Arthur asked not to concerned about his injures.

"Yes, but he is still a good distance away and will not reach the mountain for some time. And even then, he will not be able to ascend, for the barriers around Asgard keeps out dark creatures. Rest for now."

"Thank you, kind Earth Guardian. Thank you for saving my life. I am in your debt," said Arthur, laying down to rest more.

"Your thanks are unnecessary; it is my duty as a guardian of this sacred place to help those who have wandered in," said Kindle. "I wish you well, King Arthur. You are no longer lost, for your friends will soon find you."

Before he could say anything, Kindle disappeared into the clouds. A black feather then fell out of the sky and landed in front of Arthur. Arthur picked up the feather as he heard the sounds of a bird. He saw a raven fly from the Yggdrasil into the sky over Asgard.

"A feather of a raven, a sign of Odin," said Arthur, chuckling.

Arthur looked at the Yggdrasil and wished Kindle well. "I wish you well as well, kind Earth Guardian. May Asgard be forever safe by its protector."

Arthur fell asleep, grateful to have met the gentle Guardian of Asgard, Kindle.

After several hours, Arthur awoke. Standing up, Arthur walked and looked over the edge of the cliff. *I am still not fully recovered, but I have to stop Grendel here and now before he gets to close. No matter what dark magic he may possess, it will not save him from my sword.*

Down the side of the mountain, Arthur walked through the protective barrier.

"It seems I have passed the protective barrier of Asgard," he said, looking back, no longer able to see the Yggdrasil.

The clouds inside the barrier began to move down the mountain, creating a hazy mist. "This must be Kindle's magic or the magic of the Yggdrasil. A defensive warding against dark creatures and magic of the sorts. I can sense the magic in this mist weakens darkness itself, so Grendel's strength should be lessened significantly." Arthur touched his shoulder feeling the pain. "But even then, with these injuries, he will still be dangerous."

Sensing Grendel's dark mystic energy draw near, Arthur prepared himself for his final battle against the ogre.

He is not even trying to hide his presence, Arthur thought, seeing Grendel's dark shadow moving around him. *Then again, he is a mindless creature now.*

Arthur turned around, hearing a growl, saw a pair of black eyes. "You finally decided to stop running around me, have you monster?"

Revealing itself, Grendel remained silent.

"That is right, I almost forgot you are incapable of words now," said Arthur, drawing Excalibur. "Your mind is no longer your own. Now let's end this, mindless creature, so that your evil can finally be put to an end." Grendel snarled at Arthur. "And it will be ended by my sword, Excalibur."

Grendel slowly retreated into the mist. Arthur saw Grendel trying to ambush him, closed his eyes, and waited. He heard light footsteps in the snow close to him, and moved swiftly, stabbing Grendel in the back, thrusting the ogre forward into the ground.

Grendel growled in agony. Seeing the righteous anger in Arthur's eyes, Grendel tried to crawl away.

"You coward." Again, Arthur impaled him as Grendel roared in pain. "Even your cowardice knows no bounds."

The light of Excalibur glowed bright; Arthur prepared to finish Grendel. "Now you will answer for all that you have killed. Purge this evil Excalibur," said Arthur, closing his eyes. Arthur pierced through Grendel's head, killing the ogre.

The light of Excalibur purged Grendel, lighting his body on fire as it turned to ashes. Sheathing his sword, Arthur looked at Grendel's charred remains. "Now go and face your final judgement before God. May He have mercy on your soul," said Arthur, walking down the mountain as the ashes blew in the wind.

Sensing his friends close by, Arthur waited in a frozen forest.

"Ready to go?" Chase asked

"Always, my friend," said Arthur.

Later that night, while Amphion was in his tent treating Theseus, the others sat near the campfire.

"I know everyone is tired and very stressed over everything that has happened these past few weeks, but we are not finished. Until we kill Loki and take the Life-Lock scroll from him, nobody will be safe from his evil."

Chase looked at Amphion's tent. "Plus, all of this is my fault as well. I wish I had done things differently, that way, none of you would have been put in this danger."

"You have nothing to be sorry for. Battle will always lead to other battles," said Arthur, dismissing him. "It is how you learn from them, which will lead you to make better decisions. None of us here blames you for what has happened. Just focus on what you can do instead of what you didn't."

"I know, but I need to say something to you and the others. Thank you," said Chase somberly.

Arthur placed his hand on Chase's shoulder. "Listen to me, trying to shoulder the burden of everything alone is impossible. I tried once when I was king and failed. Merlin always told me this— now I'm telling you. Never bear everything, let your friends help. Only then will you succeed. Now, then, with that being said, let us eat, for we have not eaten anything in days."

After eating, they discussed Loki.

"Now then, Chase, how do you think we should maneuver in this battle against the trickster god?"

"For now, we have no choice but to wait. The deal I had with Loki fell through before everyone fought the Rökkr."

"Wouldn't you be able to find Loki's divine energy again?

"No. The reason we were able to find him the last time is that he let us find him. The scanner won't be able to find him this time since he will probably mask his divine signature. I can only track him if he unmasks it. We have no choice but be patient for the moment and see if something happens," said Chase, staring into the fire.

"I agree. As Merlin always said, patience is the key to what you seek," said Arthur as he yawned. "But what is also key before anything is sleep, and right now, I think we all could use some."

"Ya, let us get some rest first and then try to come up with a plan first thing in the morning."

Sleeping through the night after their dreadful battles, elsewhere in the far reaches of the north, Loki plotted.

"How should I go about this?" Loki asked himself, staring at an odd-shaped hammer embedded in the ice. "After all, just luring him here would be so boring."

Suddenly, sensing a baleful presence, Loki turned and saw the dark figure that had confronted him before. "They have sent you again."

"No, I sent for myself," said the shrouded figure.

"Then why are you here?"

The shrouded figure stood in front of Loki menacingly. "I am watching," it said before stepping back and dissipating into darkness.

"Then I will be sure to put on a show for you," said Loki, smiling nervously.

The next morning, Chase waited outside, sorting through his thoughts about the disturbing prophetic dream.

"How did you sleep?" Arthur asked.

"As best as I could, minus the vision I had last night."

"Vision, of what kind?"

"A prophetic one of some sort. Images of the ancient battle between Thor and the Midgard Serpent."

"What do you think this vision means?"

"I can only think of one reason—an invitation from Loki."

"Then you know where he is?"

"Sort of. All I know is that it is in an icy valley cavern beyond the Arctic Circle. I can't really explain, I just know where to go."

"There is something you're not telling me isn't there?"

"I think it is for the best that Ulf and I do this alone. I have a strange feeling that he and I have to settle this ourselves."

It is not strange all. To settle an ancient battle that was not decided long ago. The last battle of the Norse Gods, Arthur thought.

"You don't have to explain anything. I think it is for the best that the both of you go."

Walking toward Amphion's tent, Arthur stopped and looked back at Chase. "And besides, there are still too many unknowns. There could be other forces involved."

I did not even think of the possibility of that, Chase thought disturbed. Looking up at the northern sky, a slight breeze blew. *What other dark forces could be involved in this?*

A few moments later, Chase met up with Ulf outside the airship. "Let's go."

A few hours later they were in the northern region of Norway. The visibility had become steadily worse.

"This could be another trap, you know," Ulf warned.

"I realize that, but I have no choice because this is the only chance we got."

"Where did we go?" Ulf asked, as they hiked across the icy plain.

"There, the mountains of the Arctic Circle, the Icegaios Mountains," said Chase, pointing to a range of mountains in the distance.

"And you think Loki is there?"

"I know he is."

You and I have been bound together for centuries; nothing will change that. For you have my fang and I will always walk beside you, thunder god, Ulf thought, seeing Chase's confidence.

"Thank you, old friend," Chase said, hearing Ulf's thoughts.

"It's funny being here now. It feels like we have done this many times before. Always on an adventure."

"But once we get James back, then we can go on a real one."

Chapter 14: Ragnarök

After a long trek across the icy plains, Chase and Ulf arrived at the tundra of the Icegaios Mountains.

"Are you ready?" Chase asked, looking into the valley.

"Do you have to even ask?" Ulf asked sarcastically.

"I guess not."

Walking deep through the icy valley, Ulf felt a familiar but ominous mystic energy. "What is this mystic energy I am sensing? It's familiar, but it feels cold."

"You've finally come, old enemy?"

Ulf sensed someone and looked to the top of the valley.

"What is it?" Chase asked.

Ulf could no longer sense the energy—it had disappeared as quickly as it had appeared.

"It's nothing. Let's keep going."

Chase said nothing but knew Ulf wasn't being honest. There was something.

Coming to the end of the valley, Chase looked up and saw a cavern on the mountain side.

"This is it," Chase whispered, seeing an icy mist cover the entrance.

The entrance was at a considerable height, and there were no trails leading to it. Chase pulled climbing equipment from his backpack and began prepping for the climb.

"We're going to have to climb to get in, Ulf," Chase said.

"Is that the cave you saw in your dream?" Ulf asked.

Chase's eyes began glowing a lightning blue as he conjured the vision. "Look," Chase said, sharing his vision with Ulf.

Ulf's eyes glowed white, understanding the visions that Thor, through Chase, had given him. "I see."

Chase hit his ice ax into the ice and started to climb up the mountainside. "Then let's get to climbing."

Ulf embedded his claws into the ice. "Yes."

They reached the entrance of the cave after a treacherous climb. They stared into the abyss of the cave that seemed even colder than the outside temperature. Setting their fears aside, Chase and Ulf pressed forward into the icy cave. The ice inside the cave glowed a crystal blue.

"This crystal blue light keeps dimming and brightening like it is trying to speak," said Chase, touching the ice.

"Yes, the mystic energy here is mysterious. I have never sensed anything like it before," Ulf said. "The energy feels as though it is the coldness of winter itself. Can you feel it?"

Chase took his hand off the ice, unsettled by coldness from the icy mystic energy. "Ya, and for whatever reason, I don't like it."

Chase had never felt mystic energy like that before. But he also felt as though it was somehow familiar. He thought that perhaps it could be because of Thor. Chase also felt more of his own mystic energy the deeper they went into the cave.

Pondering the mystery without either one knowing, Loki watched them through one of his illusions. "I think it is time we welcome our guests, don't you?"

"Get on with it," said a figure in the darkness.

Loki tapped his snake staff on the ground, sending magic pulses throughout the cavern. "I hope they're not afraid of the dark."

The cavern around Chase and Ulf started to shake violently.

"What is happening?" Ulf yelled.

"I don't know. It must be Loki's doing," said Chase, seeing the ice begin to crack.

Ice fell from the cavern ceiling as it started to cave in.

"Move," Chase yelled, realizing they were in danger.

Chase moved fast trying to avoid a large piece of falling ice. Unfortunately, he wasn't fast enough and the ice landed on his foot. Unable to free his foot, he charged his lightning aura, but was still unable to free himself.

Ulf saw that Chase was stuck and charged his white aura, throwing Chase to the other side of the cavern as the rest of it collapsed. When all was calm, Chase opened his eyes.

"Ulf?" said Chase, looking around for him.

He remembered Ulf had knocked him out of the way and was worried that Ulf had been buried under the ice. Chase tried to move the large boulders of ice blocking the path. "Ulf? Ulf, can you hear me?"

After a moment, Chase heard a wolf's howl.

"Ulf, are you alright?" Chase yelled, relieved that Ulf was alive.

"I'm fine. I was able to run out of the way at the last moment," Ulf yelled from the other side of the cavern. The pathway is completely blocked by the fallen ice."

"Ya. I tried moving them, but they are too heavy," Chase said.

"Then maybe we can destroy them to clear the path," Ulf said, charging his aura, preparing to destroy the rubble.

"I wouldn't recommend that because we may cause this cavern to further collapse."

"Then what do you suggest we do?" Ulf asked, calming his aura.

"There are only a couple of ways to get out of this. One is to see if there's another way out, and the other…"

"I can dig you out," Ulf interrupted.

"But that would take several hours, and there is no guarantee," Chase sighed. "Trying to find another way out might not work well since we don't know how deep this cavern goes."

"I will dig through this ice then," said Ulf, picking through it with his claws. "Chase, you go on ahead and go after Loki.

"Are you sure?"

"Yes, we do not have time to waste. As soon as I dig through the ice, I will catch up to you."

"Alright, but make sure you don't take too long, or I will be done by the time you dig through," Chase teased.

"Don't worry, I will be there faster to save you in the end," Ulf chuckled.

Standing up, Chase tried to put weight on his foot but couldn't. His ankle had been broken in the chaos. He didn't have any healing stones, so he patched up his foot. Once he was finished tending to his ankle, Chase navigated cautiously through the ice and spikes in the ground.

After a period, Chase stopped to rest. He picked up a piece of the glowing ice and pondered the mystery behind them. *There is something very unusual about this ice. Not only is there a strange beckoning, but it's also so indestructible that even I cannot destroy it with my lightning, which is the power of Thor himself. Is all of the Icegaios Mountain like this?* Chase wondered. He tossed the ice and began to look around the glowing cavern. The deeper he went into the cavern, the more questions he had. But for some reason, he also felt as though he knew one of the answers. Whatever mystic energy it was, it was not the first time he had encountered it.

After a while, Chase came across a large, open area in the cave where he could see the light from the night sky above. This not only gave him a way out but a way back in if he had to come back for Ulf.

Standing directly underneath the opening, Chase saw the northern lights, which made him smile. "No matter how many times I see it, I'm still amazed by it. The Bifröst, the gateway that connects all the Nine Realms," Chase whispered as his eyes turned lightning blue.

Shaking his head, Chase felt a slight headache. "The Bifröst is the northern lights?"

Chase saw a blue spark coming from a large wall of ice and heard the hum of thunder. He could not explain what it was or how it felt. It was as though it called to him. Instinctively, Chase walked to the spark. Standing next to the large wall of ice, he looked down to see a hammer embedded in the ice. Sparks of lightning came from the hammer. Chase intuitively reached for it.

"I wouldn't do that if I were you."

Chase recognized the voice and turned to see Loki leaning up against the wall of ice.

"At least not yet."

Chase took out his rifle and fired several shots, but the bullets passed right through Loki.

An illusion, Chase thought, seeing the image of Loki fade.

"You are really touchy, aren't you?" said Loki, sitting on a boulder. "But then again, after everything that has happened to you, I can't say that I blame you."

Chase remained silent but maintained his aim at Loki. Loki waved his hand dismissively. "Please, you and I both know something like that will not hurt me. Even if you were to shoot, I would just cast another illusion, and I will continue this conversation."

"And why should I listen to what you have to say?" Chase asked, lowering his rifle.

"Because I will tell you what you don't know about yourself."

197

"What do you mean?"

"We will come to that part later, but first, I'm sure you noticed there was something mysterious about this place."

"Ya, I noticed there is a strange mystic energy here. What about it?"

"Have you really ignored what Thor has been trying to tell you from the moment you arrived here?" Loki laughed.

The odd sensations I felt when I first got here, that was Thor, Chase thought.

Loki saw Chase's hesitation. "Ah, so you have noticed."

"Then what exactly is Thor trying to tell me?"

"It is not so much that he is trying to tell you; it is more like he is trying to warn you."

"Enough of your games, trickster, tell me what you know."

Loki sighed at Chase's impatience. "It seems I have to explain it to you after all. Very well then. First, I am going to tell you the secrets behind Ragnarök," Loki said, snapping his fingers, casting illusions of day and night.

Loki slowly walked around Chase, playing the illusions. "I'm sure you haven't noticed. In fact, I'm sure none of you mortals have. Some of the written texts about Ragnarök are far from the truth."

"What is that truth?"

"Impatient as always. Ever since the end of the Viking Age, the days have been getting shorter, and the nights have been getting shorter without any of you noticing."

Loki cast an illusion of land, snow, and ice. "And with its coldness, set the world slowly into an ice age. Can you guess why that is?" Loki waited for Chase to answer before continuing when none came. "The reason for this is that certain entities were sealed away during Ragnarök, but some of their mystic energy wasn't. So, they were only partially sealed away by the All Father Odin."

Odin, the ruler of the Aesir and Norse Gods, Chase thought.

"Or maybe they were put to sleep, but over the centuries, they have been steadily awakening. This is the mystic energy that is all around here."

"Bingo! You have one of the right answers," Loki said.

"Then what are these entities, and why were they sealed away?"

"I can see that your curious now —good," said Loki pleased. "The reason why is because they were too powerful. Fearing that power, Odin used a certain spell to seal them away." Loki gestured his hand toward the wall of ice. "And the lock and key to that seal."

"Mjolnir," said Chase, looking at the hammer.

"That's right, the hammer Mjolnir crafted by the Dwarfs for the mighty god, Thor," said Loki, appearing next to it.

Odin used Thor's hammer infused with his power to put to sleep beings of winters inside this wall of ice. What the Gods called the Ice Wall."

Sensing the ice-cold mystic energy, Chase saw images of tall humanoid ice entities appear in his mind. "No, it can't be, that is not possible. They were destroyed during Ragnarök."

He has finally realized what Thor has been trying to tell him, Loki thought, chuckling.

"The Jötunn (Frost Giants)," Chase whispered in fear.

"That was one of the names they were called, but that is not their true name. The Ice Wall you see before you was made by really powerful magic, so much so that it drained away most of Odin's and Thor's strength during Ragnarök," said Loki, looking up at the wall of ice. Loki waved his hand, and an illusion of the Arctic Ocean barricades of ice all around it appeared. "It contained most of the ice in the Arctic Ocean.

"It really is pathetic. If neither one would have done so, then they wouldn't have met their fate by Fenrir and the Midgard Serpent," Loki chuckled at the irony. Loki cast away the illusions before he continued. "But then again, if that didn't happen, my escape from my bonds wouldn't have gone unnoticed.

You can't imagine the pain of having venom dropped into your eyes. Even I have to admit, if it wasn't for that outside help, I wouldn't have ever gotten free," Loki said, pacing in anger.

"It was Jǫrmungandr (Midgard Serpent) that freed you?" Chase asked.

"Oops, you weren't supposed to hear that part. Sorry," Loki said, covering his mouth sarcastically. "Well, it really doesn't matter at this point…"

Devoid, Chase thought.

"…since this is your final battle against your ancient enemy," Loki said. "Now that you know one of the secrets of Ragnarök, I think it's time you have a happy reunion with an old friend."

Eager, Loki snapped his fingers, and the sound echoed through the cavern.

"What did you do?" Chase demanded.

Loki grinned and pointed up.

Chase stared into the silence and was unnerved when he saw a serpent's tail descend.

The Midgard Serpent appeared, lowering its head. "Now it is time to meet your end, son of Odin."

The Midgard Serpent silently gazed at Loki. "As promised, I leave Thor to you. I look forward to you ripping him apart," Loki said.

"No, that's impossible, Sepher," the serpent said, lowering himself into the cavern.

"Oh, it's true. The one you see before you is the one and only Sepher Axes, your mentor," said Loki, taking delight in Chase's agony. "Or should I say, he never existed to begin with."

"No, there is no way that you are Sepher," Chase said.

"Just like that time you told me you regretted not being able to save your parents," Devoid laughed.

"How, why?" Chase said, no longer denying the truth.

"Because you and I are mortal enemies bound by Norse Gods. You mean you never questioned anything? How everything was set before you?"

Chase remained silent.

"Everything in your life has been a lie—from the moment I killed your parents in front of you to when you joined the Black Order and trained with Sepher to gain your vengeance. It was me who guided you, me who manipulated you. Think carefully now. Think back to all the moments you spent with him."

This can't be, Chase thought, remembering his time with Sepher.

"Haven't you ever wondered why I killed your parents? Why Sepher was the one who personally trained you. Why he pushed you so hard to be the very best. I will tell you that I did not want you to forget the pain and despair I caused. It was to help you awaken your power of Thor. But despite all that, you were still too weak," said Devoid, disappointed.

"I only have one question," said Chase, realizing most of his life had been a lie. "Tell me, why. Why me?"

"Why bother asking at this point?" Devoid said with a demonic laugh.

"Answer me," Chase yelled in rage.

"For what you have become now," Devoid answered. "I wanted you to be stronger than you were in your past life when you fought me during Ragnarök. I want to take away everything you care about and turn it all into nothing. To send you into absolute despair."

"Everything you have heard from him is true," said Loki, joyous by what was transpiring.

"Your fate, your destiny, was decided the moment Odin decided to reincarnate Thor through his bloodline. Of course, I played a part throughout most of the moments in your life, along with other dark forces. That is something that even I won't discuss. But I will say this with all sincerity—the moment you were born, it was already in the fates that Devoid would kill your parents. It was meant to instill hatred in your heart, to set you on the path of vengeance." Loki snapped his fingers, conjuring an illusion of Thor. "All for the purpose of turning you into him. To awaken the power that slumbered within. But with all set plans, there will always be flaws. In this case, it was your best friend, the physical incarnation of the dark flame, James Akatsuki," said Loki as he cast an illusion of James. "So, we came up with something else if you were to stray from the path we set before you. That is why Devoid called you to Iceland. To remind you of who you are. For Sepher to die and for you to cry. To help amplify your pain and despair of losing another loved one. A true eruption to remember," Loki laughed.

"You act like it was nothing. Over hundred thousand people lost their lives in that," Chase yelled.

Loki dismissed Chase's damnation. "I act like this because it is nothing. To Gods, humans are nothing more than ants. If you crush a hundred thousand, then one million will take their place. And besides, you are in no place to question my methods when you yourself used everyone in the path of seeking your vengeance."

"Shut up," Chase said. "I don't care if you manipulated my life because I am not that person anymore. I was saved by him—by my best friend, James."

Loki laughed. "Yes, he did. But yet, you let him die."

"James did die and in my arms," Chase admitted. "But he won't be dead for much longer once I get the Life-Lock scroll from you," Chase said, staring murderously at Loki.

Loki snapped his fingers, and the Life-Lock scroll appeared. "We shall see, hunter. We shall see. The finale is just getting started."

Chapter 15: Cold Descent of Darkness

"I'm curious about something, Loki. You said you and other dark forces played parts in my life. What did you mean by dark forces?" Chase asked, bothered.

Loki was frightened at the thought of the dark figure. He wondered if he somehow knew. But that was impossible. There was no way he could know.

"I don't have the faintness idea what you are talking about," Loki said, dismissing Chase.

"When I'm done killing you and Devoid, they're next on the list," Chase vowed.

"You really know how to ruin my fun—even back then," Loki said, remembering Thor. "But it doesn't matter. I will get to enjoy every single moment of your pain in return." Loki conjured a glowing mirror of water. "I just hope to make it one to remember. I will record it all. Enjoy your last moments alive, Actaeonis," Loki said sarcastically.

"I don't plan on this being my final battle but promise these will be your final moments."

"Do not underestimate me, little spark. Even after told countless times never underestimate those who are clearly stronger, you still do. But as Loki said, it will be your last," said Devoid demonically to Chase.

"That lesson I have learned. I'm just glad I didn't learn from you," Chase said.

"Still as arrogant, I see. I will be sure to strip away that arrogance when I tear you apart." Devoid looked at Mjolnir then back to Chase. "Though without Mjolnir, you will truly not awaken your power from Thor. But even with you without it, I will be sure to let you live long enough to experience the greatest despair and pain," said Devoid, relishing the thought of killing Chase.

The lightning around Chase became intense as he closed his eyes. "If my life is a lie, I don't care." Opening his eyes, the lightning enveloped the whole cavern. "But I did choose them as they chose me." Chase wielded Zeus's thunderbolt. "Just as right now, I choose to kill you both myself."

Devoid guarded himself against the sheer intensity of Chase's lightning. "Bold words, nothing more. As always, you are."

Before Devoid could finish, the thunderbolt zapped past Devoid. Stunned into silence, Devoid looked back at the thunderbolt pierced into the Ice Wall. Blood dripped from a cut on his face onto the ice.

"I'm not as weak as you think I am," Chase declared, summoning the thunderbolt as Devoid became enraged.

The battle continued as Loki looked on, clapping his hands in excitement.

"Very impressive, Chase. You may indeed hold a candle to Thor. But will see how much longer that will last," Loki declared, seeing Chase struggle.

Devoid knocked Chase against the ice. Chase feeling the aching pain from his broken foot, threw the thunderbolt into the ice ceiling, collapsing it on top of Devoid. He knew it wouldn't hold Devoid for long but would give him enough time to devise a strategy.

"Very resourceful. To think you would come up with such a plan is truly impressive. Even I, Loki, the God of Mischief, am impressed. But you should watch where you step," said Loki, smiling gleefully.

Chase felt something hard at his feet and looked down. He was horrified to find the dismembered remains of Hela. He had not seen them before.

"Don't act so surprised. I just didn't allow you to see them until now. She came here trying to kill me for controlling her, but the one in the ice took care of her.

Hela never saw her attacker coming.

Before Chase could process anything, he saw the ice rubble start to move.

"I wouldn't waste too much time with your slight reprieve if I were you; otherwise, you might die to soon," Loki warned.

"I wouldn't be so sure about that," Chase said, looking up at Loki. How else would you get me to pick up Mjolnir if I was dead."

"It doesn't surprise me that you figured that," Loki said, closing his eyes. "It is as you said, only the one who is worthy can lift Mjolnir."

Suddenly, large tremors began to shake the cavern.

"But we still have plenty of time before that," Loki said.

Chase looked back at the ice rubble as a dark aura seeped through it and enveloped the cavern while the ice rocks violently scattered everywhere.

The darkness dissipated; Loki smiled. "Now the true fun begins."

Lowering its head, the Midgard Serpent opened its pitch-black eyes.

"Your death, your true despair begins now," Devoid said, breathing its poison breath.

"I am not ready to give up yet," Chase said, pointing the thunderbolt at the Midgard Serpent.

"But I will end you, once and for all," Devoid replied.

The battle between the mortal enemies raged for a few hours with no victor. The combatants were wounded, but neither could deliver the final blow, killing their enemy.

Exhausted as his vision blurred, Chase dropped to one knee. "I won't fall."

"You truly have come a long way," Devoid said as he laid down, bleeding.

The Midgard Serpent smirked, seeing the silhouette of Thor around Chase. "You have truly awakened."

Before Chase could respond, Devoid was ripped apart. Horrified, Chase gazed up and saw a dark shroud standing over the remains of the serpent.

"Who are you?" Chase asked fearfully, sensing its sinister dark mystic energy.

The shrouded figure glanced down at Chase but did not answer. Ignoring him, the dark shroud looked at Loki in wrath.

"Why is it here? I still have... " Loki whispered, slowly backing away.

"No, you don't," said the dark shroud, disappearing into darkness.

In absolute terror, Loki frantically looked around the ice cavern for it but could not see the shrouded figure.

"We have seen enough of your failure, false God," the dark shroud whispered to Loki.

Loki jumped down and tried to escape, but the dark shrouded appeared before him, grabbed and lifted him by the throat. Staring at Loki with its pitch-black eyes, the dark shroud impaled Loki in the stomach, retrieving the Life-Lock scroll.

A shadowy pit appeared under Loki. "You were the trickster of Norse Gods, always sewing doubt and chaos. You may have been one of them, but you never were a God."

Shadowy hands emerged from the pit and grabbed Loki.

"Please, I can still be of use. Don't do this," Loki said, pleading for his life.

The dark shroud smiled at Loki's fear. "No. For your failure, you will suffer a fate worse than death." Laughing demonically, the dark shroud let go of Loki. "You will know the true meaning of terror as you will be forever engulfed by shadow. Damned for all eternity in the dark."

"Please save me," Loki yelled, reaching out for Chase.

Chase could do nothing but watch in horror.

"You never were anything. You were always nothing," the dark shroud whispered. "Forever trapped in the shadow of Thor. Steeped in the evils of envy for the admiration of the Gods you could never attain." But worry not, you will never be truly alone in the dark."

Laughing, the shadowy pit swallowed Loki and disappeared.

"How could you condemn him to such a fate?" Chase yelled.

The dark shroud turned to Chase. "Odin, Thor, and the Gods, he was desperate to be acknowledged with his trickery. It earned him nothing but their contempt and eventually, their hatred. Grendel, Sultr, the Midgard Serpent, and Ragnarök itself, he caused all of it. He whispered in their ears with his trickery and inevitably led the Norse Gods to their end. From the throwing of the serpent into the sea to the theft of Thor's hammer. He deserved his fate. And such is damnation, forever tormented by the shadows of darkness. That was his price to pay."

"It was you this whole time. You're the dark force behind all of this," Chase said.

"Yes and no. You'll know the true meaning behind everything in time. For now, you still have a fate you must fulfill." The dark shroud slowly walked to Chase. "Before the time of Norse, before they were known to Norse Gods, the ones who sleep here walked the Earth and with them, Winter itself. As destiny foretold, it brought a new ice age."

"Fimbulvetr," Chase whispered.

"Yes," the dark shroud said. "And their name is the Winter Wraiths. They are mortal entities that are the physical manifestation of Winter itself. Due to the Norse Gods fear of them and that prophecy, they were sealed away in the frozen wasteland you stand upon. These ice mountains, the whole Arctic Circle is their prison."

"Why? Why would you reveal all of this to me?"

"As I said, you still have a fate that you must fulfill. But if you really want to know, I will reveal this truth to you. There is nothing you can do to stop them. Now let me help you fulfill this part of your destiny," the dark shroud said, grabbing Chase.

Ulf appeared at that moment, biting down on the arm of the dark shroud, trying to drag him away from Chase.

"Aesir the God of all wolves," the dark shroud said, not at all wounded.

Seeing Ulf was protecting Chase, the dark shroud retreated to the Ice Wall. "As in your past life, you stood alongside the God of Thunder. Your presence here is not unexpected. But like him and James Akatsuki, your fate, your destiny has already been decided."

"What do you mean by that?" Chase asked, struggling to stand.

"Your destiny is now intertwined with James Akatsuki. But to see a part of it unravel, you must first make a choice."

Ulf had heard enough of the dark shroud and charged his white aura. "Enough of your nonsense demon, you weren't surprised by my bite. You will be this time when I rip out your throat."

"I wouldn't be so sure. Because then the object of your journey will burn to ashes," said the dark shroud revealing the Life-Lock scroll.

"Ulf, stop."

"Alright," Ulf growled, seeing the scroll.

"You know the price, Actaeonis. So, I will make this very simple for you. The dark shroud pointed toward Mjolnir. "Either you lift the hammer and break the seal with your power, or do nothing as the salvation for the ones you cherish is destroyed."

The dark shroud levitated the scroll in his hand to force Chase to make the difficult choice that would decide the course of fate. "The choice is yours, descendant of Thor."

Chase hesitated to decide.

"I do not play tricks, nor has centuries taught me patience," said the dark shroud, annoyed by Chase's hesitation. "I suggest you make your decision quickly."

Ulf growled at Chase's hesitation.

Chase looked at Mjolnir and then back at Ulf. Hardening his resolve, Chase staggered toward the Ice Wall as he thought about James.

The dark shroud smiled. "Lift Thor's hammer, save your friend's life, but at the cost of the world. This is the price you will pay."

Standing in front of the ice wall, Chase grasped Mjolnir. He was torn as he thought about the vow he'd made to James that he would save him and they'd live to have more adventures together. Chase's eyes turned to lightning blue as he freed Mjolnir from the ice. He had every intention of keeping his promise to James.

Lightning bolts ricocheted through the cavern into the night sky above as a large crack appeared in the Ice Wall.

Grinning, the dark shroud slowly disappeared into shadow. "Very well done. I just hope you don't regret it," said the dark shroud, dropping the Life-Lock scroll. "You asked before for my name. I will now tell you. My name, as it has been since ancient times, is The Shroud. As the dawn of the ice age perpetuates, so shall the cold descent of darkness."

Ulf watched Chase wield Mjolnir and was in awe. He could feel the energy surge past him, making his fur stand on end. He felt a profound joy as though he were seeing Chase for the first time. A tear slid slowly down his face.

Chase lowered the hammer, the lightning within the cavern stopped. "It is mine once more."

Possessed by Thor, Chase looked back and smiled at the wolf. "It has been too long, my old friend."

"Yes, it truly has been," said Ulf as his eyes glowed white possessed by Aesir.

Thor knelt and petted Aesir. "Even though this is brief, we will never be apart again."

"Yes, as they are together, so shall we be," Aesir agreed.

With one final embrace, the Norse god slumbered once more within their descendants. Opening their eyes, Chase and Ulf were in a daze.

"What just happened to us?" Chase asked, dropping Mjolnir in the snow.

"I do not know," said Ulf.

Chase looked at the Ice Wall, noticing the wide crack within. Feeling the cold mystic energy intensify, Chase touched the crack. "The seal is now broken."

"Yes, and there is nothing keeping the frozen ancients from awakening. Judging from the flow of the mystic energy, they will soon be upon us."

Chase saw the Life-Lock scroll and picked it up. He felt the tremendous energy it contained.

"Now we can save his life," Chase said, relieved, putting the scroll away.

Ulf saw the burden lift from Chase's shoulders. "Shouldn't you examine its contents?"

"Soon, I will. Once my mystic energy recovers. Right now, I don't think I have enough power to contain it."

"Do you remembered the last thing that dark creature told you?" Ulf asked.

"It said its name is The Shroud."

"The Shroud. What do you want to do about it?"

"For now, we will let it go. James's life is first. We will gather more information on The Shroud and find out what type of dark entity it is to hunt it down. Let's get back to the others and journey back to Shangri-La before James's resurrection."

"But first, we are not leaving her like this," Chase said, looking down at Hela's remains.

"Of course," Ulf said, helping Chase.

"There, they can stay in there for now," Chase said, storing Hela's remains into his backpack.

"So, how are you going to send her off to the next life? After all, we do not have a Viking ship."

"I took a couple of the Vikings and stored them in my pocket dimension when we were at the Viking museum doing research. So, as long as we use one of them and have her Valkyrie weapons gathered, we should be able to send her off on her journey to Valhalla."

Ulf chuckled, nodded his head yes. "Alright."

Suddenly, the cold mystic energy within the ice glowed brighter. More cracks formed within the ice wall as the cavern shook violently.

"We have to get out of here now," Chase yelled.

They ran to the exit, but ice boulders had already blocked their path. They ran back toward the ice wall. Chase looked up through the large opening above.

"We have to get up there somehow."

"How? The whole cavern is collapsing, and even if we were to climb, we wouldn't make it."

Chase, for a moment, heard Thor's voice guiding him to use Mjolnir to open the Bifrost.

"I have a plan, but you are going to have to bear with me."

Chase charged his lightning aura, held out his hand to Mjolnir, and said, "Bifrost Opið (Bifrost Open)"

A rainbow portal descended from the Northern Lights, enveloping them. Soaring across the sky, they emerged from the Bifrost crashing in the frigrid land of the Arctic.

"Next time, work on your control of the Bifrost," Ulf sneered, shaking the snow off him.

"Sorry, I'll be sure to do that," Chase said, laughing.

Hearing ice breaking, Chase and Ulf looked off in the distance, saw the Icegaios Mountains crumble as a beam of light shot up into the sky, forming dark clouds.

"So, they have awakened."

"Ya, and with them the storm," Chase answered, feeling the cold rush by him.

In the mountains, the remains of tall pale figures emerged from a blizzard. The Winter Wraiths opened their icy blue eyes.

"The ice of snow begins."

Raising their hands, the storms of winter moved rapidly.

"The return of Fimbulvetr (Great Winter.)"

Chapter 16: The Life-Lock Scroll

Chase and Ulf regrouped with the others a couple of hours later.

"Let's keep this brief. We don't have much time," Chase said, giving Hela a Viking funeral on frozen shores.

"Let us take this to give her a proper farewell to Valhalla," said Amphion, placing Hela on the Viking ship with her weapons.

Holding up a torch, Chase set the Viking ship on fire, starting the funeral pyre as it set sail into the sea.

"Farewell Norse Goddess, may you have eternal honor and glory as you did in this life."

With final farewells to Hela spoken, everyone watched the Viking ship sail as it burned upon the horizon.

One week after the adventure in Norway to retrieve the Life-Lock scroll, Chase and the others returned to Shangri-La. Not speaking to anyone, Chase shut himself into the library. For weeks in the Oracle library, he buried himself in books as he tried to study the contents of the Life-Lock scroll. In the rock training grounds of Shangri-La, Arthur and Amphion trained to hone their skills.

"I really am concerned about Chase. He hasn't come out of the library in weeks," Arthur said.

"He is just seeking answers to questions we all want answered," said Amphion, understanding Arthur's concern.

"The question was how to use the spell embedded in that scroll to break the curse of death that binds James."

"For now, just leave him be. He will come out in his own time to see him," Amphion said, slashing the rocks he'd been levitating.

"Alright, I'll leave it be for now," Arthur begrudgingly accepted.

"That is all I ask."

Timber watched the group from a distant forest. He understood their concern for their friend and went to speak with the hunter.

Chase was unhappy with his research. He was not able to decode much of the scroll, and what he had would not help break the curse on James. Chase needed to decipher the scroll before James's next revival.

"Your friends are concerned for you," Timber said, walking into the library.

"I can't stop, not now," Chase said.

"You look exhausted. You should get some rest," Timber said, seeing Chase's fatigue. "There is still time before he awakens from the curse."

"I know, but that is only a week away. He will not be able to remember most of his memories. But once he awakens, he will slowly remember them over time. And once he remembers everything, his curse will activate again, and he will die again in a never-ending cycle."

"I see, so you thoroughly researched the curse of life and death."

"I had to since I'm going to break it. It is, after all, one of the strongest magical curses. That is why I want to learn this spell. So that when I bind my life to his, he will be able to remember his past and not suffer from death because of it."

Standing silent, Timber understood Chase's reasoning but saw the flaws in his logic.

"I'm only just now barely able to understand a fraction of the scroll's content."

"What have you found?" Timber asked, looking at the Life-Lock scroll.

"Not much, if anything," Chase said, frustrated.

The illustrations and codex glowed as Chase opened the scroll. Timber looked at the codex carefully, recognizing the language in which it was written.

"It is written in ancient Sumerian," he said to Chase.

"Yes, all the texts written in the scroll are in ancient Sumerian," Chase said.

"Ancient Sumerian is no longer a spoken language, and all known texts written over the centuries have either been lost or destroyed. I see now why you struggled to translate it."

"My knowledge of the Sumerian language is not that great, but this is what I have been able to decipher."

The glowing texts levitated. "Only under the light of the full moon can this spell be cast and with it the binding of life."

"I see. That is plausible given the type of spell it is."

"What do you mean by given the type of spell it is?"

The Earth Guardian closed his eyes briefly and sighed. "Life spells, especially ones that commune with the soul, can only be cast with the full moon's light. Only then can the spell work successfully."

"This spell is a life spell," Chase said, looking at the scroll again in amazement.

"In a sense, yes. But given its power, it would be more accurate to say it is a soul spell."

"Do you know when the next full moon will be?"

"No, but you will be able to tell with this."

Timber snapped his fingers, and an astronomical calendar made of stone appeared.

"This is a Mayan calendar. There aren't any left in the world," said Chase, studying it. "How did you get something like this?"

"This place is special. It houses all of the world's knowledge. Here in Shangri-La, knowledge is never lost."

Chase pushed past his enthusiasm and re-focused on his task. He studied the Mayan astronomical calendar closely and realized the next full moon would be soon.

"The next full moon is in a week. The same day as James's revival."

"Then if you want to stop the curse before it begins again," Timber said, waving his hand, making the Mayan calendar merge back into the stone floor. "You must learn this spell in that time. You will find texts here written in ancient Sumerian, but none that will aid to decipher the complexity of this codex. Before you try to read them, you should seek the one whose knowledge exceeds even mine. Only she will be able to help you," said Timber as he opened the doors to the library.

"Master Shinko," Chase whispered.

"She's lived here since ancient times, acquiring every piece of knowledge on this Earth. I'm sure Master Shinko will impart her wisdom of lost languages to you if you were to ask."

If only I could, Chase thought, disappointed.

Timber saw Chase was not amused by his short-sightedness. "If you weren't so focused on trying to decipher the scroll yourself, you would have realized not everything can be done yourself. You are not the only one trying to save his life. After all, he is her disciple—Master Shinko and mine."

"I am sorry. I promise you something like this will never happen again.

"Your apology is unnecessary," Timber said, dismissing Chase. "If you understand your mistake, then improve yourself. Focus on what you can accomplish, not on what you cannot."

Chase was grateful for the wisdom of the Earth Guardian and bowed his head in respect. "If you don't mind me asking, how is Theseus?"

"For now, he is stable. The regenerative healing process takes time. If you want to know more of the particular details, you will have to ask Master Shinko. She can speak better for him than I can. I am not his healer; I am an Earth Guardian charged to protect this sacred land of Anki," Timber said before departing to continue his watch over the Himalayas.

After Timber left, Chase wrapped up the scroll, knowing he couldn't solve the problem without the help of his master. He left the library, determined not to waste the time he had left.

Walking through the castle halls, Chase was annoyed by the structure's constant change. "I remember Timber once said the halls and stairways rapidly changed to help get to your desired location, but I can never get used to it."

Suddenly, the halls changed. Chase stood in front of James's room. "Is this truly where I have to be?"

"You are," said Shinko, opening the door.

"Master Shinko."

"You desired to find me, so the castle led you here."

Before Chase could say anything, Shinko closed the door behind her. "Not here."

"I know the reason you have come to see me. I will answer your questions, but not here. I know you want to see to him, but for now, let him rest."

Back in the Oracle library, Shinko asked Chase, "Now, you want to learn how to translate the scroll?"

"I need to learn the spell contained within this scroll before James's resurrection. That's two weeks' time."

"I already know. You don't have to repeat it," Shinko said, annoyed.

"Right, sorry," Chase said, handing her the scroll.

Shinko ignored Chase's apology and opened the scroll. She smiled, looking at the illuminated codex and illustrations within. "This is very impressive even by my standards as the knowledgeable one. I will tell you what is written within this scroll, but first, I will need to know everything that happened to you and your friends in Norway. Including the cold darkness you mentioned that has awakened from its slumber.

Chase tried to speak, but Shinko placed her finger on his forehead. "There is no need to explain. I'll be able to see it for myself," Shinko said as her silver eyes brightened, witnessing everything that Chase had experienced in Norway.

Shinko felt genuine sorrow for the hunter after seeing the dark events that Chase had endured. "You poor boy. None of this should have happened to you."

"It is alright. It is all in the past now anyway. Sometimes, you have to let the past go in order to move on."

"I have seen what I needed to," Shinko said. "The entity in your memories is called the Shroud. I want to hear your thoughts about what its purpose is."

"I don't know much if anything at all. All I know is it manipulated Loki for the purpose of me lifting Mjolnir to break the seal on the Winter Wraiths. That is why the Shroud used that scroll against me."

"I see," Shinko said, opening her eyes. "Are you sure there wasn't anything else?"

"There was one other thing that bothered me about it," Chase said, remembering. "It mentioned twice about me carrying out my role that my destiny was only partially fulfilled. I don't know what it meant by that, but I know for sure it wasn't anything good."

"Yes. Until we can uncover what it intends for you and James, I suggest you move carefully," Shinko advised.

"That is what I plan on doing."

"As far as the Winter Wraiths with the removal of Thor's hammer Mjolnir, the seal that locked them in the Arctic Circle is now broken," Chase told Shinko.

Shinko waved her hand, and a three-dimensional map of the Earth appeared.

"Most of the world is covered in snow," Chase said, staring at the map in shock.

"With the seal broken, the northern hemisphere is locked in an endless winter. I speculate it will cover the whole world in a matter of months once the Winter Wraiths have recovered their full strength," Shinko said.

"It is like an ice age."

"That is exactly what it is," Shinko agreed.

"If I had done things differently, knowing what I do now, none of this would have happened."

"None of this is your fault. You couldn't have predicted all of this chaos would have happened, nor could you have prevented it," Shinko soothed as she waved her hand, sending the map away. "You heard it from Loki, didn't you? The world has been steadily getting colder ever since Ragnarök. That means the seal that was put in place by the Norse Gods would have broken anyway. All of this was inevitable. Not all prophecies are false—some of them will come to pass. But regardless how things may seem, there is always hope," said Shinko, standing at the library entrance. "You are still alive, and you hold the object that will save your friend's life. So, I ask you this, are you going to keep your promise?"

"I made a promise to James, and I'm never going to break it," Chase said without hesitation.

"Good, because if you had broken it, I would have killed you right here and now," Shinko told a frightened Chase.

"Why did you bring me here?" Chase asked, standing under the raging rapids of the Nirvenus Waterfall.

"This place is one of the most sacred places in the world," Shinko said, enjoying the breeze. "Here, mystic energy is calm and full of life, allowing one to achieve enlightenment. It will help in your meditation. Only under the light of the full moon can this spell be cast and with it the binding of life. To bear the mark, the wearer and the caster must each be pure of heart—a soul with strength that knows no fear, not even death."

"I see, but I know that can't be all. What does the rest of it say?"

"The rest is the incantation for the spell. I will reveal it to you when you are ready. But first, in order for you to perform the Life-Lock spell, you must train your soul to endure its power."

"Is that why you told me to sit under this waterfall and meditate?" Chase asked curiously.

"Yes, this place is very spiritual in nature. As I said, it will help you during your meditation. You must meditate and focus on your fears. Face your darkest fears, conquer them, and then let them go, like a flow down the river. Only then will you have the strength to endure the spell and bear the mark with James. But be warned, training the soul to conquer is dangerous, for it is fear itself that keeps us from our worst impulses. Once the training of the soul has begun, it cannot be stopped until courage or fear conquer the other."

"And if I fail to conquer my fear?"

"Not only will you die, but your soul will cease to exist," said Shinko, warning of the grim consequence.

Chase, fearful, nodded his head as he sat under the waterfall, meditating. He'd come that far. He wasn't going to stop then.

"No, no, I'm not going to lose, not again," Chase whispered, focusing on his darkest fears from Devoid killing his parents to James lying dead in his arms.

Shinko observed Chase struggle for hours. "You will realize this in time. To save James, you must let go of your fear of losing him. Only then will you have the fortitude to endure the binding of souls."

Days passed as Chase tried to vanquish his fears but failed. Opening his eyes, he breathed heavily, no longer able to bear the pain of his terrors. "I am still not able after all that I've been through."

Shinko walked along the stream. "As I said, conquering your fears is not easily accomplished. I'm sure you're now aware you felt the tremendous pain of remembering them."

"I'm aware now. It is just painful to let them go. I can't get over my fear of losing him again."

"That is understandable, but you must overcome it nonetheless."

"Then you tell me how to overcome this?" Chase yelled in anger. "How to let go of the fear of losing the ones you love?"

"Only you will be able to find that answer. But I will tell you this. To face one's fears takes courage and to conquer one's fears takes conviction," Shinko counseled.

"And how does one have that courage and conviction?"

"By focusing on what matters most to you," Shinko answered as her eyes turned to silver, and she disappeared into the night.

Chase closed his eyes and focused on what mattered most. He saw James and Ulf in his mind and smiled. Then he focused on his fears, facing them once more, attempting to conquer them.

Shinko observed Chase from the waterfall and saw he was finally trying to overcome his fears. She knew it would take everything and more for Chase to subjugate them.

During the night, Chase slowly but valiantly overcame his fears. In the morning, he felt a change within him. He felt a peace, a calm, a happiness from deep within. Chase wondered if those feelings had come from overcoming his fears. The effort had exhausted him, and he quickly succumbed to the drain on his body, almost falling into the stream.

Shinko smiled, watching her young student. She waved a hand and easily laid Chase down on the shore, allowing him to rest.

That evening, Amphion walked toward the waterfall after a day of meditation. Seeing Chase asleep, Amphion knelt down to him. He could see that Chase's efforts had brought him to the point of exhaustion with his efforts. Amphion didn't want to wake Chase and made himself comfortable under the waters of the fall to rest.

Hours later, Chase finally awoke.

"What happened?" Chase asked, grabbing his head as he sat up. "I know I finished the training, but after that, everything went black. How long was I asleep?"

"For the fatigue that you possess, I suspect almost a full day."

Chase looked at the waterfall and saw Amphion meditating under it. "Then was it you that pulled me to shore?"

"No, I was not the one who saved you. By the time I arrived, you were already asleep where you lay."

"Do you know where Master Shinko is?"

"I do not," said Amphion, levitating rocks from the water.

"Come, I am in the library. It is time for you to learn the incantation for the Life-Lock spell," came Shinko's voice in Chase's mind.

"I know where she is," Chase said and then rushed back to the castle.

"He seems to be doing fine now," Amphion said.

In the Oracle library, Chase found Shinko reading ancient Celtic at a table.

"You have done well. Your soul is now strong for the binding ritual."

Chase stumbled against a bookshelf, knocking over stacks of books.

"But it seems you have not fully recovered your stamina," Shinko said, closing her book, looking at him. She waved her hand and levitated Chase to a chair. "You should rest a bit more before you learn the incantation." Floating an ancient book, Shinko placed it in front of Chase. "But in the meantime, you should read that book on ancient Sumerian in-depth."

Chase sighed and opened the book. He noticed he was now able to read the Sumerian codex. "*Magical translation,*" it read.

"Why didn't I find this book before?"

"Because it is from my personal collection that I keep in my dimension room."

"Oh," Chase said, continuing to read.

Chase read for a few hours and then started to stretch. "I may be exhausted, but I haven't felt this good in a while. Like I don't have any worry at all."

"That is what courage is, to stand and overcome the darkness within the heart. Right now, you're in the spiritual state of contentment."

Shinko stood and handed Chase a written note. "I have to leave now, for I need to stabilize the borders of the dimensions within Shangri-La. I translated the incantation on that note for you to learn," said Shinko revealing the texts. From here, you will have to learn the rest on your own. Learn the spell and save his life, not for my sake but for his."

"You don't have to ask because I will," Chase whispered, reading the incantation.

After a few days of studying and learning the spell, Chase was surprised at how powerful and complex it was. He realized what Timber had told him about the spell was true—it was a soul spell first, then a life spell.

"It looks like it's almost time," said Chase, seeing the night set in.

"The light of the Moon is faint yet, but I feel its power," Chase said, placing his hand over his heart.

Chase picked up the Life-Lock scroll and headed to James's room. He looked down at James and said, "Have you not revived yet?"

As he reached down to touch James, blue flames suddenly emerged from James's body. Chase was surprised that the flames didn't burn him. He was so absorbed, he hadn't heard Shinko come into the room.

"The flames don't burn because they are the flames of life, and they sense the pureness of your heart," Shinko explained.

"Master Shinko, do you know what is happening?" Chase asked as the flames appeared to intensify.

"His resurrection has begun," Shinko answered. "The flames you see are the flames that will revive him from his curse."

"These flames are the flames of life?"

Shinko nodded her head yes. "While you were on your journey to Norway, I thoroughly analyzed samples of these flames. From those tests, the flames started to pulse."

"Pulse, what do you mean?" Chase asked, confused.

Shinko reached to James and took a piece of the blue flame. "This flame is like a heartbeat. Those beats burn fire into his body, giving him life. The blue flames are one aspect of his soul." Shinko then held up the black flames in her other hand. "The black flames are the other. One flame gives him life while the other slowly takes it away, inevitably leading him to death."

The flames of life and death, Chase thought.

Feeling the warm essence of life, the flames pulsed louder and louder.

"It is almost done," Shinko said quietly.

The flames slowly laid James back down as they merged back into him. Chase could see that James was breathing, so he stepped closer.

"James," Chase whispered.

"You're late," James whispered back.

Chase tearing up, embraced James. "I know, I know, but I'm here now."

Chapter 17: Light of The Moon

"Easy James, you just revived," Chase said, helping James sit up. "You have not recovered your mystic energy."

"The flames of life took most of your magic to revive you," Shinko said, happy to see James alive again. "But do not worry, you will recover the magic with time."

"Master Shinko," James whispered faintly, looking up at her.

Shinko placed her hand affectionally on James's cheek. "It's nice to see you again, James.

"Your hair is silver now," James said, noticing the change in Shinko.

"I'm so glad you noticed. Magically changed it, of course."

Teacher's pet, Chase thought, sensing something between James and Shinko.

"James, how much do you remember of your past?"

James took a moment, trying to remember but couldn't. "Not much. Nothing but nightmares," said

James as his eyes turned red.

Chase seeing the darkness within James again, showed him the Life-Lock. "I made you a promise, and I intend to keep it."

Crying, Dark James smirked. "You always do."

James relinquished control and his eyes returned to normal. "To both of us."

"And I always will," Chase said, shaking his head, yes.

"The spell written in this scroll will bound your soul to mine. If you die, I die, but it will release you from the curse."

"How do you know the spell will work?" James asked, happy but having doubts.

"Because I have faith, James. And because I had to conquer my fear to strengthen my soul and..."

Shinko interrupted Chase. "You can tell him about what you went through after the spell is cast. First, I needed to tell you some things, now that you have the scroll. The Life-Lock was written by God himself," said Shinko, revealing one of its secrets. James and Chase were both shocked into silence.

"It was specially written for the one who has both life and death within. Which means it will only work for you, James, and the person who your soul is connected with. And with it, bear the mark of the soul."

"He foresaw all of this?" asked Chase. "But how did God know the one of life and death would appear?"

"I am not sure, but God is infinite. He foresees many things and foretells all truths. He alone created this universe and this very Earth."

Casting images of Earth, Shinko showed the beginnings of humanity. "Setting all of creation and focusing into to balance, to be free." She waved the images away then said, "That is the meaning of life. The time draws near; you know what must be done," said Shinko, instructing Chase.

"Of course," Chase answered.

Shinko smiled and walked over to James and kissed his forehead. "I really am glad to have you back, my little flame."

Definitely, teacher's pet, Chase thought, watching Shinko leave.

"James, we need to go to the waterfall. Only under the light of the moon will the spell work."

"Can you go on ahead? I will meet you there," James asked Chase. "I need a little time alone if you don't mind."

Chase looked outside at the moon and then back to James. "Alright, but don't take too long because the moon is about to set."

"I know you are there, so you might as well come out," James said after Chase left. He sensed a presence in his room. The little girl who'd been coming to him over time appeared.

"I see that you are different now," James said,

surprised to see her as an adult with long dark hair and piercing red, slitted eyes.

"What gave me away?" the girl asked, giggling.

"I've sensed your presence since I woke up, and I'm familiar with it now.

"Your powers are improving—that is good," the girl said.

"I don't have time for these games that you play. I have been meaning to ask you this since I first saw you. Who are you exactly?"

The girl smiled. "It's too soon for you know my true name, for you will not be able to understand it. For now, you can call me Zet," she said as she gently touched James's cheek. "As far as what I want, I only what's best for you."

Reaching to grab her hand, James stopped as he stared into her eyes. He grabbed his head in pain.

"What am I seeing?" said James in agony, seeing memories of a woman holding a baby.

"Who are you?" James said, staring at Zet in anguish.

Zet saw James's eyes turn slitted red. She placed her hand on his head as a blue ember appeared. "It is still too soon for you to remember. For now, just sleep and build new memories with the ones you love. I will always be with you," Zet said, sorrowfully kissing James on the head before fading away. "Always."

James cried while he slept, then woke with a

headache. He wondered if he had blacked out but couldn't remember. James shook himself wide awake then rushed outside to meet Chase.

"Am I too late?" James asked, arriving at the waterfall moments later.

"No, you're just in time," Chase said, looking up at the moon.

"Are you sure you're ready? The pain you are about to endure is going to be tremendous," Chase cautioned.

"I am, I felt the worst pain of all, so I think I can take it."

"No, you haven't—not like this," Chase said, stepping into the water. "The pain that this spell will inflict will be completely different."

"Different how?"

"Like having your soul ripped apart."

James was fearful but did not cower. "I don't care. I'll take it all."

"I had a feeling you'd say that," Chase said, opening the scroll.

James stepped into the water as Chase unlocked the scroll's power.

"Lux (Light)," Chase said.

The codex writing and illustrations within the scroll glowed. The scroll levitated and was illuminated by the light of the moon.

"What do we do now?" James asked, mesmerized by the light in the water and the falls.

"Now we endure the pain together," Chase answered, charging his lightning aura and placing his hand over James's chest.

James charged his blue-flamed aura and placed his hand over Chase's chest. "Together, then."

"Together," Chase said, nodding his head yes.

"Cor meum et animam meam (Heart and soul.)"

The light of the moon reflected off the Life-Lock onto James and Chase, burning into their chests. They collapsed into the water in tremendous agony as they started to lose consciousness.

Chase struggled to stay conscious and placed his hand back over James's heart once again. He would not give in until James was saved.

"James, you have to stay with me. Hurry, place your hand over mine."

"Just get on with it," James said as he painfully moved his hand to Chase's heart.

"Just hold on a little while longer, James. I'm now going to start the incantation."

Chase looked up the written scripture of the scroll. "We the ones that hold the lives that God gave us. Our souls are bound as one. Mine to his and his to mine."

Orbs of water from the waterfall and the rocks from the ground levitated. "We pledge our lives to this mark. To the mark of the Life-Lock. While one lives, the other shall live. When one dies, the other shall die. His fate and mine. We swear on these words

241

to you as we have no fear. As we tell only the truth."

Chase finished the incantation, and the light of the moon enveloped them both as the Life-Lock began to burn.

"Chase, what is happening?"

"The binding of our souls," Chase said, feeling their spirits connect.

In the Oracle Forest, Shinko watched the soul binding ritual.

"This is beyond anything I could have foreseen."

Her silver eyes glowed, seeing James and Chase thrash in the water. "Their pain must be unbearable."

"Even so, they must endure it," said Timber, joining her.

"The way you phrased that, its sounds like you're also concerned for them."

"A bit perhaps," Timber admitted.

"As far along as they are in the soul binding ritual, even we couldn't stop it."

Timber nodded his head yes.

Shinko looked on in amazement. "Their souls are starting to bind."

"Are you sure?"

"Do you question me?"

"Not at all, Master," said Timber, coughing.

"The Life-Lock spell—it is powerful magic indeed. The spell that God left behind is in worthy hands."

"Yes, and with the dark forces now in motion

from the Winter Wraith's awakening, those are going to be crucial to stop it. When the time comes, the Order must be maintained at all costs," Shinko said.

"Indeed," Timber agreed, shaking his head yes.

"It seems it is all coming to an end," Dark James said, appearing before James and Chase within the light.

"Our pain, our suffering. In a moment, it will all be over."

"And what will happen to you?" James asked, feeling sorrow.

Dark James smiled. "Simple."

Fading away, Dark James walked into James. "We become one again."

Ignoring the raging pain, James stood.

"Is it you?" Chase asked, staring into his eyes.

James smiled. "No, it's me. I'm all here."

"You better be, after all the trouble I went through."

"The moon is beautiful this time of year, don't you think?" Chase whispered with his vision fading.

"Ya, it is," James whispered back.

The Life-Lock scroll burned to ashes, and dark tattoos appeared on their chests, signifying their souls were now bound together. Suddenly, James and Chase were violently knocked back from the sheer power of the spell. James landed against a tree and Chase behind the waterfall.

Zet appeared to James as he lay unconscious.

"Now it begins. You are whole again. Sleep well, my son," said Zet, crying as she placed her hand on his cheek. Zet looked up at the night sky. "For you are a star in the night in the sky of the heavens."

Three days later, James awakened in his room.

"About time you woke up."

James saw Chase sitting at his bedside. "How long have I been out?"

"Three days is what Master Shinko said. I just woke up this morning myself."

"How are you feeling?"

"In a little pain but like before from that ritual. So, what about you?"

"The same. More of a headache than anything else from being propelled back into the waterfall."

"Did it work?" James asked, looking himself over.

Chase lifted his shirt, revealing a dark tattoo on his chest. James lifted his shirt and saw the same tattoo.

"It worked. Our souls are now bound together," said Chase happily.

James was overwhelmed with emotion. "Then that means?"

"Ya, your curse is now broken, James."

Later that day, after training in the Oracle Forest, James walked slowly back to the castle. He sensed a presence as he approached the outer wall of the castle.

"Why are you hiding behind these vines?" James

asked, barely seeing Chase.

"No reason," said Chase, noticing Shinko watching from a distance.

"Well, you'll see," Chase said as he jumped from the bushes and ran.

"What was that about?" James asked aloud before continuing to the castle. He had a question for Chase, but he'd ask him later.

James caught up with Chase in the courtyard.

"Hey, I need to ask you something."

"What is it?" Chase asked, catching his breath.

"Well, I have sensed the others, but not Theseus. Do you know where he is?"

Chase remained silent for a moment. "It is best you follow me for that."

James and Chase encountered Shinko when they arrived where Theseus was. She'd been waiting for them.

"Master Shinko, what are you…"

Shinko interrupted James. "Just wait."

Shinko placed her hand on the wall, and the stones moved apart, revealing a double door. "It is best that we go inside. There you'll find Theseus. This is the medical lab, where the curation is done," Shinko said, revealing the vast laboratory to them. "There are many different books and equipment, healing scrolls, and so much more from the Asklēpiós."

"Where is Theseus?" James asked, looking at all

the flasks with strange liquids.

"He is there," said Chase, pulling back a curtain.

"What happened to him?" James asked, noticing that Theseus' hand had been severed.

"When you were still dead, Ulf, some of the others, and I journeyed to Norway to bargain a deal for the Life-Lock with the Norse God, Loki." Chase sighed. "Unfortunately, the deal did not go as we'd hoped. We were thrown into battle against many different creatures of Norse myth. During one of those battles, Theseus was heavily injured with many broken bones and that severed hand."

"Then he is going to…"

"No, Master Shinko and Amphion managed to save his life just in time. But if it would have been any later than it was, he would be dead now. All of his broken bones have healed, and his severed hand…"

Shinko used her magic to pulled Chase back. "As far as his severed hand, it will have to be regenerated. With my knowledge of alchemy, only I can rejuvenate the cells needed to grow the tissue."

"You guys went through all that just for me?"

"You are an important friend to us James, nothing will change that," said Arthur, walking in.

"King Arthur, is that you?" James asked, surprised.

"It is, but please call me Arthur. I am no longer a king, after all. There is no need for such formalities."

"How did you come back to life?"

Arthur gestured toward Shinko. "Your Master was the one who brought me back. She recreated this body of mine with the highest level of alchemy using my flesh and soul."

"Master Shinko, how long do you think it will take?" Chase whispered.

"If you mean for the regeneration process, then no," said Shinko focused on creating the regenerative elixirs.

"Alchemy on this scale takes time, and recreating tissue on a cellular level is not so easy. But compared to the complications it took to propagate Arthur's body, the timetable will not be as long."

Shinko heard Chase's thoughts. "Indeed, alchemy is always difficult even for the most trained of eyes." She looked through a flask of the regenerative elixir. "Knowledge of alchemy is not just obtained through effort; one must also have patience."

Laying down the flask, Shinko poured strange roots into the elixir. "I'm never wrong, and if you don't want your thoughts to be heard, you should learn how to conceal them."

Trying to focus on her alchemy, Shinko nodded her head and opened the laboratories' doors. "Timber will arrange for lessons for you to study, but for now, I need you and the others to leave so I can concentrate on my work."

"Of course," said Chase, nodding to James and

Arthur.

The laboratory doors shut and disappeared, leaving only the stone wall as they walked away.

"Will he be ok?" James asked.

"Of course. His life isn't in any danger, and he is in the hands of your master, the best alchemist in the world. There is no one in the world who has her vast knowledge, so don't worry."

In the library, Chase sorted through the books. James helping Chase, looked down at Ulf, surprised by his new appearance. "Since when does Ulf have white fur?

"Oh Ya, I forgot to mention. Ulf merged with one of his ancestors. That's why he looks different. He still needs to recover his mystic energy, so for now, just let him sleep."

"You two were always loud," Ulf snarled, hearing them.

Yawning, Ulf looked up at James. "Seeing your blank face, you don't seem surprised at all by my appearance."

"Actually, I am somewhat surprised, but it doesn't matter to me what you look like. You are still you, that is all that matters. Besides your white fur, only your mystic energy is slightly different."

He hasn't changed at all, Ulf thought, laying his head back down.

Letting Ulf sleep, James and Chase went to a different section of the library. "I think you should hear about what happened in Norway. But I warn you, it's all very dark. Even now, I'm still trying to deal with it myself."

James, ready to know the dark truths, silently nodded his head.

"Everything about us is dark. It is nothing new. So, whatever it is, you can tell me," James said.

Chase saw that James was ready and told him the hidden secrets that had haunted his life. James was shocked and deeply disturbed by what he'd heard.

"Sepher was Devoid this whole time?" James asked.

"As much as I don't want to believe it, it is true," said Chase sorrowfully.

Chase remembered the visions Thor showed him. "In fact, probably a part of me always knew. I just wanted to deny it."

"I'm so sorry," said James, angry with himself.

"I should have done more for you. I should have been there to help."

"You were dead, James. This would have happened even if you had been there. Besides, the entity called the Shroud would have used them differently to get to me."

"But they killed your family and twisted your whole life."

"It is true, they did. My family and my whole life. I can't keep dwelling on what happened, James. But I have to disagree with you—they haven't everything from me. The one thing they couldn't take away from me is you. You, my closest friend. With all the darkness that ruled my life, you were the light that saved James, that guided me away from the emptiness of vengeance."

"That's what friends are for, to be there for each other through anything."

Chase silently shook his head yes. Closing his eyes, he called upon Mjolnir. "Come."

"What's with that hammer?" James asked, seeing the sparks flow around it.

"It's Mjolnir, the hammer of Thor," said Chase as his eyes turned lightning blue.

"To get the scroll, I had to lift it, but in doing so, I broke a seal on the frozen ancients of winter—the Winter Wraiths. The Shroud manipulated everything from the shadows to ensure the seal was broken. For what purpose, I'm not sure."

"The Shroud and Winter Wraiths, what are they?"

"I am not too sure about the Shroud, for I have never encountered a malevolent entity like it before. But what I sensed from it was sinister. All of it was evil." Chase remembered the Shroud became scared. "It was absolutely terrifying. The Shroud used the Life-Lock scroll against me and gave me a choice. Break the seal to the scroll and save your life or save the world from the great winter. I have Mjolnir, so you already know what choice I made," said Chase, putting it away. Pulling out his scanner, Chase displayed a holographic map of the Earth. "And for that choice, that is the consequence."

"What is that covering the upper part of the world?" James asked, seeing the northern hemisphere blanketed. "Is that snow?"

Disconnecting the digital map, Chase nodded his head yes. "Yes, all of it caused by the Winter Wraiths."

"What?"

"The Winter Wraiths are the cause of these powerful winter storms. They are the ancients of winter, frozen beings that are made of ice. Ever since the age of Vikings ended, the world has been steadily moving closer toward an ice age."

James fearful remained silent as Chase showed an image within his mind of the mythical Norse prophecy of Fimbulvetr (Great Winter.) "And now it is here."

"A new ice age," James whispered.

"Yes. When you were still asleep, I knew we would eventually have to confront them." Chase walked to a bookshelf and set ancient scrolls on the table. "That is why I decided to do more research on them."

Pointing out the ancient texts in codex, Chase revealed it to James.

"As I said, the Winter Wraiths are beings completely made of ice that can take on a humanoid shape. They are capable of manipulating cold weather on any scale. Ever since the dawn of Earth, whenever the Earth went through its cooling phase, they blanketed it into a glacial period for a time. That is why there so many throughout time. They are also immortal as they are the physical manifestation of Winter itself. But that is only one of the dangerous capabilities they possess, I'm sure. They could have other terrifying magic," Chase warned.

Chase placed the scrolls back on the shelf. "Inevitably, we are going to have to stop them before this ice age becomes any worse."

"How are we going to stop them? I mean, you just said they are the physical manifestation of winter, so wouldn't that make them part of nature?"

"Like we always do. We stop them, even if we have to kill them," Chase reassured James.

"We can't just leave the world covered in ice and snow."

It is my fault that this ice age has happened, so I will make amends for it, Chase thought, clenching his fist.

"Indeed, you shall. But unfortunately, with the weapons you certainly possess," said Timber overhearing them, "you will not be able to do them any harm."

"Master Timber, what do you mean?" said Chase, not realizing Timber was there.

Waving his hand, the Yeti summoned alchemy scrolls. "You are not the only one who has been in this library learning. I've found the hidden texts in those codexes that described how when normal metal clashed against their skin, it shattered."

"In the scenario your bullets with your lightning or your sword with the black flames, you will not be able to kill them. Only die a pointless death."

"Then what weapon can kill them?"

"Only weapons made of sveiða (burn) steel can kill the frozen ancients," said Timber, highlighting the written texts.

"This steel is one of the rarest in the whole world, and it cannot be gained easily."

"Are you saying we won't be able to find any?" James asked in frustration.

"I did not speak of any such thing, but there is a way to obtain what you seek."

Summoning another scroll, Timber gave Chase the sveiða (burn) steel codex. "You shall forge it from alchemy."

Transcribing the texts of the codex, Chase was shocked by what it contained. "The forge to make sveiða (burn) steel."

"The principle of alchemy is turning raw metals into gold. But instead of gold, you shall turn metals into the rarest one of all. And once you have accomplished this, forge weapons from them."

"I will do as Master Shinko has instructed me to. What is written in that scroll is your next lesson. I shall make all the preparations. In three days' time, come to the forging chamber when you are ready. There you will learn the proper steps of alchemy," said Timber. "Which, fortunately for you, is metal."

"Where is the forging chamber exactly?

"Well, I guess we will go there once we find it," said Chase, seeing Timber was now gone.

"Alright, at least we have the solution now. We will need those weapons made of sveiða (burn) if we are to kill the Winter Wraiths."

"You mentioned a dark entity called the Shroud earlier," said James. "What do you think is the reason why it set all of this in motion?"

"I don't know, but I do know one thing. It is not the only one."

Chapter 18: The Grim Visitor

A few days passed as James and Chase waited for Timber's preparation for the lesson on the alchemy to forge the sveiða steel. In his room, James sat around thinking. *Are there really others, and if possible, could they be?*

"I see you're in deep thought," said Chase, walking into the room. "What were you thinking about?"

James sat up in his bed. "I was thinking about what you told me. With the Gods that we have encountered, do you think the Shroud is one as well?"

"It is possible, but it is too early to draw conclusions about what they are. What I do know is their dark plans evolve around you and me."

"Alright, I guess we'll have to wait for now before we know more. You're usually never wrong with these things."

"Until we gather more information to determine what type of entity the Shroud is, let's focus our attention on the Winter Wraiths."

"Alright," said James, getting up. I've seen

everyone since I awakened, but not Amphion. Have you seen him, Chase?"

"Amphion is in Shangri-La, but he is either meditating or assisting Master Shinko treat Theseus and Beowulf."

"Beowulf, who is that?"

"He is a legendary hero from Scandinavia. He helped us in Norway get the Life-Lock. Oh, and he is technically a dragon since he is fused to one."

"What, dragon?"

"I guess it's best for you to know more about him to understand. Beowulf used to be an ordinary Viking warrior. He answered a king's plea and battled the monstrous ogre Grendel, and what we thought at the time, killed it. After Denmark was terrorized by Grendel's mother, Beowulf killed her as well. After this, Beowulf returned to his own kingdom and fought in many battles, and eventually became a king. One day, his kingdom started to be terrorized by the ice dragon, Fýri. Once again, forced into battle, he fought the dragon. Instead of dying, they ended up merging together. Eventually, he and the dragon reached a compromise and slept for centuries within a cave in Norway. Only until encountering us, though. I don't know everything about Beowulf's life, but I told you the short part of it."

"Wow, that's amazing," said James as Chase walked into the hallway.

"Always be aware of everything around you,"

said Chase, looking back at James. With the shadows moving in the dark, we must be careful now more than ever."

James smiled at Chase's warning. "No matter what darkness lays ahead, we will rise above it."

Chase smiled back but noticed James's eyes turned slitted blue. "Chase Actaeonis."

Chase rushed back into the room, and checked on James. "James, are you alright?"

Not getting a response, Chase gazed past James as he saw Zet sitting on the bed. "That was your voice."

"Who are you, and how do you know my name?"

James grabbed his head and looked at her. "You're…"

"Sleep," said Zet, laying James down.

Chase, unnerved that Zet effortlessly put James to sleep, cautiously stared at her, realizing her power.

Chase looked into her eyes. "Slitted red eyes, that long black hair. You are…"

Zet waved her hand and cast a spell to prevent Chase from speaking further. She giggled at Chase. "That would be telling."

"I prefer you not say my true name, for sometimes he can hear while he is asleep. If you accept my request, I will release you from your silence."

Chase witnessed the power of the woman, nodded his head yes. Sensing Chase's sincerity, Zet released him from her spell.

"I know who you are. Why would you appear

now?" Chase asked, pointing at James. Do you know how much he has suffered because of you?"

"I have known longer than you can have ever imagined, but that is the reason I am before you now," said Zet, understanding Chase's anger.

"What do you mean?"

"With the curse no longer able to inflict harm on him, his memories will slowly be restored. But before that happens, it is imperative that I pass something important to you, his best friend."

"And what would that be?" Chase asked, not trusting her.

Zet held out her hand, and a small blue flame appeared. "Hold out your hand."

Holding his hand out, Zet levitated the flame to him.

"What is this?" Chase asked.

Suddenly, Chase grabbed his head in pain, and he began to have visions. *What am I seeing?* Chase thought, seeing deathly visions. *It's too painful.* Breathing heavily, Chase dropped to his knees when the visions stopped.

"These memories, they are?"

"They are James's memories," said Zet, confirming Chase's suspicions. "His darkest ones."

The blue flame faded into Chase as he looked fearfully at Zet. "Why would you give me something like that? Those memories belong to James. They don't belong to me."

"Because you are the closest one to him. That is why I can entrust his memories to you, Chase Actaeonis. But there are two other reasons why I have given them to you. You've seen the darkness of those memories yourself. If James were to remember them in his current state, his soul and mind would break. Even with the Life-Lock that binds both of you, you wouldn't be able to save him."

"You know about that spell?" Chase asked, standing up.

"And much more, for I have seen everything from within him."

"And what was your last reason?"

"You already know the answer, for you have already witnessed it. Just remember," Zet said, speaking in a deep voice as her eyes glowed.

Chase witnessed the memories his time with James in the Sanctuary. Seeing the dark blue flames envelop James, the vision broke. "Solideth."

Zet acknowledged what Chase remembered. "That is why I have taken his memories until he is ready for the transcendence."

"What is this transcendence, and what are those dark blue flames that I saw around him in Sanctuary?"

For a moment, Zet remained silent. "I cannot reveal any more than what you know now. Once you have seen it for yourself, you will understand. James trusts you with his life, so I will as well by giving you his memories. The memories will eventually need to be returned to him, but only when it's the proper moment." Sensing her time was at its limit, Zet started to fade away. "So, I ask Chase Actaenois, will you accept these memories?"

"If it means protecting my best friend, then I'll accept it," said Chase without hesitation.

Zet was relieved as she faded away within James. "Thank you. I am glad James was able to make a friend like you. You will know when to return them to him."

James then awoke. "What happened?"

"You fell asleep talking too much," Chase lied.

"Well, it's not the first time."

"Ya, I'm sure it's not going to be the last," Chase said, chuckling as James got up.

"Here, let's go get something to drink to take our minds off things. The wine cellar here has all the best alcohol from all over the world."

"And how did you know there was a wine cellar?" James asked.

"I may have heard Master Shinko mention it before, and I may have followed her to the lower levels of the castle without her knowledge," Chase answered nervously.

"Alright, let's go then."

As they left for the wine cellar, Shinko observed them from her personal study.

"Are you sure you want him to have James's

memories?" Shinko asked Zet.

"You have seen him and his love for James as well as I have," Zet said, sensing Shinko's presence. "They are best friends, and with their souls now connected, he is the only one who can carry them."

Shinko sighed. "Alright, I will trust your judgement for now. But only because of the millenniums we have known each other," Shinko agreed.

Shinko was hopeful for James. "He may not be aware now, but he will always be loved."

"Always," Zet agreed with a smile.

After raiding the wine cellar, James and Chase met up with the others. For the remainder of the day, they drank together.

Late into the night, with James and Chase passed out from the alcohol, Arthur and Amphion helped them to their rooms.

"Hahaha, this reminds of the times of drinking with the knights—always passing out from drinking too much," Arthur laughed.

"Yes, but it seems today's generation has not learned how to hold the alcohol," Amphion said, mumming in disappointment.

"Hahaha! Indeed, my friend, very well, indeed."

Later that night, as James slept, a dark-cloaked figure appeared at his bedside.

"You are no longer going to collect him, Death,"

Zet said, grabbing its skeleton arm as it reached for James.

"Do not interfere with what must be done," said Death in a grim voice.

Refusing to stand aside, Zet pushed Death back with a gale pulse. "I will not."

Death, angered, summoned its scythe and pointed it at her. "You dare to defy Death? To defy me is to defy the Order itself."

"I am not afraid of you, Death. If it means protecting him, I will gladly stand against you."

Recognizing Zet, Death remained silent for a moment. "So, it is you. The one who has done the forbidden. But it does not matter since it is already done. What lives must die, and what dies must stay the same. That is one of the rules to uphold the Order." Death lowered its scythe and pointed at James. "By his resurrection, you violated this truth and distorted the balance."

"And you what you know about James, you are just a soul collector in the end," said Zet angrily. "You expected me to sit back and do nothing, to accept his death. You're the one who cursed him. You're the one who made him suffer endlessly with the cycle of life and death. The love you feel for him is irrelevant to me. Chaos must not reign, the cycle of the curse placed upon him kept the scales in balance. That is the price for seeking the forbidden." Death pointed at Zet. "That is your sin." Looking back at

James, Death sensed a change within his soul. "But it seems now that it can no longer be kept."

Tired of Death's presence, Zet's body shined bright.

Death was shocked seeing her appearance. "I see, so you are one of them. That explains everything. But even you know there are no…"

Zet interrupted Death. "I know the Order cannot be changed, but you have my promise it will be restored. I'm not asking for forgiveness. All I ask of you is that you do not meddle in James's life until his time comes."

"Very well, but only for this once," Death agreed. "For your sake, they better survive the cold darkness that awaits them, otherwise, I will collect their souls," Death warned, fading into darkness.

"Not while I am still," Zet said, returning to her normal appearance. "No matter what darkness or chaos comes, I will always protect and guide him through it."

The next morning, Chase had a severe headache but went to James's door anyway. "I shouldn't have drunk that much last night. I can't even remember what happened last night."

"Hey, James, you up?" Chase asked, walking inside.

Chase suddenly stopped as he saw Shinko sitting at James's bedside. "Master Shinko, what are you doing here?"

"I'm just waiting for James to wake up, but it's good that you're here because I wanted to ask you something. I was waiting for you. I checked last night and noticed some of the alcohol was missing from the cellar. You wouldn't happen to know anything about this, would you? After all, some of those are one of a kind."

Chase became extremely nervous and hesitated to answer. "Ah, no, nothing."

Shinko crookedly smile, "Is that so?"

Chase nodded his head yes.

"Well, I'm sure it's somewhere. If not, I can brew more since I have the recipes," said Shinko.

Huh, that was a close one, Chase thought, breathing a sigh of relief.

Blue and black flames suddenly emanated from James as Chase walked over to wake him. The sight reminded him of what he'd seen in Sanctuary but different in that the flames were not merging as one. They were two distinct flames.

"Elemental Unison," Shinko said, staring serenely into the flames.

19: Principles of Alchemy

"Elemental Unison?" Chase asked.

"It is a rare state, and only a few mystics have achieved it throughout the millennia—a metamorphosis of those who possess dual mystic elements. The elements combined all at once and increase the destructive power of the mystic dramatically, but in exchange, it consumes most of the mages' mystic energy," Shinko said as the flames died.

"Is James alright?" Chase asked, noticing that James's breathing was heavy.

"Yes, he is, but if enough of his mystic energy is drained from that state, he will die."

"And what are the specifics for this risk?"

"With the aura of both elements around the individual, the demand of the mystic energy becomes more, and in turn, painfully increases the stress on the body. And after a time of being in the rare state, they will collapse from exhaustion from the depletion."

Chase was shocked to discover the heavy risks the Elemental Unison spell carried. He looked back down at James. "And what would happen if he tried to force it?"

"Well, for one thing, it wouldn't work. In his current state, he would only be able to maintain it for about ten seconds at most. If he tried to force it again beyond that, worst-case scenario... he will die. To have dual elements is extremely rare. Not even the most refined of masters have more than one." Chase remained silent, accepting the risks. "Only let him use that power when it is most dire."

"I will."

Before Chase could awaken James, a large hand grabbed him by the back of the neck, lifting him up.

"Oh Ya, I forgot to mention, Timber is here," said Shinko giggling.

"You are late," Timber seethed.

Before Chase could speak, the Yeti threw him out into the hallway with great force.

In pain, Chase looked from the stone floor at Timber in James's room. "I thought you said when we're ready today."

"I did speak that yes, but it is not wise for you to keep an Earth Guardian from his sacred vigil," said Timber. "But my patience is at its end, so I decided to come for the both of you for your alchemy training."

Is this what James had to put up with this whole time? Chase wondered.

"Be fortunate that was your only punishment," Timber said to Chase. "Master Shinko, I have come as you have instructed."

"Do what you must to craft the weapons they need," said Shinko with an amused smile before disappearing.

"Very well," said Timber, turning his attention toward the sleeping James.

The Yeti grabbed James and threw him into the hallway next to Chase. James woke in pain and looked over at Chase.

"Not how I expected I would wake up."

"Ya, I was just about to wake you up too."

"Enough of your greetings. You have wasted enough time already," Timber said, pulling the boys to their feet. "I shouldn't have to remind you that time is not with us."

James and Chase remained silent, nodding their heads yes.

"Good, now, follow me. It is time to instill within you the principles of alchemy," said Timber as they headed to the alchemy room.

"I know what you said before, but do we really only have two months?" James asked.

"Even though the seal was broken, the Winter Wraiths didn't have their full strength. I know because when I picked up Mjolnir, all of Thor's wisdom passed to me. But by the rough timeframe, it will take the Winter Wraiths less than a few months to fully recover their strength. That is why it so important for us to learn this alchemy," Chase reminded James. "To forge the weapons of sveiða steel that will kill them. Remember, James, these are entities that even the Norse Gods feared."

"But you don't have to carry the burden alone," James said, assuring Chase.

"I know. That is why we will do it together."

Timber pressed his hand against a stone wall on the upper floor, and a wooden door appeared. As they stepped in, the room began to change.

"This is the Alchemy Room of the Oracle. The room changes to sot the needs of apprentice or grandmaster, depending on the lesson of alchemy that is to be learned."

"Here, you will learn the fifth level of alchemy, Pure Metals," said Timber, snapping his fingers, lighting the fire pits under the forges. "Normally, it would take an apprentice ten years to fully comprehend this lesson, but we do not have that kind of time. Chase, you learned all the way up to the fourth level of alchemy, this would be the natural lesson for you, but we must diverge from that path for now."

"James, you are not an alchemist at all. But since the need is dire, you have to forgo the other levels for now."

Timber turned from them. "This is a special occurrence, so learn everything in time that is spared to you, for this lesson will cause much hardship and even failure. But if you persevere and dedicate yourselves to the craft, I know you can both succeed."

Timber waved his hand, and stone tables with stacks of metal appeared at the forge. "Only weapons forged of sveiða steel are capable of destroying a Winter Wraith. It is essential for you to make weapons of this rare metal if you are to fight them in the winter storms. Sveiða steel is one of the purest metals. It will not freeze or break as it always stays hot and burnt," said Timber, placing blacksmithing tools on the anvils.

"These tools and those pits are your sanctums to craft the sveiða steel. But what sort of weapon you make will depend on you."

James and Chase approached the forges as Timber stepped back to observe. "But given your temperaments, I'm sure you already know what it would be."

Timber summoned the scrolls at their forges. "Those scrolls are alchemy codexes you will reference for the sveiða steel. But remember, arrogance is the first step toward failure. If you pass this lesson, do not think that you have accomplished anything. The fifth level of alchemy is just starting at the basics. As you advance as alchemists, the levels of alchemy will be more complex and difficult. To learn them all would take no less than thousands of years, even for a grandmaster to master. True lessons like this are not available to the average mystic or alchemist. Now, open up the codexes and follow the instructions to the letter, for there are no shortcuts. The codexes have been translated into English, so make sure you read each and every step. There is no time limit on this, so take as much time as you need."

Chase studied the codex and placed the metal pieces into the pot according to the instructions. He noted that the fire was not an ordinary one. Timber noted Chase and was pleased to see Chase's observation skills at work. Chase was young, yet he learned quickly. Timber knew that even the most prodigious alchemists didn't possess Chase's natural abilities. James was not as bright as Chase, but he knew instinctively and understood what he needed to do.

You two are truly one of a kind, but there are still many trials ahead, for you must learn failure before you can succeed, Timber chuckled as he thought to himself.

For the next week, James and Chase tried to complete the first lesson but failed as they could not fully melt the rare metal.

"Master, if I may ask, what are we doing wrong?" Chase asked as he and James looked to him for guidance.

"The metals that are within those containers are Alterian steel, the hardest and rarest metal in the world. And the other Tamahagane (jewel steel), which is what ancient Japanese katanas are made of. These two metals will melt and combine into liquid metal. The fire in the pits is a special flame that will melt and evenly balance it. Now continue, and do it until you pass the first step," said Timber bluntly.

"Hey, Chase?"

"James, I know what you want to say, but complaining about it now won't get it done. Just keep trying like me. I know you will succeed," Chase said, trying to melt the metal into liquid.

"Ya, together we will," James encouraged.

Hours later, Chase sensed a change in the fire.

"Chase, look here—my metal is starting to melt."

"This is no place for yelling, so I advise you to use an inside voice," said Timber, smacking James on the back of the head.

James remained quiet as Chase nodded his approval at James's progress.

Timber checked on their progress. They had both made enough progress to impress even him. He knew they didn't know that it had been their mystic energy that had caused the flames to become more intense. Only the flames of mystic energy could melt the purest of metals. They had passed the first step.

"We finally did it," James said after a few days of trying.

"Ya, the metal is fully melted now. I don't know about you, James, but I am tired."

"Well, working non-stop would do that."

Chase saw the fire die out and if it had somehow absorbed their mystic energy.

"I know you are both tired, but this is not the time to rest," said Timber, waving his fingers, highlighting a passage within the scrolls. "For the next step, I must directly guide you."

"I see," said Chase, pouring his lightning element into the liquid metal.

Nodding his head in approval, Timber turned to James as he did the same. "Good, now keep the channel of your mystic elements flowing. Once the elements are fully bound into the liquid metal, then you will be able to forge your weapons."

After a few hours, Timber noticed Chase lose concentration. "You seem to have a question, so I suggest you ask before you lose complete focus."

"Right, well, I noticed in codex it didn't mention why our elements are needed."

"It does but at the same time does not, for the metal that you will make will neither freeze nor break. But the purpose for placing the mystic element within it now is because it is impossible once the sveiða steel is forged. Only mystics with tremendous magic can forge this metal. If one with low magic were to try, not only would it end in failure, but also it would strip away all of their magic never to practice it again."

"I see," said Chase, seeing the dangers as he saw the mystical lightning mold with the liquid metal.

"Until you feel your mystic elements have fully bound to the sveiða steel, you will continue to let it surge, even if you fall," Timber warned, looking back.

A day later, seeing a drastic change in James's progress, Timber walked over to him. "James, what are you doing? I did not instruct you to pour the flames of death within the metal."

"I don't know. I was charging the blue flames, but then the black flames started to pour out as well," James said, confused.

Intrigued, Timber looked in James's forge. "Interesting, perhaps your powers are trying to commune with you. Very well, I do not foresee any difficulties for you. Continue to channel both flame elements into the sveiða steel."

"Can you explain the reason why, Master Timber?"

"Because you are to forge a weapon like no other."

Waving his hand, Timber cast an illusion of a dual elemental weapon. "A dual elemental weapon forged from sveiða steel with both the flames of life and death channeled through the sword."

"How will I know it will succeed?" James asked, channeling both his flames.

Timber cast aside the illusion and placed his hand on James's shoulder. "Because you are my apprentice. Clear your mind, and the answer will come to you."

His instincts are becoming sharper the more he

channels his flames, Timber thought, walking away as he looked over his codex. *It won't be too much longer until he succeeds in binding the fire elements into the metal. And Chase as well. It is likely they will succeed in this, but only their minds and wills will dictate that. Channeling that much elemental power is difficult and takes a heavy toll on one's body. But the weapon that you will forge will be one of your own power.*

After a few weeks, James and Chase were almost finished channeling their elements. Feeling immense mystic energy, it surged, knocking them both back from the forge.

Timber walked over to the forge, looking into the containers. "I commend the both of you. You have succeeded."

"The flames of life and death elements have perfectly infused," James said excitedly.

"Do not get carried away. There is still much more to be done," Timber cautioned.

"Right."

"Your thanks are unnecessary; you have achieved this on your own."

Chase felt his lightning power within the sveiða steel. "I did it."

Timber observed the lightning perfectly bonded into sveiða steel. "Yes, you have. I'm proud of both of you. The synchronization is now complete. Now it is time for the final step," said Timber, pulling out vials filled with magical lava.

Chapter 20: The Three Crimson Blades

"How is the lava not melting the glass?" asked Chase, puzzled.

"These glass vials are made of special magical properties," said Timber, handing them to James and Chase. "Special properties that can contain high temperatures. Now, take lava from those vials and pour them into the containers."

Pouring the lava into their containers, Timber gave them their next instructions. "The layers of the lava will mold with the liquid metal. Continue to stir the contents until it has done so."

For several days, James and Chase stirred until the lava merged with the liquid metal. Timber, seeing the lava and liquid metal merged, moved on to the next step.

"Now that the lava and the liquid metal have merged, channel all of your mystic energy."

As they channeled their mystic energy into the liquid metal, Timber set an hourglass for how long they needed to work. "You will continue to channel your magic until the time is up in this hourglass. But once you completed this task, the sveiða steel will be ready for you to cast your choice of weapons."

Realizing they were close to the end of the alchemy lesson, James and Chase persevered as they vigorously channeled all their magic until the time in the hourglass was up. After one day, the last grain in the hourglass dropped. Exhausting their mystic energy, James and Chase collapsed.

"It's glowing brighter than it was before. Does that mean it is now complete?" Chase asked, noticing the light from the sveiða steel glimmer even more.

"It is for the alchemy, but not forging," said Timber checking on their progress.

"The first glimmer you saw is your mystic energy channel through the metal. The second brighter one illuminated and enhanced it with its lava. That is why it is called sveiða steel, for the burnt glimmer of it."

"The mystic energy now within will continuously flow through the metal and radiate heat. It will do so even in the coldest temperatures. Neither freeze nor break," said Timber, waving his hand through the smoke over the pot.

That is the reason why sveiða steel can kill the Winter Wraiths, Chase thought, realizing the steel's purpose. *Weapons forged from it will never shatter from the cold due to the extreme heat it radiates.*

"The sveiða steel will glow brighter and radiate more the more the mystic energy from the maker is channeled through it," said Timber, feeling the tremendous heat in James's sveiða steel. "Ones' magic acts as both a conductor and amplifier all at once. Any weapon crafted from this steel is a masterpiece of alchemy. Now, it is time to forge your own personal weapons of sveiða steel. Chase, I will leave your weapon to you since you have the experience." Timber turned his attention to James. "James, since you do not, I will forge the weapon for you personally. I know swords are your preference, but the decision is yours to make."

James thought for a moment as he imagined an image of a katana. "How about a katana?"

Waving his hand, Timber levitated the liquid sveiða steel out of the container. "A Japanese sword, a very interesting choice."

As he levitated the sveiða steel, Timber formed it into three casts of katanas. James watched them gently land on a stone table.

"They look amazing, but why three?" James asked, confused by the number.

"For the different flames you possess," said Timber, pointing at them. "One blue represents the flames of life. The other black represents the flames of death."

"Then what about the third? It's blue and black?"

"You were able to synchronize your flames into the metal. The third blade is a merge of both of your flames. It will help your Elemental Unison to prepare to control it."

I can control it with this katana, James thought, holding the weapon.

Timber turned to Chase. "Have you decided what you will forge?"

"A revolver," said Chase, already starting.

Timber shook his head yes. "I see."

Pulling a blueprint, Chase used it to help him with the design of his revolver. "I already have the measurements and everything else I need."

Timber waved his hand as a blacksmith hammer made of elvenian steel appeared on Chase's anvil. "Almost everything."

"I do now," Chase chuckled, pouring the liquid metal into the cast.

"Master Timber, thank you."

Timber shook his head, pointed to the katanas, instructing James. "Pick up each katana individually and charge your mystic energy into them."

"I thought you said you could only charge your mystic energy during the forging process."

"I did, yes, but now that your element is in the katana and already contains your mystic energy, you are able to channel more into the blade."

Wielding the blue katana, James charged his mystic energy into it as it illuminated into a blue flame. "Wow. This one holds the blue crimson, so I think I will call it Sapphire Shard."

James picked up the black katana and channeled his mystic energy, a black flame illuminated from it.

"And this the black crimson flames." James stared intently into the black flame. "I know, I'll call this one Shadow Meteor."

Putting the Shadow Meteor katana down, James picked up the last katana.

"Firmly grasp it and calm your mind. For you to bring out both flames together, your mystic energy must be perfectly controlled," said Timber, instructing James.

"Ok," said James, closing his eyes, flowing his mystic energy through the katana.

Timber sensed James was in perfect synchronization. "Good, bring forth the flames of life and death."

Suddenly, blue and black flames blazed from the katana. James felt his mystic energy draining from the flames, and they grew out of control into an inferno.

"Stay focused, control them, do not let them control you," Timber yelled.

James tried to regain control but couldn't. "I can't."

Seeing the flames out of control, Chase tried to help James but was knocked back by Timber.

"What are you doing?" Chase yelled.

"If we don't do something, the flames will grow further out of control and incinerate everything."

"No, they will not. The castle and Shangri-La are protected by warding against destructive forces such as this," Timber said calmly.

"Then what are we supposed to do, just let him burn to death?"

"I will handle this," Timber said, walking to James.

"If you get any closer, the flames will engulf you too," said Chase, warning Timber.

Dismissing Chase's worry, Timber summoned a golden cloth. Wrapping the cloth around his hand, he reached into the fire, snuffing the flames. Letting go of the katana, James started to fall back.

Chase rushed over and grabbed James before he could fall. "James, are you alright?"

"Ya, just in slight pain," said James weakly, drained of strength.

Chase looked at James's arms, noticing the severe burns. *There are only burns on his body, but his hands and arms are burnt pretty badly.*

Chase pulled out a Sapphire Healing Stone and treated the burns. *I am surprised that he didn't get more burnt than this. Perhaps his mystic energy ran out before it could, or maybe it was her,* Chase thought, thinking about Zet. He dismissed the thought when he saw how destructive the flames were. Chase knew now the danger. *It is just like Master Shinko warned—this is extremely dangerous.*

"I'm sorry, Master Timber, I couldn't control it," said James, thinking the yeti was disappointed in him.

"There is no need to apologize. I never expected you to control the flames for a long period of time,"

Timber said, wrapping the Katana in the golden cloth. "You did well, in the beginning, to conjure both flames together, but you require more concentration if you are to control them."

"I will keep training until I do."

"Of that, I have no doubt," Timber said, smirking, leaving to make the sheaths for the katanas.

Later that day, Chase finished healing James's burns. "Are you sure you're going to be alright?"

"Ya, I'm fine, just focus on forging your gun," said James, recovering a little of his mystic energy.

Chase resumed his work to forge his revolver. A few hours later, Timber returned to show James his finished katanas.

"You will be able to tell the difference between each one by the blaze elements they now possess, but I took the care and decorated each one in colors for you. The Sapphire Shard katana is clothed in sapphire. The Shadow Meteor katana is clothed in shadow black. And the last katana, clothed in midnight blue."

James was amazed by the beautiful texture of the sheath and hilt. "They all look amazing."

Timber held out the last katana. "You didn't give a name to the third katana.

"Oh, Ya, I forgot. Can you give it to me for a second?"

"I'm afraid I cannot allow that. You are not yet ready to wield this sword. But I will unsheathe it to show it to you."

Unsheathing the katana, Timber showed its blade to James. James was again mesmerized by its glimmer and felt the heat it radiated.

"Have you decided upon a name?"

Staring into the burnt blade, a voice appeared in his mind. "Solideth."

"How about Solideth?"

"Solideth is definitely an odd name for a sword, but it is a name nonetheless," said Timber, curious. "Does it have any meaning to you?"

"I don't exactly. It was just a feeling I had," said James nodding his head.

"Very well."

Chase had overheard their conversation. *Is he starting to realize the truth? Is he summoning both his flames together and naming that sword Solideth, acquaintance? No, it may be a sign, but it is still early*," Chase thought, recalling James's memories he'd received from Zet.

Timber handed Chase the Solideth katana. "I trust that you will know how to handle this."

"Of course."

"Only give it to him when he is ready," Timber whispered before leaving.

"How's your progress going?" James asked, knowing the reason why Timber had given Chase the solideth katana instead of James.

Chase showed James the unfinished revolver. "I'm about halfway done. I just need to craft and groove the barrel. Oh, and I also need to make bullets."

"I see. I will leave you alone then so you can concentrate."

"James, why did you name that katana Solideth?"

"I don't know, it is just a word that appeared in my head," said James, stopping at the door.

"Does that word have a meaning to you?"

"Why do you ask?"

"Just curious, that's all."

James knew immediately that Chase was hiding something but did not question him. "Well, I can't really say there is a meaning. It is more like a feeling actually."

"A feeling," said Chase, confused but having somewhat understood.

James placed his hand over his chest. "Ya, like a burning feeling within my chest. It happens every time I use either flames."

"Chase, what do you think this burning sensation I feel is?"

For a moment, Chase remained grimly silent. "I can't really give a definite answer, but I can tell what I feel. One day, you're going to become something truly unique. And the burning sensation you feel must be a sign of that," said Chase, turning around smiling.

"Ya."

Chase, what are you trying to tell me? James thought, walking down the stone hallway.

I'm sorry, James, but I cannot tell you the truth, Chase thought. *I cannot stand the pain of losing you again.*

Wiping his tears away, Chase resumed working his revolver. *I cannot tell you the truth, for it is not yet time, but for now, the least I can do is stand by your side. And to that, I will fix this somehow, by stopping the Winter Wraiths before they blanket the world in an endless winter.*

A day later, Chase scoured through his encrypted emails. Getting a new email, Chase jumped from reading it. "The Black Order base was found destroyed."

Chase rushed into the Oracle, looking for more information.

"Why am I not seeing it," Chase asked, looking through the archives. "It has to be here somewhere."

Sensing Chase's thirst for knowledge, a dark cloaked phantom appeared before him.

Chase, startled by the cloaked phantom, took a few steps back. "Who are you?"

Looking down at its feet, Chase noticed it was hovering above the ground. "Or maybe I should ask what are you?"

The cloaked phantom moved away from Chase but stopped, looking back at him. "You want me to follow you?"

The cloaked phantom remained silent. "Alright, show me what you want me to see."

Following reluctantly, the cloaked phantom led Chase further into the library. Deeper inside, Chase looked around and saw more cloaked phantoms archiving.

"More of them?" Chase asked.

"All secrets lay here," said the cloaked phantoms as they turned toward Chase. "Both ancient and present. We, the Philosopher Phantoms of Knowledge, are the guards that protect this sacred sanctum. The algorithm that records all comprehension and wisdom."

Chase was shocked into silence. The floors of the library shifted under Chase, lifting him to the upper floors. The Philosopher Phantom floated to a shelf and levitated a scroll down to Chase.

"You record and protect all this knowledge?" said Chase staring at the Philosopher Phantom before him.

The Philosopher Phantom nodded yes.

"Then how did all of this get here to start with?"

Seeing the Philosopher Phantom gaze up, Chase looked up and saw a fresco mural of Shinko and her people.

"Master Shinko and Light Elves."

Chase looked back to the Philosopher Phantom, but it was gone without a trace.

"Thank you," said Chase, leaving the Oracle library.

Back at the Alchemy room at his forge, Chase read the scroll's contents. "The Black Order has been disavowed by the European Union."

"Is it because of us?" Chase asked.

"The European Union has determined the Black Order has failed to uphold the standards dignified by Radix Magic Accords section three: To minimize lives and damage during the execution of contracts for the supernatural. As such, it was unanimously decreed by the council of the European Union and the Mages Association the Black Order is disavowed and is to be disbanded, effective immediately."

"There has to be more than this."

Without Chase noticing, a phantom hand appeared, placing a piece of paper at his forge.

"That wasn't here before," said Chase, picking up the paper as he felt a chill.

Status report dated January 12, 2036. Agents of the European Union went to deliver the paperwork to the hunter organization the Keepers of the Black Order. Before paperwork could be issued, the Black Order was found destroyed by fire. An investigation was launched as more agents were sent out.

After a long search, the remains of chairman Leon Black and other members of the organization were recovered. The cause of death is still unknown, and cause of the fire also remains unknown. The remains of Leon Black and the others were sent to a coroner to determine cause of death.

The investigation is still ongoing."

Chase was shocked that Leon was dead. "Leon is actually dead." Shaking in disbelief, he dropped the paper. "Who could have done this? Why kill Leon and destroy the Black Order? I'm going to have to look at what I know to help make a good assessment," said Chase, thinking of too many possibilities.

Chase continued to sort through the information. In the inner ward of the castle, James trained to sharpen his swordsmanship.

"I wonder if Chase is finished with his revolver," James asked out loud. He tried to leave to the inner ward, but before he could, he sensed Chase's mystic energy was close by.

"Hey, what are you doing here? I was just coming to see you," said James, running into him.

"Do you have a minute?"

"Ya, what do you need?"

"Good, follow me," said Chase, walking past him before he could finish.

James was worried by Chase's weird behavior but followed him into the Oracle forest. *This must be pretty bad.*

Chapter 21: History Untold

"I don't know the full details yet, but I need you to listen," said Chase, standing at the edge of the waterfall. "There really is no easy way to say this, so I'll just be blunt. The Black Order has been disbanded."

"Disbanded, why?" James asked as questions raced through his mind.

"Because of us, James. From all the recent catastrophic events that we have been through over the past year. The United Nations, the European Union, and the Mages Association holds the Black Order personally responsible for the lives lost and all the destruction caused by our battles with the Gods."

"I don't really care since it was the Black Order who tried to kill us. But why did the European Union do this? We may have acted on our own, but we were only trying to stop the Olympians from destroying the world," James said.

"I know, but unfortunately, with bureaucracy, that's irrelevant. They see two rogue hunters who have violated the rules causing nothing but destruction. That is why we have been marked for death."

"Is that all you have to tell me?" James asked, annoyed.

Chase sat down on the rocky bank. "Unfortunately, you might not care as much for this part, but you should know anyway. Before the Black Order was to be officially broken apart, their base was found destroyed."

"Destroyed?"

"It was burned to the ground, and during the search of the wreckage, the remains of Leon and many other Black Order officials were found."

"Leon is dead. You're sure?" James asked in disbelief of the man he hated most.

"It is best that I show you," said Chase, standing up.

In the alchemy room, Chase showed James the status report.

"The details of Leon's death are still vague, but there will be an autopsy to determine the cause of death. See.

"When did all of this happen?"

"According to report, just little over a month ago."

James realized it happened when Chase was in Norway when he was still in his "dead" state.

"Knowing you, I'm pretty sure you have an idea of who is responsible," James said.

"Ya, I might have an idea, but it is hard to say for sure."

"What do you mean?"

Chase sighed. "It is best I go over everything in order first. After you left to train with Timber for the first time, Leon was visited by the third vampire Primogenitor, Adrian Abel."

Him again, James thought, gripping his hand tightly.

"Not knowing your affiliation with the Black Order at the time, Adrian approached Leon regarding you and Rin Zetsumei. Leon refused to give him any information since he saw a valuable asset."

"Valuable asset. I highly doubt that. Based on the conversation I had with him, he only saw us as expendable." James said coldly. "You know that as well as I do since he betrayed and tried to kill us."

"True, but there is no sense in holding onto that hatred since he is dead," said Chase, understanding James's feelings.

"I guess you're right," said James, trying to dismiss Chase.

"Alright, let's put that aside for now and get back to what I was saying. Leon refused to give any information regarding you. Adrian wasn't pleased by that refusal and threatened Leon and the Black Order."

"Threatened him how?"

For a moment, Chase didn't speak. "It was more of a threatening promise. He told Leon, 'The next time we meet will be your own destruction.' Adrian disappeared after that."

"Then it had to be the vampire Primogenitors."

"More than likely, but if they were, then there is no way to prove it," said Chase, still having doubts.

James was frustrated that the vampires continued to conspire against them. "I have been meaning to ask you this ever since we observed the true events of Titanomachy. How did Gilgamesh become the first vampire Primogenitor?"

"That I don't know. I think I know something about him and the other eight. Gilgamesh is immortal."

"Immortal," said James, taken back. "Does that mean the other vampires are too?"

"No, from the research I have done, they are not," said Chase, showing James his notes. "They just have longevity from consuming Gilgamesh's blood. Gilgamesh is the only one among them who is immortal, but it is not complete immortality. He is ageless, meaning he cannot die from old age or disease. But he can still be killed through unnatural means. All documents, texts, scrolls, books, any type of information in the world are recorded here and archived. Every subject of Gilgamesh is recorded here except what I just told you. The origins of Gilgamesh come from the oldest heroic tale, the Epics of

Gilgamesh. But there are no other texts of him beyond his rule as king of Ancient Sumeria. But remember what Cronus told us before," said Chase, showing Chase artwork of the gods.

"Originally, there was a being imprisoned in the underworld since the first civilization. He was the first demi-god and the one king of the world. But for his lust for immortality, he became cursed by the very thing he tried to attain. Transformed into immortal yes, but also a creature with an unquenchable thirst for blood."

"Ya, but why create the other vampires?" James asked, worried about what Gilgamesh was plotting.

"Gilgamesh would keep those goals either to the vampires or to himself. But if we are going to one day kill him, we will need to find what those are."

"I think a good place to start on that is uncovering the identities of the other vampire Primogenitors," James offered.

"That's a good idea coming from you," said Chase surprised.

"Gee, thanks. Well, we already know one, which is Adrian Abel. Have any ideas who Adrian truly is?"

Chase thought for a moment as something about Adrian bothered him from the moment they'd met. Suddenly, a disturbing thought came to Chase's mind.

"Wait here, I need to go get something from my room," said Chase, rushing out of the library.

Chase returned with a Bible in hand and turned the pages to a passage. "From the Bible in the Book of Genesis, there were the first two sons of man. One was named Cain, and the other was Abel, Cain's younger brother. Cain was said to have murdered his brother because God favored Abel's sacrifices over Cain's. Cain then lied to God about what happened to Abel, and God cursed him to wander the Earth for all eternity. Cain is regarded as the first murderer and Abel as the first victim of murder."

"Are you saying Adrian is actually Abel from the Book of Genesis?" James asked, poking his finger on the Bible.

"I'm not at all sure, but with his name being Abel, it is in line with the Abel from the Bible. And we saw how he looks."

Chase pulled out an ancient scroll painting from the library and showed James.

"What's this?" James asked.

"This is one of the very first painted passages painted for the Bible. It has been lost since the ten Lost Hebrew Tribes."

Taking out a photo he had taken of Adrian, Chase placed it next to the scroll on the table. He pointed to the photo and to the man in the painting. "Look closely."

James looked at both closely and was shocked by their similarities. "It looks just like him."

"That man in the painting is Abel from the Bible with his family. There is little doubt in my mind that they are one and the same." Chase pointed out their eyes. "The only difference is his eyes, but they could have changed once he became a vampire. But it is also possible that Adrian could be someone else entirely," said Chase, rolling up the scroll. "With events that we have recently witnessed, history is sometimes not truthful and other times distorted."

Chase gazed upon all the written texts in the great Oracle library. "It really does make you question about everything to its foundation. What is true and what is a lie. All the texts in the Oracle library may have all true written history, but what about the history that isn't written?"

"I know what you mean, but are you saying the Bible is not true?" James asked.

"There have been verses of the Bible that have been omitted, and other scriptures that have been lost over time. But despite all that, I am still a firm believer in it and God. I am just saying due to what we witnessed and learned recently with the Titans, Olympians, Norse, and now the Winter Wraiths, we should not believe everything and keep an open mind on what's true and what's not. You can find the original scriptures of the Bible in the Biblical section here that has not been altered over time. Abel could very well be dead as the scriptures states, but I'm not going to dismiss the possibility either of him being Adrian, the vampire Primogenitor."

If Abel is Adrian a vampire, does that mean Cain is too? If they both are, how did they survive for so long before meeting Gilgamesh? Chase thought disturbed by the possibility.

Chase grew even more frustrated with the deepening mysteries of Gilgamesh and the vampire Primogenitors. *It is possible they could have met during the first civilization of Mesopotamia. But there are too many questions to say for sure. For all I know, I could be completely wrong, and there could be no connection at all.*

"Let just say this, James. If we are going to stop Gilgamesh, we need to kill all of the vampire Primogenitors."

"You have no disagreements from me on that. The encounters we have had, and all that we have learned about them, the Wraiths are dangerous, and they need to be stopped."

Chapter 22: Lesson of Balance

A few days later, James and Chase received a summons from Shinko for them to train to properly wield their sveiða steel weapons. On their way from the keep, they ran into Arthur and some of the other Demi-Gods in the basilica who were on their way to learn alchemy from Timber.

"Arthur, you are learning alchemy from Timber?" Chase asked.

"Yes, he requested us to ask you to meet him this morning for the next steps in how to make sveiða steel."

"Are you close to the last steps?" James asked, seeing Arthur progressing fast as them.

"Unfortunately, no. But we are making steady progress with the lessons so far. I learned some alchemy from my teacher, Merlin, so I know that it is extremely complex and difficult. It is what makes it worthy of the challenge."

"I see that you have already completed this task," said Arthur, noticing James's sheathed sveiða steel katanas.

James unsheathed his black katana, showing the blade to Arthur. The king was amazed at its burnt luminous texture, and he felt the radiating heat from the weapon. "Through all my life of seeing swords, I have never seen such craftsmanship. I have also never felt this heat emanating from a weapon before."

"It really wasn't that easy," said James, sheathing the katana.

Arthur, seeing James's fear, tried to speak but stopped as a big, white, furry hand grabbed his shoulder.

"I do have patience, but time has not taught it to me that well," said Timber, glaring down at him.

Timber pressed down hard on his shoulder as the king dropped to his knees in pain. "The pain you just felt is only a fraction should you test the limits of my patience again."

"You have you my deepest apologies, great guardian, you have my vow it will not happen again," said Arthur, standing up, bowing his head.

"I expect nothing less from a Knight of Britannia. I will hold you to that vow. Now, go wait with the other Demi-gods in the alchemy room until my arrival. I need to speak with my disciple."

"Of course, right away," said Arthur, leaving.

"He really is humble with words and actions, probably the most courageous person in the world," said James.

"I did not ask for your opinion on the matter," said Timber, not caring but knew the truth in those words.

Without warning, Timber smacked James into a tree. Leaves from it tell as James looked up in pain at the yeti who was glaring down at him. "With the time that is left, you don't have the luxury of it."

Helping him to his feet, Timber scolded James. "When the master summons you, it is expected to heed it without delay."

"But I was just…"

"Enough, there are no excuses for your delay to the master. Before you go to Master Shinko, I shall impart these words to you, James. Winter waits for no one, for the storm it brings is here. To survive it, you must endure it."

"Thank you, Master Timber," James said, bowing his head.

"If you understand, then go. Master Shinko is waiting," said Timber.

"Right," said James, leaving to catch up with Chase.

"Now then, I should be on my way as well. For this world to survive the winter, we need more wielders of the rarest metal," Timber mumbled to himself.

In the forest of Shangri-La, James tried to find Chase but found no sign of him. "Where could he have gone? I know we are in a race against the clock with the Winter Wraiths and all, but I wasn't wasting time."

Suddenly, Shinko appeared behind James as she whispered in his ear. "You can't really blame him, though, can you?"

James, startled, looked behind him but did not see Shinko. "Where did she?"

"Up here."

Looking up, James saw Shinko sitting in a tree. "After all, he did teach you and Chase the sveiða steel alchemy." Shinko jumped down in front of James. "And you shouldn't forget he forged your katanas."

"I realize that, Master Shinko, it is just with everything that has happened and..."

Before James could finish speaking, he became more uncomfortable as Shinko got closer to him.

"Don't stop midway. Tell me what is on your mind," Shinko asked, teasing him.

"That this place, and even you, know what I'm thinking without me saying anything."

"I see that you're not surprised. Maybe you sensed it the first time you came here. The place of knowledge, Shangri-La, I know everything that goes on here. Knowledge is the key to enlightenment."

James was still flustered by Shinko. "You are something, Master Shinko. It must not be easy keeping an eye on all of this place since it houses all of the world's knowledge."

"It has moments. The only thing I can say is that it is difficult to maintain and reinforce the gateways to the magical dimensions that are connected to Shangri-La."

"Dimensions," said James, confused. "What are they for?"

"It is difficult to explain, but in short, they are called the Arcane Dominions, and each space keeps a different aspect of knowledge."

"Like the library?"

"Yes, the Oracle Library is one of these dimensions. It is called Cŏdexis, the dimension that holds all written knowledge."

"Then what are the other dimensions?"

"Those can wait," said Shinko. "You will learn of one very soon, but first you will need to meditate on the balance of your katanas if you are to master them. Do you mind showing them to me?"

James complied, showing her the katanas. She was impressed by Timber's craftmanship and with James's hard work. "This is very fine. Timber was always the best blacksmith, even among the other Earth Guardians. You have done well too, James. I can see the rune lines on both katanas from your elemental flames."

"Thank you, Master Shinko. Coming from you, that really means a lot," James said, sheathing the katanas. "Have you seen Chase? He went on ahead after I got stopped by Arthur and Master Timber," James asked.

"You do not need to concern yourself. I have already instructed Chase on what he must do, for he will endure the same struggle just separated from you. Focus on what I instruct you in without worry. Now the time has come for you to learn how to properly wield those katanas with your own strength."

At the waterfall, Shinko pointed toward the ground. "Place both of katanas there on the ground."

James did as he was instructed, and Shinko tapped them with a light glow. "Now try to pick one up."

James tried to pick up the Sapphire Shard katana but struggled. "It's heavier than it was before. What did you do?"

Smiling, Shinko placed her hand on the hilt, helping James. "Just like this."

James dropped the katana when he became flustered, looking into Shinko's beautiful eyes. "Ahh."

"I am just teasing you," Shinko giggled. "I dispelled the lightness spell that Timber placed upon it before he gave it to you."

"Wait, you mean the reason why the katana felt so light was because of a spell?" said James, looking at the katana.

"Yes, but now it weighs as it originally did." Shinko picked up the katana and held it in front of James. "You will need to learn the balance before you can wield this katana. Once you learn how to wield both together, they will become light as a feather. But first, it seems you need to learn how to lift one," Shinko laughed.

James, not deterred, lifted the katana. "There."

Shinko was impressed to see James had learned the balance of one.

James was smug as he pick up the second weapon. It didn't take long before he dropped them because of the pain.

"My hands," he said, letting out a deep breath.

Shinko knew James would not be able to wield both katanas. He still hadn't learned to balance the two.

"Brute strength alone will not help achieve the balance that is needed. Remember, those are the only weapons on this Earth that can kill the Winter Wraiths. This battle will be more dangerous than all of your previous ones with the demi-gods and the Olympians."

"I know. That is why I will not fail, not again," James said, ignoring his pain, remembering Timber's words of warning.

Smiling and pleased at James's conviction, Shinko affectionately kissed him. "You are one of the very few people who are precious to me, so make sure you come back alive this time."

James felt a comforting warmness that seemed familiar to him somehow as he hugged Shinko. "I will. You do not have to worry about that this time."

After Shinko left, James looked down at his katanas. "So, to find balance between them, I will need to wield them until they are light as a feather."

For days, James struggled to lift both katanas but could not achieve the balance to wield them. Frustrated, James dropped to his knees in exhaustion. "What am I missing?" Thinking back to what Shinko had told him, James closed his eyes. "Could it be that?"

Concentrating, James's mystic energy flowed throughout his body. He placed his hands back onto the katanas' hilts. "I know now what I must do."

For several hours, James held up the katanas better than he did before. "No, it is still not enough. I need to increase my innate mystic energy."

James concentrated harder, creating more mystic energy to flow through his body. "One more."

Pushing himself to his limits, James momentarily attained balance but could not maintain it. He dropped the weapons again.

"I will not rest until I have attained balance," James declared.

Timber was working in the alchemy room and could hear the intensity of James's concentration. He walked to the window and stared out toward the waterfall. He knew James was working on increasing his innate mystic energy. It was the second lesson Shinko wanted him to learn. The lesson of balance was a difficult one and could only be achieved if you did not allow your mind to limit the possibilities. If the mind perceived an object as heavy, then it would be. To achieve the balance to wield the katanas, James would have to expand his thinking. Only then would he be worthy to wield the sveiða steel. Once he'd mastered that, there would be one more lesson to learn. Timber was impressed by James's sheer endurance and will.

"Wait, there is something I must attend to," Timber said to Chase, walking toward the door, realizing what Shinko intended for James.

"Master Timber, if I may ask?"

"You do not need to be concerned with where I am going," Timber said, stopping at the door. "Just focus on the task that I have given you."

Timber left the castle and went into the forest. He did not fully comprehend the master's intentions for James and his newly awakened power, but he would carry them through regardless of his apprehension of the danger ahead.

James and Chase continued to train with their new weapons. On the other side of the world, dark forces conspired.

Cain knelt before a man on a long-staired throne. "Master Gilgamesh, I have returned."

"I see that," Gilgamesh said, awakening from his slumber. "But I am not one to complain about something that is beneath me, so you may speak."

"It is just as you have summarized, My Lord. The winter storms that plague the northern hemisphere are magical in nature. But forgive me for saying this, I have been unable to find the entities responsible," Cain gave his report.

Gilgamesh was pleased with the report. He knew who was responsible for the storms, and it was confirmation that the seal had been broken.

"Master Gilgamesh, if I may ask, what are your thoughts on this matter?"

"It is of no interest to me. The great winter and the creatures behind it are only a minor hindrance. As such, it is beneath me to act, but something worthwhile to let unfold."

"Then may I ask what is your will?"

Thinking about the two hunters who had defeated the Greek Gods, Gilgamesh grinned. "Send a message to the tenth Primogenitor, inform him to have those two handle this matter. Use whatever persuasion you deem fit, for I will tolerate his petty bureaucracy this time."

"At once, Master Gilgamesh. I will see to it personally," said Cain, standing.

"Be sure that you do," said Gilgamesh as Cain left.

Gilgamesh had been bored waiting for his vision to materialize. He was anxious to rule over Order and set an irredeemable work back to its proper state.

James sat, exhausted after hours of training. He'd even diminished the remains of what mystic energy he had.

"What is it that I am not getting?" James asked, giving in to frustration.

"Every time I increase the flow of my mystic energy, I'm able to lift the katanas but only for a short while. I know that I am close, but what is it that I am not seeing?"

"To attain balance, you must see in your mind," Zet's voice came to James. "Clear your thoughts and visualize. Only then will the requirement be fulfilled."

"That was Zet's voice just now, but why would she help me?" James asked, confused.

Not wanting to dwell on the reason, James took her advice. Holding the katanas in front of him, he closed his eyes. "I think I understand now. Instead of using my strength or my mystic energy, I need to use my mind."

Focus, imagine them, James began. See yourself wielding the katanas together as they become light as a feather.

James saw himself wielding the katanas, and they had become light in his hands. He was able to swing them around.

"I did it. I finally did it. I can now wield them."

Shinko, and all of James's friends, sensed he had passed the lesson of balance. They all smiled as they could hear his happiness at his success.

"Alright, now I need to practice on different dual wielding forms," said James, standing under the waterfall.

Slashing through the water, James felt the light and swiftness of each strike. *They're light as a feather.*

"You're really loud, you know," Chase said to James from the bank of the stream.

"Sorry, I couldn't help it," James said as he sheathed the katanas,

"I know," Chase chuckled.

"I guess you being here means you succeeded too."

Chase wielded Mjolnir. "Ya, but I only achieved balance a short time before you did just now."

"With your revolver," James asked, confused at seeing Mjolnir.

"Not just that but Mjolnir as well."

"How is that possible? We were supposed to achieve the balance of our sveiða weapons."

"Ya, Master Shinko wanted to see Mjolnir and said that it was made of sveiða steel. She said Mjolnir was crafted by the dwarfs from Norse myth. They were the first forgers of sveiða steel.

"Perhaps I already knew there were similarities since I felt and saw them, but I dismissed it at the time," said Chase, remembering the characteristics within the runes of Mjolnir were the same as his new revolver. "But with Mjolnir being made of sveiða steel, it probably was one of the reasons why it was used to seal away the Winter Wraiths in the Arctic Circle."

"Well, that's good to know, and since you're a descendant of Thor, your mystic energy is already contained within it."

Chase examined the hammer closely. Tiny sparks emitted from it. "True."

But I'm actually slightly bothered that it is made the same, Chase thought, staring into Mjolnir, disturbed by questions for its use against the entities of winter.

Because if they knew, why didn't Thor or the Norse Gods use it to kill the Winters Wraiths instead of sealing them?

Chase became more disturbed by the mysteries behind the Norse Gods. *But as I learn more about either one, I am left with more questions than answers.*

"Hey, Chase," James yelled, trying to get his attention.

"I can hear you; you don't need to yell."

"Oh, sorry."

"James, I think we should use this time to train more with our weapons until Master Shinko calls us for the final lesson," Chase suggested, not wanting to get distracted by his thoughts.

"Good idea," said James, running back to the waterfall.

Chase watched James before beginning to wield Mjolnir. He could see that James was truly getting the grasp of the katanas.

"James, let's call it a night," Chase said several hours later.

"Alright."

Walking back toward the castle, James and Chase went over the experiences they'd gained.

"How are you handling your katanas?"

"I still need more time dual wielding, but I think I will be able to train with my crimson flames through them soon."

"Good call. Even though I have gained Thor's experiences, I don't have much experience with hammers, so I could use some as well."

After eating dinner, they met up in the Oracle library, sitting at a fireplace.

"What are you reading now?" James asked.

"I am reading one of the fifth level of alchemy lessons—how to turn base metals into gold and silver. The concepts have been around since ancient times, mostly for more people to become rich or something.

But other times, it was either for sorcery or academical."

"You sure like to read," said James, poking fun at Chase.

"I do, but without it, everything would be too boring," said Chase, closing the codexes.

"I only became an apprentice alchemist during my school years with the Mages Association on a whim. But now, seeing the importance and complexity of it, I should forge ahead and strive to become a grandmaster alchemist. And besides, everyone here in Shangri-La has to learn at least the basic principles of alchemy, which is first through fifth levels. "According to Master Timber, that means you too," said Chase, smiling.

James grew annoyed. "Thanks for the reminder, and how I am not looking forward to it?"

"We all have to learn sooner or later. It might as well be sooner since one day all of this can save our lives."

"Good point," said James.

"Hold on, what's this?" said Chase, receiving an encrypted email.

"What is it?"

"It is an email from a high official from the European Union. It says the representatives would like to discuss a deal about the warrants of the mark placed on us."

"Are you sure? That's the organization that wants us dead."

Chase showed James the email, pointing out the symbols of the E.U. and the Mages Association. "Yes, you see these symbols are right here? This email was both corresponded by the representatives of the E.U and the Grand (Crown) Magus of the Magi's Table from the Mages Association, so it is official. And besides, this email is top-secret. The way that it's written, it is used only for business purposes with paladin hunters in Europe. It says further they would like to schedule a meeting later in the week to discuss the matter along with other concerns in Brussels, Belgium."

"I'm not really convinced. This could be a trap," said James.

"I don't think so. Ever since World War II ended, the E.U. helped establish the contracts for supernatural threats. So, killing two hunters, even though we are fugitives in the Europa building where European leaders meet, won't be easy. And even if it was, we could use a mystica jewel to teleport away. So, what do you think, James? I think it is worth it for us to at least listen to what they have to say."

"I'll go along with whatever you think is best, but just make sure you have those jewels on standby if things go bad."

"I can do that. Let's just keep this to ourselves for now, alright."

Chase responded to the email, agreeing to meet. James was still not convinced but would follow Chase's lead. He bid Chase goodnight and left the library. Chase stayed on, thinking the situation over.

Nothing made sense to Chase. The Black Order had been disbanded, Leon was found in the ash of a fire, and now he'd received a strange email. He realized that whoever had sent the email was after something more than he and James. There was a good possibility they didn't know that Chase was aware of the fate of the Black Order. He needed to find out who had sent the mail and not let on to what he knew.

Chase spent the rest of the night trying to uncover the answers to the conspiracies.

Chapter 23: Projections of Thought

The following morning, James and Chase were summoned by Shinko.

"Arthur, how are your lessons on making sveiða steel going?" James asked, running into Arthur on the stairs.

"I will say it was rough, my friend, but as Merlin once said, tough is one of the keys to magic, or something like that." Arthur suddenly stopped, seeing Timber on the stairs behind James.

"I am sorry, I didn't mean to interrupt your conversation, please continue," said Timber, looking at Arthur blankly.

Arthur sensed Timber's animosity toward him and fearfully turned back to James. "If I have time, I'll tell you more later, but I still have a lot more alchemy that needs to be done."

"Be sure that you see to it, for you still must make up for the last time you spoke to him."

Timber turned his attention to James as he passed him. "Don't you have somewhere to be?"

"Right."

Walking down the hall to the library to meet up with Chase, James stopped and looked back at Timber. "Master Timber, what would I do next?"

"That is up to you now," said Timber, leaving.

As one of your mentors, it is my responsibility to guide you along your path. But there are times where you must seek the answer yourself, Timber thought going to the Himalayas.

"I know that it is up to me now, but I still must thank you, Master Timber and Master Shinko, because even though you are both my mentors, you are still my friends too," James whispered in gratitude.

Wanting to see what Shinko had planned for their final lesson in training with their sveiða steel weapons, James met up with Chase outside the library.

"Are you ready?" Chase asked.

"As ready as I'll ever be."

On the upper floors, they met with Shinko as she stepped out of one of the Arrayal gateways to the Arcane dominions connected to Shangri-La.

"Shall we?" said Shinko, inviting them.

Walking through the door, they stepped into the dimensional space connected between Shangri-La and the Arcane Dominions. James and Chase were amazed by the different galaxies and stars.

"Are those galaxies? Are we outside of Earth?" James asked.

"Master Shinko, what is this place?" Chase asked.

"What you see is called the Arrayal Gateway, a magical space in the universe between Earth and the dimensions of the Arcane Dominion. It is one of many gateways that connects all knowledge."

Nearing the end of the gateway, Shinko heard James's thoughts. "Yes, just like the Oracle library but just the aspect of knowledge."

Through a lightened doorway, James and Chase were in awe as they found themselves standing atop a raging waterfall with many more beyond the horizon.

"This place is the dominion where imagination becomes reality, the Arcane Dominion, Beo Noros (Beyond Horizon)," said Shinko, revealing the identity and purpose of the magical dimension.

"In this dominion, Chase, you and James will achieve your final lesson to unlock the full potential of the sveiða steel. There is no time limit for this last lesson, but I assume you want to complete it quickly since you are leaving soon. To unlock the true power of your weapons, you will need to unleash the true power of your mystical elements."

"Master Shinko, if we did, what would happen to this place?" James asked, concerned.

"This space is full of infinite magic to prevent such instability and destruction," said Shinko, easing James's concern.

Holding out her hand, Shinko briefly closed her eyes. Suddenly, the day over the waterfalls turned into night with moons and nebulas in the sky above. Snapping her fingers, the waterfalls and the night sky faded away as everything turned dark.

"James, do not worry, for this magic is in its purest form."

"Why did it become so dark all of a sudden?" James asked.

"Let me enlighten you," Shinko laughed as the dominion changed once more becoming a golden grassy plain. "As I said, this the dominion of imagination." Shifting one last time the dominion changed into a rocky plateau with multiple moons in the sky. "Where the environment you imagine becomes reality."

"Is that…" Chase asked, seeing something familiar in the night sky.

"Correct. That familiar glimmer you see is Earth."

"Then this a different planet we are on."

"Yes, but just an imaginative version of it," said Shinko, correcting Chase.

"The planet you now stand upon is Gaia in the Milky Way galaxy."

"How are we able to see this planet's surface. Humans haven't even advanced beyond our solar system."

"There is more to magic than what you can comprehend. With it, anything is possible. The magic uses the images of the environment within your mind and casts an astral projection of it within this dominion. But your mind cannot overwrite the existence of the universe, for we are all bound to it. Even God must follow the balance set in place."

"Are we supposed to think of ourselves as some kind of ghosts?" James asked.

"In a sense, everything here is still real," Shinko answered, picking up a rock and tossing it to James.

James was surprised that it was real.

"Even from the air you breathe to the ground you stand upon."

"Just how many galaxies and planets have you seen?" Chase asked curious.

"Millions upon millions, so many that even I have lost the exact count," said Shinko.

Shocked by the sheer number of galaxies and planets she had seen, Chase knew such a feat of knowledge could not be accomplished even in multiple. Wanting to not make her angry, he hesitantly tried to ask her age. Chase stopped him as she intercepted his question.

"I know what it is you want to ask, but I cannot give you a direct answer. Even if you had a hundred lifetimes, one will still not be able to comprehend my knowledge. So, let me just say, I have been around far longer than you could possibly imagine. Now, it's time to let your imaginations takeover, for this is your last lesson before you face the Winter Wraiths."

Holding out her hand, Shinko challenged the hunter and her disciple. "Whatever environment you astral project to, you two must decide what will be your training guard. Be it be a valley of mountains or the sand seas of a desert."

Chase understood what Shinko was asking of them, and couldn't help but think about going on a galactic adventure. Suddenly, the dominion changed to what Chase had imagined as it changed to many different small and larger galaxies.

Shinko was pleased that Chase was able to expand his imagination.

"I see many different , both big and small," Chase said.

"What do they mean to you?" Shinko asked.

"It is what I want to see James and me do one day," said Chase, walking around looking at the final frontier.

A star floated into Chase's open hand. "To be able to travel to the many galaxies and to many different planets where life is. To experience what no one has experienced before. This is my dream that I want to share with you. An adventure of many lifetimes."

James remained silent as he was overcome with emotion. Chase smiled at James's silent acceptance.

"But before I can make dreams a reality for the both of us, we must defeat the enemies within the darkness."

Ready to move on to their final training, Chase closed his eyes as he thought of the land where they would train.

"Think not of what you dream. Focus your thoughts on a place for you and James to train," Shinko advised. "It can be of anything one of mountains, skies, and rivers, anything you can imagine."

Focusing his imagination, the dominion changed to a rocky mountain landscape with many rock plateaus in a sunset sky.

"Whoa, that really is a long fall," said James, stepping away from the edge.

This is what I imagined—this is my reality, Chase thought, opening his eyes, looking at the rocky landscape.

"Very impressive. I see that time you spent learning the full implement fourth level of alchemy went well," said Shinko, congratulating him.

"At first, I had a hard time grasping what Timber was saying, but now I understand. He meant being creative to succeed in my alchemy."

"Correct. The main lesson in the fourth level of alchemy is to use your imagination to create. Imagination itself is the most underused and hardest to grasp in the mind. It is one of the reasons why most humans cannot use it and results in their short-sightedness."

Shinko held out her arms. "In this dominion, the two main requirements to use its magic are visualization and creation. Without either one, and if one has ill intent, the dominion will cast out the person. But one can't use its power unless they have vast amounts of mystic energy."

"There is no need for you and James to worry about that."

"This is your creation from imagination Chase, this is your reality," said Shinko as the lighted Arrayal gateway to the dominion appeared behind her.

"Even though this is serious, try to have fun. For joy is one of the greatest strengths of all. And your smile can help you both shine through the darkest of shadows and keep you warm through the coldest of nights."

Shinko winked at James and spoke telepathically to him. "Like a phoenix being reborn from its own ashes."

James and Chase took their place on different rock plateaus as they both took their respective weapons.

"What's wrong? Normally you're more upbeat," Chase asked, seeing James's blank expression.

"It's nothing," said James, remembering Shinko's words of phoenix ringing familiar to him.

"I made my choice long ago, and remembering my past only reaffirms my conviction. As long as and you and I stand together, nothing is impossible. And besides, we can't break our promise to each other."

James and Chase trained with all their might for several hours before they began to feel the balance of the weapons.

"This is really well balanced," said Chase, resting while examining Mjolnir.

Chase closed his eyes and focused his mystic energy on the hammer. Lightning erupted from Mjolnir as it shot into the sky, creating storm clouds. Satisfied with the power of Mjolnir, Chase dispelled the lightning.

"You done?" James asked, seeing the clouds clear above.

"Ya, let's rest for a little while longer."

Feeling strain on his body, James sheathed his katana. "I was just about to suggest the same."

James and Chase sat on the edge of the rock plateaus eating together. "We are going to have to push ourselves like we never have before. With our current level of strength, we would barely stand a chance against the Winter Wraiths if at all."

"Ya, this is the only chance we got," said James, not satisfied with his strength.

"We have to push ourselves past our limits."

Knowing that there was not much time left before the Winter Wraiths regained their full strength, James and Chase hardened their resolve to become stronger to stand against them. Chase held out his fist to James. "No holding back."

James bumped fists back with James as he promised. "Never, if you did, I would hold it against you."

"If you did, I would hold it against you too," said Chase joking back.

The next morning as their meeting the E.U. drew near, James and Chase dedicated their remaining time to training individually.

It is lighter than it was before, Chase thought, noticing a subtle change in the hammer.

Swinging his hammer again, Chase began to levitate from the sheer lightness of Mjolnir. Chase broke his concentration as he gently stepped back onto the rock plateau. Smiling that he was starting to grasp its power, Chase felt Thor's experience flow through him. *One more.* Chase held Mjolnir above his head as he levitated even higher than he did before.

On another rock plateau close to Chase, James continued to practice his dual wielding with steady progress. He stopped for a moment when his hands cramped up.

I'm gripping the hilt too hard, James thought, bleeding from his hand.

Loosening his grip, James noticed he had more swift movements with the katanas dual wielding. *There, my movement is more fluid and swifter. I need to remember this feeling and imprint it into my muscle and memory.*

After half a day of their individual exercises, James and Chase were in the castle's kitchen as Chase made them dinner.

"Is it almost ready?" James asked, getting impatient.

"Almost. With food like this, the more you take your time, the better it will taste, so just be patient."

"You have been saying that for the past three hours."

"What is this delicious smell?" Arthur asked, walking into the kitchen, smelling the aroma. I haven't smelled something so delicious since the grand feasts of the Round Table. Ah, my friends, you are having a feast together."

Chase finished cooking and pulled it out of the oven as he sat down to eat. "I wouldn't really call it a feast, but you are welcome to us."

"I don't think that would be very appropriate of me. After all, you cooked that meal to have together."

"Nonsense, come and eat with us," said James.

"Ya, we don't mind. You've been working just as hard as us, so you deserve to have a great meal too," said Chase.

Arthur, happy and hungry, joined them. "Very well, if you insist."

After eating their meal, they all walked through the basilica and discussed their progress. "It was by Merlin's grace that I was fortunate to meet you, my friends. Were it not for that, my soul would still be bound to the sword."

It's what friends are for. Is that your new sword?" James asked, looking at Arthur's sheath, seeing heat come from it.

"Ah, my friend, so you have noticed."

Pulling out the sveiða steel sword from its sheath, Arthur showed its burnt blade. "I have completed the alchemy task and have made my new sword.

"That is great. That means you can now train with us."

"Of that, I am not sure," Arthur said, nodding his head.

If I'm not mistaken, it looks just like Excalibur, Chase thought, seeing the familiarity of the sword.

Chase pulled out a notebook from his backpack and took notes on Arthur's new sword.

"What are you writing?" James asked.

"Nothing important. I'm just making a note on Arthur's new sword."

James chuckled at Chase. "You like to make notes of everything."

"I do all the time, that way, I can refresh my memory with important things, especially the codexes and scrolls in the library."

"If you're going to do that, then you really should write down everything Master Shinko and Master Timber tell you about important stuff," James joked.

"I do, unlike you, at least I can remember it," said Chase.

"What is that supposed to mean?"

"Nothing, it is just you do forget a lot of stuff."

"It truly is refreshing seeing both of you argue," said Arthur, laughing at them.

James and Chase were confused as Arthur placed his hands on their shoulders to assure them of their friendship. "That is a sign of strong friendship and brotherhood that can never be broken."

It seems they are overcoming their limits, Timber thought, watching over them from a tree. Choosing not to interfere, he saw their cuts and bruises from their final lesson. Proud of their hard work, Timber disappeared from the tree.

James sensed the familiar presence and looked over Arthur's shoulder and saw the leaves fall from the tree. *Was that?*

"Now, my friends, if you will excuse me, I need to get some rest."

"We are leaving in a few days, be sure that you are ready," Chase whispered to Arthur.

"Have you told Ulf? Wouldn't he like to go too?" asked James as they walked to the upper levels of the castle.

"He wouldn't be able to even if I would have told him. He is still strained from his spirit fusing with his ancestor, Fenrir. And since he pushed himself more in Norway, it will take more time to recover than we have. Remember James, this is a fight against beings made of pure ice. Our weapons are the only things that kill them. Ulf only has fangs and claws. We would only be putting him into needless danger," said Chase, stopping at the door. "Anyway, we're here. Let's use the remaining time we have left before we leave for the meet with the E.U."

Back in the Arcane Dominion of Beo Noros (Beyond Horizon), James and Chase used their remaining time to finish their training.

Hours later, Chase satisfied with his results, stopped.

Should I allow him to use the Solideth katana, Chase thought, wanting to escalate James's training.

Taking what he had seen and Timber's warning into account, Chase pulled out the katana, "Hey, James."

James looked to Chase as he threw him the Solideth katana. "Why are you giving me this?"

"Because we are going to use the remaining time for you to train with it."

"I don't know," said James, remembering what happened before.

Chase understood James's reluctance. "At least try, that's all I ask."

Putting aside his fear, James unsheathed the Solideth katana. Responding to James's mystic energy, the black and blue flames emanated from the katana. The flames were calm as both formed around him in an aura.

Elemental Unison, Chase thought, surprised at seeing the flames.

"I'm able to wield it this time, look, Chase," said James, swinging the katana fluidly.

Chase remained silent, observing. *Did she do something to James for him to control the form?*

Chase noticed James struggle to maintain the form. *His mystic energy is dropping.* The crimson flames died as James collapsed.

"Are you alright?" Chase asked, grabbing James before he fell.

"Ya, just drained."

Suddenly, the sound of bells rang throughout the dominion.

"What is that sound?" James asked.

"I don't know," Chase replied.

The Solideth katana took flight into the air, seemingly on its own. Shinko had summoned it to her telekinetically, and it flew with great speed to her.

"Your training is at its end," said Shinko, grabbing it.

Shinko looked around at the destroyed landscape. "You two altered the area quite a bit, I see that none of you held anything back."

Chase tried to speak, but before he could, Shinko used her telekinesis to lift James and Chase, hovering them over the steep drop below. "As I said, your training is at its end."

She let them drop, and they splashed into the river below.

"Why did you do that?" Chase demanded, lifting his head out of the water.

"You two have completed what Timber and I have set forth before you," said Shinko, hovering over them.

Holding out James's katana, Shinko summoned its sheath to cover it. She then summoned Chase's backpack and put the katana in it.

"Since we did, why did you drop us into the river?" Chase demanded again.

"For a reward and punishment," said Shinko, smiling. "One, for defying Timber's instruction, and two, I thought you could use a refresher. And given his current state, I'd say it was warranted."

Snapping her fingers, the imaginative projection of the dominion disappeared as everyone within disappeared into gateway space between it and Shangri-La. In the Arrayal Gateway, Shinko affectionately tapped James on his head, putting him to sleep. "Now it is time for you to rest."

Unlike before, even though it was only for a brief moment, you were to attain the balance of the flames of life and death, Shinko thought, levitating James behind her. *But it is still too soon for you to understand that power. Its power and the experiences that you had with it are now engraved into your memory and body.*

"I suggest you get some rest as well," Shinko said to Chase. "After all, you both will depart the day after tomorrow."

Waving her hand, Shinko opened the gate to Shangri-La. "You may have only scratched the surface of your true potential, but if you dedicate yourselves and strive beyond the horizon, you will inevitably attain it and ascend to places you never imagined."

Chapter 24: Business of Magic

James and Chase slept the next day, recovering from Shinko's grueling training. Early in the morning, before they departed, Chase walked into the medical laboratory.

"What are you here for this early in the morning?" Shinko asked, looking over the regenerative codexes for Theseus.

"I came to ask more about alchemy," said Chase, wanting to learn more.

"By alchemy, you mean the Sapphire Healing Stones?"

"Yes. When I used them in Greece and Norway, I could tell they were inefficient somehow."

Shinko showed Chase the different codexes of alchemy on the healing stones. "Your instincts are correct. You realized that they were incomplete. The second level of alchemy, Remedy, is only the first of many lessons in healing alchemy. Judging by your silence, you're not surprised," said Shinko, pointing out the different steps. "To make the healing stones from second level alchemy can heal some injuries but all due to its limitation. But that limitation can be overcome by refining its healing properties and capabilities with the higher healing lessons."

"I suspected as much, so the refinement quality of my stones is at the lowest levels," said Chase, understanding why the healing stones were lacking.

"Correct. I would allow you to learn the higher levels, but you're at the level of an alchemist you need to be. Each step of alchemy needs to be learned in order, for it takes time and it teaches something important about the next."

Setting aside the alchemy codexes, Shinko handed Chase a vial with a red stone inside. "But worry not, for I have refined a more potent healing stone for you."

"Why is it red?" Chase asked, confused by the color.

"It is refined due to the different ingredients used to enhance it. The ingredients give it its different color. That stone is called a ruby helix stone, an enhancement of the sapphire healing stone."

"A ruby helix stone."

"Yes. Use it carefully. I was only able to create one stone," Shinko warned. use it only when the need is most dire."

"I understand," said Chase, putting the stone away.

"Now, if you have nothing else, I ask you to leave," said Shinko, as the doors to the laboratory opened on their own. "This regenerative process is delicate and requires my full attention."

"Thank you for your help, Master Shinko."

Wanting to get underway for Brussels, Chase went to James's room to wake him up.

"You're awake," said Chase, walking into James's room.

"Ya. Why wouldn't I be?" James asked sarcastically. "You said we're leaving early in the morning so we can get to Belgium later today."

"Smartass," Chase whispered, not taking too kindly to James's sarcasm.

"You say something?"

"No, just get your stuff together and meet me in the courtyard when you are done."

Waiting for James in the inner courtyard, Chase met up with Arthur.

"Morning, my friend," Arthur greeted.

"Morning. Do you have everything together?" Chase asked.

"Of course. I gathered everything needed."

"Alright, all that leaves is James."

Amphion appeared, walking past them on his way to the upper floors. "

Amphion, where are you going so fast?" Chase asked.

"Master Shinko has requested my presence, now if there is nothing else, I must be on my way," said Amphion, moving up the stone steps.

"He really likes to stay busy," Chased laughed.

"Indeed, such is the role of Medjay, to help all who are in need," Arthur agreed.

James got his stuff together and met up with Chase and Arthur. "Alright, let's go."

In a clearing in the forest, as Chase pulled out the airship, he magically altered its size back to its original form. Αcαλλοίωση (Alterization Mass)."

"Do you just…" asked James, watching.

"It is called Alterization Mass, it a spell that I learned while you were still asleep. It allows me to alter the mass and size of any inanimate object."

"Can you explain in simpler terms, so I can understand?" James asked, confused.

"Alright. It basically shrinks and enlarges anything. How's that?"

"Oh, now I get it."

If you read and learned more, you would have caught it the first time, Chase thought, opening the back of the airship.

"Anyway, let's get going. We have a long flight to Brussels."

Later that day, a few hours away from Brussels, the weather turned for the worst as Chase struggled to fly through the winter storms. "This is rough."

"All of this is being caused by the Winter Wraiths?" James asked, staring into the storm.

"Yes, but it is not just happening here in Europe. The whole northern hemisphere is covered in darkness and snow," Chase reminded him. "I suspect the more north we go, the worse it will become. The storms themselves will not just become stronger, but inevitably colder.

"You're kidding?"

"You already know James. The Winter Wraiths are manifestations of winter itself. They are strong. The archived records in the Oracle library show all of the ice ages there have been since the creation of the Earth."

"All the ice ages?"

"Ya, some lasted for a few decades, others centuries. This one is ominous for it lasted for over a thousand years—since the age of Vikings ended, we just didn't know it."

"You're holding back something. What aren't you telling me?" said James, seeing Chase's disturbed expression.

"I wouldn't say I was holding back something since I just learned about it a couple of hours ago," said Chase.

Chase pulled up a holographic map of the Earth, showing the northern hemisphere blanketed in snow and pointed to a holographic temperature gauge, showing its negative degrees.

"They're causing all of this?" James asked.

"Yes,"

"All of them?"

"Most of the northern hemisphere has below-freezing temperatures. The intensity of winter storms, the freezing temperatures, all of it is the supernatural powers of the Winter Wraiths. It's not that they caused the storm; it is because they are the storm."

After several hours, they landed at the airport in Brussels.

"James, Arthur, you two might want to put some thick clothes on because it is really cold outside. Have these on you in case something goes wrong," Chase said, handing each a mystica jewel. Good. Now let's go meet them, but remember, stay vigilant for anything."

In the city of Brussels, James, Chase, and Arthur got out of the cold as they waited in a restaurant for an official from the Mages Association.

"How much longer do we have to wait?" James asked, waiting for hours.

"According to what the email said, it will be another hour," said Chase, drinking his coffee. James, have some patience and eat your meal in the meantime."

James glanced around to see if anyone was watching them. "Do they know what we look like?"

"You and me, yes, but not Arthur. When a hunter is given a contract by the European Union, they are required to give their personal information and I.D. Right now, they have our past information. I'm sure they shouldn't have information on Arthur and the others because there is so little information, and they have been thought long dead."

"It is our best-kept secret," said James, smiling at Arthur.

"Indeed," said Arthur, smiling back. "Coming from this king, that is a very wise decision of a leader.

"It's the right the thing to do. For those you don't trust to begin with, if you can, give as little information as possible," said Chase.

To pass the time, Chase looked over their equipment. "Well, since we have to wait here a little longer, we might as well talk about our plan."

"That reminds me, Chase, how do we afford everything we do?" James asked, curious.

"Most of it was covered by the Black Order from profits the organization made from the contracts. But I have for a long time never relied on it since I have my own fortune."

"Wait, fortune?"

"Ya, it basically means I'm rich. How else do you think we were able to do all that goofing together; the Black Order wouldn't have covered that.

"Oh."

Pulling schematics of their Stealth X suits, Chase showed them the upgrades that Shinko magically enhanced. "Well, anyway, that's not important right now. I need to tell you about the upgrades that Master Shinko made for our Stealth X suits."

"Improvements, like what?" James asked.

"I'm not sure of all the details since Master Shinko said they needed beta testing to ward out any flaws. But the invisibility function of the suits has been improved slightly. Oh, and also, the scanner has been improved as well."

"You mean the device we used in Norway?" Arthur asked, remembering finding Beowulf with it.

Chase pulled out the scanner and mystica jewel. "Ya, the functions are still the same, but when you sync a mystica jewel to the scanner and mark a coordinate, it will better map the location using magic."

"Basically, like a map as a guide from one place to another?" said James, confused.

"In a sense, yes. The mystica jewel is the key, and the scanner is the guide," said Chase, putting them away.

"That really is something, but with you, you are always working on something to improve," James said.

"Of course. How do you think we survive sometimes? I will do anything within my means to improve our survival and success. There is a saying that can back this: Expect the worse, so prepare for the worst."

"It is getting worse out there," said Arthur, feeling uneasy.

"Ya, it is a good thing we're prepared for it," James said, lightening the mood.

"You were always the one to see the good before the bad," said Chase, chuckling. "That and your smile are enough to keep me going."

"Indeed," said Arthur, agreeing with Chase.

"And your smarts keeps me going," James said, smiling at Chase.

With the blizzard raging on, James, Chase, and Arthur shared a laugh together. Sometime later, the door to the restaurant opened, and a man in an overcoat with armed personnel behind him approached them.

"Excuse me, gentlemen, pardon my delay. Are you Chase Actaeonis and James Akatsuki?"

"That depends on if you are enlightened," Chase replied, cautious of the man.

The man remained silent as he rolled up his sleeve and showed Chase his magical crest tattoo of the Mages Association. "Indeed I am. I have been given the honor of escorting you and your friends to the Europa building to meet with the representative of Mages Association for the Europe Union."

They must be mages as well, Chase thought, studying the mage.

"You have nothing to fear from us. Our only task is to escort you to Mr. Caldor Grifton, nothing more," said the mage, trying to calm their wariness.

Hearing that name, Chase paused for a moment. "Caldor Grifton, the archmagus that sits on the Magi Table."

"The very same. The man whose magical bloodline goes back ten generations and who oversees the Radix Magic Accords."

"Who is Caldor Grifton? I've never heard of him before," James asked, not recalling the name.

The mage looked at James and enlightened him. "I am surprised by your lack of knowledge since there are still so many mysteries about you, demigod."

Demigod? Why call me that? Is it because I have the blood of Gilgamesh? James thought.

"To put it simply, he is whose name you see on all Mystics & Magic contracts dealing with the supernatural and magical orders throughout Europe. He is the representative of the Mages Association in the European Union that oversees every mage, paladin, and hunter alike. To monitor delegation between the two organizations."

"You surely speak highly of him," said James, annoyed by the long explanation.

"But of course. He is, after all, what every mage strives to be, and his name is known throughout the secret world of magic," said the mage.

"It is only befitting that we respect him, even when his name is mentioned."

I can't say I'm not surprised. Mages throughout the world think highly of him, Chase thought, seeing the mage's high reverence of Caldor. *After all, it was his magi family that helped the Mages Association and E.U. establish the Radix Magic Accords after the end of World War II.*

"Excuse me, gentlemen, but we really must be on our way, or we will not meet the timeframe set before us. I'm sure you're aware, mages do not like to be kept waiting, especially highly revered ones."

"Of course, I don't want to keep him waiting either. He is the one who arranged this meeting," Chase agreed.

After driving through the hazardous blizzard, they arrived at the Europa building for the difficult meeting with Caldor Grifton.

"All of Europe's business is done here," said James, seeing all the different businesses as they walked through the lobby.

"Pretty much. Almost every European deal is run through this building at some point, and all must be proved here as well. Trade, stocks, money, immigration, you name it," Chase explained as they rode the elevator up.

"Well, almost everything as far as the public eye is concerned," said the mage, magically coursing the elevator to a secret floor. "As I'm sure you are aware." The mage looked intently at James for a moment. "Or at least some of you, the magic deals of magic and supernatural are kept under extreme secrecy. We mages do not concern ourselves with the everyday business of E.U. and Europe as a whole, but we still must be in compliance with their regulations."

"Well, even though I know some of the European Union's dealings, if it is to keep the continent safe, I'm more than willing to put up with it," said Chase, not letting his resentment of the system be known.

"For one so young, you are very wise and informed. Most mages are novices who do not understand the trueness of magic and the business side of it. They think they would be able to practice magic without care or restrictions, but, sadly, that has not been the case since the fall of most kingdoms from the 1800s. In Europe now, people may think they are free, but in truth, they are not, for the concept of it is irrelevant. They are incapable of making the right decisions for their safety and security."

"I disagree with you on that. Freedom is something a country and its people need to help them make those right decisions. If you take it away, even though they don't know it, it will lead to oppression and despair."

"I truly envy your youth. If immortality was possible, I would seek it," said the mage, chuckling. "When I was young and knew little, I used to think the same as you. But once my family sent me to the clocktower to learn, my perspective changed drastically. So, take some advice from this old mage, the curtains of Europe would unfold if its people knew everything."

"What do you mean?" Chase asked, annoyed.

"Europe's history is nothing more than powers rising and falling, failing to create the stability it needs. They are countries that amass too much power and people within them that amassed too much influence. Rising tension befall those countries on many different things. Inevitably, those same tensions would lead to something more catastrophic. Do you know what it was?" the mage asked jokingly. The man held up two fingers. "Two World Wars that not only devastated Europe but almost the whole world. Those wars left countries with weak militaries and unable to handle the aftermath. If that is not proof enough of their poor judgement over the centuries, then I don't know what is. But that does not include the secret side—magic and supernatural. Without accords in place, all of Europe would be a hunting ground for monsters of every legend."

"I know all too well what those accords have done," said Chase, disagreeing, sticking to his convictions.

"When it comes to that, I do agree with you, but the choice of the people must be given to them. The people of Europe are given a choice. The European Union not only looks at the past history of Europe but the whole world. That's why the people in power, their representatives, will make the right choices for them."

"And if the people of Europe disagree with their decisions?" Chase asked.

"Objection is irrelevant in their eyes," said the mage as they stopped in front of a stone door at the end of the hallway.

"If there is such thing, then the truth will be shined upon on them until they see it."

Chapter 25: Trades of the Contract

"We will have to agree to disagree, but I will respect your position nonetheless if you respect mine," said the mage respectfully as he opened the door.

"With that said, please wait here while I inform Mr. Grifton of your arrival."

As the mage closed the door, Chase clutched his fist in frustration. "It has always been like this, James. Even when we were a part of the Black Order."

"Ya, but we're free and able to make our own choices," said James, trying to remind him of their freedom.

"Remember, we are only here for one last deal to clear our names, and after that, we are done with them," Chase said.

"Take this advice from an old king. I never liked any of the nobles in my court. But never let the animosity of that hierarchy cloud your judgement. As Merlin once said, most problems in life have easy solutions. We are blind to most of them," Arthur counseled Chase.

James looked down the hall to a group of mages who'd gathered and whispered amongst themselves at the mention of Merlin's name.

"Did he say Merlin?" one mage spoke.

"The man must be mental or something. He acts like he knows the great sorcerer personally," another said.

"Yes, it is truly insulting," said a third.

"Hey, guys, I think other people are spying on us," James whispered, warning them.

"Then why don't we use our inside voices?" Arthur encouraged as he formed a telepathic link between them. "Inntinn (mind)," he invoked.

Arthur continued to counsel Chase as they waited for their meeting.

"To change something that you know is wrong takes time. Believe me, I tried to change many things while I was king but failed as I realized it is impossible to change everything in one lifetime."

"I know, but it can be frustrating sometimes because you know you can do a lot, but it doesn't work out that way," said Chase, seeing the truth in the king's words.

"Then we'll do what we always have to bring about change," James said, reminding Chase of their one true mission.

"We hunt," Chase agreed.

"First, the Winter Wraiths, then the vampire Primogenitor. If power struggles are all that's happened in Europe since the Dark Ages, then there has been only been one country in the world that fought for its freedom. And that country was the United States."

"Oh ya. I remember seeing that name on maps, but you didn't really hear about it before," said James remembering seeing the country on maps.

"It is a really nice country, one of many different cultures and places. A country that was, at one time, under the rule of the crown but fought for its freedom."

"It sounds great. I would like to visit there sometime."

"I have only been there once before, so I promise to take you once the ice age is over."

"It is a promise then," James said, bumping fists with Chase.

"Yes, a promise."

"You better keep it."

"I always do."

The doors to Caldor's office opened. The group saw a man dressed in a black mages' robe approaching them.

"This is Caldor Grifton, ranked archmagi of the Mages Association, representative of Deglaciation of Mystics & Magics and member of the European Union council," the mage who'd accompanied them introduced.

"Please, Mr. Ashton, there is no need to introduce me so formally," said Caldor. "After all, a mage should not care about titles, just magic itself and our values to maintain it."

"That is very wise of you, sir, for you do let triviality cloud what mages stand for, but forgive me for saying, it is standard practice to give one's titles and name before any business proceedings for European Union," Ashton said, bowing.

"I understand, and that may be, but this is not a deal. It is more of a compromise given the peril the world is in."

"Then you know this winter is magical in nature and the entities behind it?" Chase asked.

Caldor turned his attention to Chase. "Not in full detail. That is why I hope you will enlighten me. But before that, where are my manners? I am Caldor Grifton."

"Pleased to meet you. May I ask what you meant by compromise?" Chase said.

"I'd rather not discuss that matter here in the open. I'm sure you have noticed they're eyes here that watch."

"Ya, I have more than I thought we would," said Chase as he glanced around at the mages staring back at them intently.

"Then, all the more reason to continue these discussions elsewhere. I assure you, there is significant benefit for you and your friend." Then to

Aston, "Mage, I'll handle matters from here. You may leave, and thank you for completing this assignment."

"Very well, Archmagus," Ashton said, bowing once again.

"Now then, gentlemen, shall we?" Caldor said, extending his arm to show the direction.

What is an Archmagus?" James whispered to Chase.

"It is the fourth rank in the Mages Association," Chase whispered back. "The ones who are at the lower ranks are novices. They are the new practitioners of magic. Paladins, which is our rank, have few years and merits. The higher ones the magus, archmagus, grand magus, sorcerer, and the last the rank is overlord. Few have ever achieved this rank over the centuries."

"They must really be powerful at magic," said James, amazed by the depth and prowess of the mages of the Mages Association.

"Yes, but even the magic of the most powerful ones pales in comparison to that of the gods."

In a tribunal conference room, everyone sat down to discuss the matter of the ice age and the offer Caldor had for James and Chase.

"Now, before we get to matters at hand, I must inform you that the other members of the European Union council do not know what I'm about to offer you. I prefer to keep it that way since the marks are still on you to be dead."

"Of course, but let me say this, I don't trust you or the Mages Association after all that has happened," Chase said, letting his thoughts be known.

"Given all that has happened, I can't say that I blame you for feeling that way, but I do not ask for your trust, just your cooperation," Caldor remarked, understanding Chase's mistrust. "Before you hear my offer, tell me what you know about this mystical winter."

"This winter is the ice age of Ragnarök, the Fimbulvetr (Great Winter), and it was cast by the Winter Wraiths immortal entities of frost and ice. Ever since the age of Vikings end, the world has been steadily getting colder as they slept, and it wasn't until a few months ago, when they finally awakened, that the great winter was unleashed."

It is just as Master suspected. I can tell he knows more than he lets on but as long as they are of use, it does not matter, Caldor thought, knowing Chase was withholding information. Caldor smiled inwardly at the thought of what was to come. *Now, I will know why the master has his almighty eyes on them.*

"Is that everything you know?"

"Just about, but if we don't act soon, the world will be forever frozen."

"I see. If this is an ice age, as you say, then it would be natural to have freezing temperatures. Since

350

everything is hitting record lows and given your track record, I have no reason to disbelieve you. Very well, this is what I will offer you. Succeed in stopping these Winter Wraiths, and I clear the marks off your heads," said Caldor firmly, coming to a decision.

"How can you guarantee something like that? After all, it was the European Union along with the Mages Association that ordered our deaths," Chase said, unconvinced.

"Of that, you do not need to worry. I have tremendous influence in both organizations, and I am the one that oversees the accords."

Chase was uncertain as he still did not fully trust Caldor. "And you can grant this?"

Caldor chuckled at Chase's mistrust. "Even now, you still have your doubts. That is fine, for I will prove it to you once it is done. And besides, the way you talked about them, it sounds like you were already going to handle the matter. Judging by your silence, I am right. That is why I said earlier this is a compromise, and given the threat to Europe and to the world as a whole, I see no reason why they wouldn't agree despite your recent activities."

"But you still haven't explained the reason why you would give this task to us," Chase said.

"It is simple, really. It's because you both have killed gods," said Caldor, placing files in front of Chase.

Chase remained silent as Caldor read off their records. "Demigods in England. The Beast of Gévaudan in France that you failed to kill. 200 people dead since. Your unauthorized mission in Iceland, 100,000 dead. Next and finally, Greece, Titans and Olympians, that left 2,000 dead. Regardless, act or principle, you two have left a substantial body count."

"If we hadn't stopped them, Zeus and the other Olympians would have still slaughtered innocents," Chase argued.

"You do not get to make that judgement, but I'm not going to argue about what has already happened. What is seen or unseen, it is your duty as a hunter to fulfill all the obligations of the contract given to you, nothing more—not go against it. But you two achieve results, and right now, that is what is needed. No other hunter or mage has the will or strength necessary to do this, only you do. Now, what is your decision? Will you accept my request?" Caldor asked, wanting an answer from Chase and James.

"Before we agree to this, tell us what do you get out of this? I know it is not simply for one less danger in the world."

"Well, no, not just that, but my associates and I have to fulfill the tasks given to us."

"Associates, you mean the European Union council?"

"No. Ones that I think you are very familiar with," said Caldor, snapping his fingers, causing the doors to the conference room to open.

Confused, James and Chase stared back at the door and were stunned when they saw Adrian Abel walk in.

"It's been a long time, fellas," Adrian said.

"Adrian, what are you doing here?" James asked.

"That really hurts. Is that any way to say help to an old friend?" said Adrian, smiling.

"You're no friend of ours," James said, staring Adrian down.

"True, but I am an old acquaintance."

Chase, unnerved by the third primogenitor's sudden appearance thought, *Adrian being here could only mean one thing.*

Chase turned his gaze toward Caldor then back at Adrian. *The vampires have gotten their hands in the Mages Association and European Union.*

Knowing that they were in danger, Chase looked at James and Arthur and nodded his head slightly to signal them to teleport. Chase reached for his mystica jewel but couldn't find it. *Where is it?*

"James, Arthur, do you have yours?"

"I had it on me, but I can't find it anywhere," Arthur said.

"Nor I," James chimed in.

353

"I am sorry, but I cannot permit you to leave," said a bald man sitting next to Adrian. "At least not yet."

I didn't sense his presence at all, Chase thought, looking at the man.

Chase, James, and Arthur were shocked as they saw a shadow conjure from the man and hand him the mystica jewels. "Were you looking for these, perhaps?"

In an instant, the man crushed the jewels into dust.

Chase knew that their escape was now impossible and pondered the man's identity. *That shadow is familiar. Only a few vampire Primogenitors have them. We were so focused on Adrian that we didn't even notice the shadow. It is so silent, and it took our mystica jewels like it was nothing.*

"Who are you?" Chase demanded.

"Forgive me, I am called Jonathan Cain," said Cain, adjusting his shades.

As you know of Adrian, like him, I am a Vampire Primogenitor but of the fourth blood."

Chase was surprised by the name. He knew now, without a doubt, Adrian's and Jonathan's true identities. He tried to say something, but Adrian held out his hand to silence him.

"Allow me."

"Schatten (shadow)," said Cain, dismissing his shadow familiar. "The shadow itself lives within mine."

His name is Abel and this is Cain, Chase thought as he looked at the vampires.

"Chase?" James asked, knowing what he was thinking.

Adrian chuckled at Chase's silence. "What is wrong? Why did you go all silent? You were so talkative earlier."

Cain smacked Adrian on the back of his head and reprimanded his behavior.

"What did you do that for?"

"Adrian, how many times I have reminded you of your behavior?"

As Cain and Abel bickered, Chase looked at them. *There is no doubt now—it is them.*

"You are Cain and Abel from the Bible," said Chase. "The first sons of humankind."

"Impressive, you're the first person to guess that," said Adrian, clapping his hands. "From what my brother said, you have summarized correctly," said Cain, taking off his shades. "We are Cain and Abel, the sons of man."

"How are you still alive? You should have died long before you even met Gilgamesh for him to give you his blood for longevity," Chase asked.

"I see. You know about our master do you?" Cain said, amused by Chase's knowledge. "But you should if you are a reader of the Bible, then you should know the reason why we have lived for so long."

Rolling up his coat sleeve, Cain showed them a brand mark on his arm.

"That's…" said Chase, recognizing the mark from the Bible.

"It's exactly what you think it is, the mark of Cain, the very same that cursed me to walk this very Earth for eternity," said Cain, confirming Chase's thoughts.

"There is really nothing to be surprised about since you discovered who we are," said Adrian, laughing in amusement. "Allow me to indulge you in something. Those verses where my brother killed me are true as the story is told. But the part left out of the final draft was me being dead for only a short time. By the time my brother revived me, it was already too late as he was therefore cursed by God with the mark. And I, being his twin, was cursed as well."

"That is enough Adrian, you have spoken enough, Cain commanded, waving his hand at Adrian.

Adrian sat back and relaxed as he finished talking. "Alright, I was finished talking anyway."

"You have to forgive Adrian; he can be overzealous at times."

"I don't care about apologies. Tell me about the one who turned you," James demanded, wanting to know more about Gilgamesh. "Why become vampires?"

"Ah, so the successor to the ninth has spoken fully. I will speak on the matter no more, for we are not here about us, only you, James Akatsuki and Chase Actaeonis. Now, it is time for you both to decide. Accept the task to destroy the entities of winter or not. It would be wise for you to accept as I would rather not forcefully convince the two of you otherwise."

"Just try it," said James boldly.

Before either one could act, Caldor clapped his hands together to dissuade them from using magic. "There is no need for such crude methods since we all have a common goal at this particular moment."

"Very well tenth, since you oversee this, I will leave it to you," Cain conceded.

"James, don't—not here," said Chase, discouraging his best friend.

"Well, now that old and new friends are acquainted, I think we should focus on the compromise. Chase, I have told you everything that you will gain. And since your means of escape is now compromised, what is your decision?"

Caldor is a vampire as well. We really have no choice, Chase thought, unnerved by the three vampires before them.

Looking at James and Arthur, he nodded his head in approval.

"If it means clearing our records, even if we have to deal with you and these vampires, then we will accept. But know this, this isn't over between us. Once we're done with the Winter Wraiths, we're coming for you," Chase threatened, looking at the brothers menacingly.

"Don't make promises you can't keep, kid, for many have tried and failed. I have been alive for centuries," said Cain, impressed by Chase's bold defiance.

"Oh, I'll be sure to keep this one for you, trust me."

"I look forward to it," said Cain, putting on his shades.

"James, Arthur, let's go."

"Before we take our leave, would you permit me to ask a question?" Arthur asked, gazing at Caldor.

"Of course, as long as it's within my knowledge," said Caldor, obliging the king.

"Your last name is familiar to me. What is your connection to my teacher?"

"I expect nothing less of the legendary king of knights. So, you have noticed my family name," said Caldor, smiling.

"You know who I am?" Arthur asked.

"But of course, historical records and paintings of you have passed down secretly from my ancestors to me and my children. Everyone in my family recognizes and knows your appearance. Not to mention, I also know your magical energy from the samples that my ancestor left behind."

"Of course, I also expect nothing less the great wizard of Britannia. He was, after all, my teacher," said Arthur, laughing at their fateful meeting.

"What is he talking about, Arthur? And what does his ancestor have to do with you?" James asked.

"It's simple. Caldor's ancestor was also Arthur's magical teacher," said Chase, explaining the magical ancestry.

"Merlin," James whispered.

"Correct, my ancestor was the great wizard Merlin, as is my middle name," said Caldor, acknowledging the pairs' deduction.

"I know Merlin did not possess a last name, for even his father and mother were unknown to him," said Arthur. "But I know his son did, and if I remember correctly, it was Grifton. And I know my teacher well enough that he would be disappointed that one of his blood would align with such miscreates like you. Why have you abandoned his legacy and aligned yourself with such villains?" Arthur asked, turning his gaze back to Caldor. "What have they done for you?"

"Well, there's no answer that will satisfy you, but if you really want an answer… It was for my family and power, nothing more."

Arthur stood in silence.

"I can see why you are confused, so let me put it in a story that you can understand. My grandfather fought in World War II for the British and nearly died. At the war's end, he wanted my father to take up our legacy and tradition of magic."

"But my father was alive during such savage times and saw many monsters rise to power. This caused him to not only practice it but to come up with a permanent solution to end all wars. Knowing that his power was inefficient and one of the influencing members of the E.E.C., he was approached by my master, Gilgamesh, who offered him guidance and answers to his questions. With the blessed blood, he became the tenth and final vampire Primogenitor at that time," said Caldor, cutting open his hand, showing Arthur the blood. "The price for that power was to remain and for the blood to pass down to the next in line. The next person in line was me. After my father died, I continued his work for master Gilgamesh. Overseeing the policies he put in place from the Mages Association to E.E.C., which is now the E.U. for the safety and security of magic in Europe. We wanted full cooperation from all sides for the threats of monsters and magic, but the United States refused to provide their personnel from D.A.M. But with such responsibility as I grow old, I struggle to decide between my two sons who are both exceptional mages to succeed and inherit my blood and status."

"I can understand your decision, but to give in to power is never an answer, only a betrayal," said Arthur. "It is only a surrender."

"And what do you know about it, old king? Your time has long since passed," Caldor asked.

"It is true, I am from the past, here now in the present alive again. But it is because I am one from the past and have been one to hold power to know its temptation. As king, I had to stop endless hatred and wars time after time. I never once submerged myself or aligned in its evil."

"And that conviction of yours led to the end of Britannia," said Caldor, laughing at Arthur.

"That may be, but I never once regretted any of my decisions. It is only through one's honesty and strength can their ideals for peace come to pass."

"You say I have aligned myself with evil, but it is because of that evil that peace, for the first time in centuries, has been achieved. No more wars, no more famine, peace in Europe is here."

"And no more freedom to choose," Arthur retorted.

"That peace to which you speak to is false. You and everyone here only use that word to amass influence and wealth at the expense of the people. It is just another form of evil itself."

"Another form of evil, you say. I may be still human in a sense, but that's precisely why humans should not have the choice to decide for everything will be deemed evil. The only matter humanity is capable of, is self-destruction that would destroy the whole planet."

"And you think your manipulation of them is justification?" Chase argued, hearing enough of Caldor's poisonous talk.

"Better to be manipulated and controlled than to let humanity's impulses run wild and destroy everything to see or fail to understand. But we were not the ones who set these rules in place. They have been around since ancient times—put in place by the Anunnaki (Gods of Mesopotamia) from Sumer. Even though Master Gilgamesh had contempt for them because of what they did to him, he still upholds those rules to this very day. And for that, you should be profoundly grateful."

"We're not grateful. We're disgusted," said James.

So, that's why, Caldor thought, smiling.

"I can see the reason why he chose to spare the both of you, but..." Caldor shifted his gaze back to James. "But I cannot think of the other. Anyway, I'm done speaking, so I suggest you all hurry and complete your mission before the world becomes Jǫtunheimr from Norse myth."

"Every single one of you will be hunted by us, including Gilgamesh. Enjoy what time you have, for it will be your last," Chase warned before leaving.

"On that, you made a mistake," said Cain.

Chase looked back at Cain. "And what would that be?"

Popping his knuckles, Cain did not hide his killing intent. "Your mistake was threatening the master in front of me. Normally, I would kill you where you stand, but it will go against the master's wishes. Be fortunate that your life will be spared this time, for you will not have another."

"I will keep that in mind since there is not going to be a next time for you either," said Chase, smiling.

"Just make sure your threats aren't empty because I look forward to our next encounter, fleckless neophyte," Cain whispered, watching them leave, eager for their next encounter.

James Akatsuki, I wonder why Gilgamesh is so interested in you," Caldor thought curious. *And what is your connection to the ninth Primogenitor? Why did she choose you? James Akatsuki, what is your connection to the ninth Primogenitor, and why did she choose you? Regardless, once the master sets his sights on anything, his fate was already sealed, for the Demi-god's blood runs through that boy's veins.*

"Do you know the master's intention?" Caldor asked, looking at Cain.

"It is not our place to question the master's intention," Cain said outraged by Caldor's question. "We, as his loyal subjects, are to carry them out without fail. I do not have to remind you of that, do I?"

Sensing Cain's murderous aura, Caldor cowardly agreed with him. "Of course not. Whatever the master wishes, I will follow. If it is his wish, giving those two a pardon is a small price to pay to see his visions through."

Cain was not impressed but rather disgusted by Caldor but accepted his answer. "Then you will do well to remember that."

Once this winter is over, everything will change. So that this world will reborn anew by Master Gilgamesh's mandate, Cain thought, leaving with his brother, relieved to no longer have to hide in the shadows.

Chapter 26: The Arctic

After they left Brussels, James, Chase, and Arthur planned their strategy against the Winter Wraiths.

All of this is becoming more complicated, Chase thought, steering the airship through the storms.

"Are you sure they won't be able to follow us?" James asked, worried.

"Ya, I'm sure," Chase snarled. "Even the vampires would not be able to send out their familiars in these storms."

"Alright, alright, I believe you."

"It's good that you do believe me, otherwise, you would have been dead a long time ago."

But didn't I die before? James thought, laughing inside as he remembered dying on Olympus. "Have you been able to find anything?"

Looking at the dimensional map, Chase highlighted the winter storms in the north.

"I have been trying, but not with much success. They could be anywhere in the northern hemisphere. It is hard to narrow a location since we cannot track anything through these storms."

James looked at the map closely. "What about Norway or the other Scandinavian countries? Do you think they would be there?"

"Not likely since they would want a place more secluded to recover their lost strength. And if I were a creature of winter, I would not return to the same place I was locked away," said Chase, not dismissing the possibility.

"Good point."

That could be it, Chase thought, pulling up a weather chart.

"What are you checking?"

"I can't say for sure, but something just occurred to me. The Winter Wraiths are beings capable of manipulating cold weather on a global scale. Since they radiate sub-zero coldness, I figured to check different territories and counties for the coldest temperature."

"Why?"

"Maybe by measuring the coldest temperatures in the northern hemisphere, it could narrow down where we need to look."

"You think Winter Wraiths will be in the coldest temperature?"

"There is a high possibility, but it is a long shot at the most."

Looking at the different freezing temperatures, Chase narrowed their search to the Arctic in North America. "Got it. I found the coldest temperature."

James clapped his hands. "Alright, where are we looking?"

"Canada in the territory of Nunavut," said Chase, showing James the location as he put the coordinates in the airship.

"Are you sure about that because that's a lot of ground to cover?" James asked.

"I'm sure. The temperature is negative 30 in Nunavut, almost 10 degrees colder than anywhere else. And when I look more closely, the winter storms are more intense around there. It might not be much to go on, but we'll figure something out when we get there."

"You're right, and it is just like you said, we really don't have anything else to go on. How long will it take us to get there?"

"From our present course from Europe to North America over the Atlantic and with the storms, about ten to twelve hours."

Annoyed by how long the flight would be, James looked outside and saw the intensity of the blizzard. "Good point."

"So, my friends, do we know where we are heading?" Arthur asked, walking into the cockpit overhearing them.

James pointed to Nunavut on the map. "Here in the northern part of Canada."

Looking at the continent, Arthur was intrigued. "I've never seen such a mass of land before, even on all the maps I possessed during my time as king. Compared to this, England is just a sliver piece."

"It is land that was undiscovered for the majority of human history, at least for the Europeans," said Chase. "Centuries after your rule, the Vikings were the first Europeans to land on the New World soil but were never fully acknowledge until a century ago. But centuries after the Vikings' discovery, in the 15th century and beyond, other Europeans discovered it. Many countries started to claim the land to expand their maps."

Arthur was amazed. "The New World, a great discovery of a lifetime. How I wish this discovery was known during my time, that would have been such an adventure. But by your tone, I can tell it wasn't always like that."

Turning off the holographic map, Chase nodded his head. "For the Europeans perhaps, it was great but not the Native Americans."

"I see."

"I don't mean to interrupt your history lesson but let's talk about something different," said James shifting the conversation.

Chase and Arthur both agreed. "When this is all over, I'll tell you more. We'll finish this conversation then," Chase said to Arthur before he left the bridge.

Later that night, the winter storms still raging, they arrived at the frozen shores of Nunavut. Chase touched the airship down deep into the snow.

Opening up the back of the airship, Chase placed a protective barrier around it to protect them from the elements.

"Better put on some thicker clothes because the cold of Norway is nothing compared to this," said Chase feeling the cold.

"On that, my friend, I agree, but only so much."

While the others were still putting on their sub-zero coats, Arthur walked outside into the blizzard.

"You don't have enough gear on. You'll freeze if you stay out there too long," James yelled, trying to stop Arthur.

Stepping outside, James could barely see Arthur. "Arthur."

With visibility from the blizzard getting worse, James could not see Arthur but could hear his voice echo through the storm. "Nonsense, I should feel it for myself."

James, shivering, stepped back into the airship. "Burr, that really is cold. Arthur. Arthur, come back."

"What's wrong? Why are you yelling?" Chase asked, running back, hearing the commotion. Looking around, Chase did not see Arthur. "Where is Arthur?"

James silently answered Chase by pointing into the blizzard.

"He walked out there?"

James nodded his head yes.

Chase rushed to put the rest of his sub-zero gear on. "Why are the people from ancient times always the most thick-headed?"

"James, snap out of it, finish putting on your gear. We're going out there to look for Arthur."

"Right," said James, rushing to get his gear.

"Remember, it is sub-zero temperatures out there, and visibility is almost zero, so be sure to stick together."

"Are you sure this gear is enough?"

Pressing forward into the storm, Chase looked back at James. "They're enough. You'll barely be able to feel anything. Master Shinko made them personally."

After a few minutes of searching, they found no sign of Arthur. "We have to keep searching before he freezes to death."

Suddenly, an image appeared in their line of vision through the blizzard. Walking slowly, Arthur, shivering from the cold, stood in front of them.

"You were right, James; it was not enough."

Back inside the airship, Arthur, still shivering tried to warm himself. "I have been in many winters, but nothing like this before."

"Hey, easy, you're still shivering," said James, giving Arthur more blankets.

"I am sorry, I should have heeded your warning."

"Not just his but mine as well," said Chase lecturing Arthur. "I warned you about going out there without enough gear."

Closing the back of the airship, Chase sighed as he placed a heater by Arthur. "You're almost as bad as James for not listening. It's a good thing we were prepared for such cold weather, otherwise, you would have died from severe hypothermia if you were exposed to the freezing temperatures long enough."

"Thank you, my friend."

With Arthur warmed up, Chase handed him the rest of his sub-zero gear. "Don't thank me just yet. We still have to survive the winter first."

"It will be dawn in a few hours. We'll begin our search once we have more light," said Chase, looking into the blizzard, not wanting to take any more chances.

As Chase walked away to wait with the others, without them knowing a glimmer of pale blue eyes looked at the airship through the blizzard before fading back into it.

At dawn, the back of the airship opened and Arthur approached. "I am sorry, my friend."

Chase, keeping track of the storm on his radar, dismissed Arthur's apology. "There is no need to apologize, that's what friends are for."

"Indeed, though I must say, my friend, I'm impressed by your vast knowledge of winter and what you call hypothermia. Even with the best teachings of Merlin, I have never heard of such a term."

"Well, when you live in cold weather like that of Iceland most of your life, you pick up a few things. And what I learned from places like the Clock Tower and Shangri-La doesn't hurt either. Ever since I was young, I read every book I came across, studying many different subjects, including science, history, alchemy, and magic. I do my best to be prepared."

"If only you were around during the time of Britannia, I could have used your counsel," said Arthur, impressed by Chase's dedication. "If it wasn't for your knowledge and preparation, many lives would have been lost, including ours."

"Ya, but the same goes for you and the others as well. I wouldn't be here without him or you," said Chase looking at James getting ready. "But despite all that, there are some things that are beyond your control."

Arthur nodded his head yes. "As Merlin once told me, that which is uncontrollable is but one of the true cycles of destiny. That which is called fate. It is what we all must inevitably accept if we are to change it. But like I said before, I do not regret my fate nor that of Britannia. People do not know what type of people they have been until the moment of their death. I reflected on my life at the time of my death to see if there was something I could have done differently to prevent my country's destruction."

"And were you able to find your answer?"

"No, not one. But it was truly one of greatest and joy as Merlin said it would be. That alone is enough for me."

"Why are you telling me all of this?" Chase asked.

"In order to change your own fate and those of the others around you. And for you not to test it, for if it is placed on the scales, it will only lead to death and destruction. That is why God is the only one who controls fate. The rules he placed are guides to help better ourselves and to live good, honest lives. From someone who was once a king, that is wisdom of life and fate, I, Arthur Pendragon, give to you, Chase Actaeonis. And also, for you, James Akatsuki. For the fate of the world right rests on the decisions you will make," said Arthur.

Chase sighed in reluctance. "I've never really been the leading type, but I'll accept if I have to."

"Yes, I know, but it is those who do not want the burden of leadership who are usually the ones most capable of it. And after everything I have witnessed of you so far, I am confident of the depth of capability—even when the odds are against you. Too rarely you let your emotions overcome you. You learned how to keep them calm in battle. Those traits make you more than qualified by not just me but all of us who reside within Shangri-La. And you, James, you are more in tune with your emotions than anyone

I ever met. You show compassion even to those who are not worthy of it. With all the obstacles put in front of your path, you have proudly overcome. The depth of your magic and mystic powers is far beyond that of my teacher Merlin. But the true merit is your ability to bring people together, which is really inspirational. Regardless of what your former compatriots have said to you, you two have nothing to be ashamed of for the decisions you have made, for you have seen many horrors—more than the average one could bear. You know the truth that's beyond the shadows that blanketed the world for millennia, and now you both are trying to solve why it was intended. With the lives you and the powers you possess, not one can stand in your way, not even Gods."

James and Chase were thankful but slightly embarrassed by Arthur's long praise of them. "Well, thank you for your kind words, Arthur. I think I understand how you felt when you were king of England. But all I wanted to do was the right thing," James said.

"On that, my friend, James, I agree. I want the same thing as far as you both are concerned. You two are just as worthy and valiant as the Knights of the Round Table," said Arthur, placing his hands on both their shoulders.

James and Chase smiling back at Arthur, placed their hands on his shoulders in a show of brotherhood.

"That's what friends are for. We look out for each other always."

"It's dawn," said Chase, noticing light outside.

Walking out into the storm, Chase looked back at James and Arthur. "Let's get hunting. Remember, this winter storm isn't going to die down, so we're going to bear with it."

The violent winds pushed back against them when they stepped outside,. "Stick together and move slowly."

Chase and Arthur struggled to track through the knee-deep snow.

"Chase, do you see anything?" James yelled, barely able to see.

Chase looked at his scanner. "No nothing, just pure white emptiness all around us."

"What do you want to do? Keep pushing ahead or head back?"

"Since we are not picking up any signs of the Winter Wraiths in this direction, let's head back to the airship and try another route. Arthur, what are you stopping for? We're heading back," Chase yelled, noticing Arthur stand still.

Arthur felt uneasy and waved for them to come to him.

"Look closely," said Arthur, pointing forward.

"I don't see anything; this blizzard is too thick," said James.

An eeriness crept in as the blizzard suddenly eased. Everyone was disturbed by the sudden change and the ominous feeling they felt.

"James, do you see that?" Chase whispered, seeing a pair of pale glowing eyes staring back at them.

James nodded his head silently as the wind howled loudly.

After several minutes, the eyes started to move closer to them, and they heard its faint footsteps.

"Is that an animal?"

"No, it isn't," said Chase as a pale, humanoid figure appeared, stopping yards from them.

"There's no mistake about it. That is one of the Winter Wraiths."

Chapter 27: The Frozen Mark

The blizzard stopped abruptly.

"What is going on?" James asked.

Chase, feeling even colder, felt it radiate from the Winter Wraith. "It's the power of the Winter Wraith. The power of winter itself."

Unnerved by its power, the Winter Wraith shifted its frozen gaze toward him.

Þórr (Thor). The Winter Wraith thought blankly, staring at Chase, recognizing the mystic energy of the thunder god.

For some reason, every time it stares at me, I get this uneasy feeling, Chase thought fearfully. *Could it be Thor is warning me? On top of that, it stopped the blizzard without even looking at the sky. To manipulate weather on that scale with magic is truly frightening.*

"What is going on? I'm not able to sense its mystic energy at all," said James.

Shocked by James's statement, Chase tried to sense its mystic energy but to no avail. "I sensed the mystic energy before, but that could be because they're awakening from their slumber. If we can't sense their mystic energy, the scanner itself would be useless."

"So, that is a Winter Wraith known to the Norse Gods and Vikings as the Jötunn from the frozen realm of Jötunheimr," said Arthur solemnly, staring at it. "From its appearance and power, it is truly a frightening creature. Perhaps even more so than that of Cath Sit, the trickster black cat that stole souls."

Chase acknowledging the danger, pondered about the Winter Wraith. *Does that mean their magic and mystic energy are undetectable? The codexes did not mention anything about them having such an ability. But then again, there are still too many unknowns about the Winter Wraiths. Those unknowns make them all the more dangerous and unpredictable. That aside, that is not what's bothering me the most. Why did it appear before us, and why did it stop the blizzard just now?* Chase thought, staring into the pale blue eyes of the frozen entity.

"Chase, what is it?" James asked, seeing the Winter Wraith's eyes trained on Chase.

"James, Arthur, listen closely to what I'm about to tell you. The Winter Wraiths can erase their mystic energy signature."

"What? Are you saying that we can't even sense them if they are close like this one is?"

"Even if it was suppressing its energy, we would still sense it, but since we can't, it is the only possibility. And the fact the scanner did not pick up this Winter Wraith in front of us further supports that theory."

I know it could manipulate the cold, but to erase your mystic energy to where you can't sense it, that is just insane," James thought, staring at the Winter Wraith.

"Was there anything else in the codexes about them and their abilities?" James asked.

"Not beyond what I already told you. It really means we know nothing about them." Pausing for a moment, Chase remembered. "Wait, I think there was something. One time, when I was alone in the Oracle Library, I studied the origins of all cyprid creatures and how they came to be."

"Ok, I understand that, but what does that have to do with the Winter Wraiths?"

"That's just it. It has nothing to do with it, but at the same time, it does. I discovered that the first gods, or the Mesopotamian gods, were responsible for creating all creatures and monsters. They were also responsible for giving them names, but there was no mention anywhere about the creation of the Winter Wraiths and how they came to be."

James was shocked about the origins of the cyprids as he remembered seeing them all imprisoned in Tartarus. "I know that Zeus freed them from the underworld, but if that's true, why would the gods create them in the first place?"

"Fear itself, to keep humans in line. For them to be feared to prevent a rebellious defiance."

"Fear, but why? You told me the first gods loved humans in ancient times."

"For a time, yes, as was one of the charges God himself tasked to them. But that is not what's right now. As I said, the fact the Winter Wraiths weren't created by the gods could only mean one thing. They existed before even the gods themselves."

"How is that even possible?"

"Right, James, they are the physical manifestation of winter itself, so it's not that hard to believe they came before the gods. But what that also means is that they are a part of nature too."

"Was that one of the reasons why they were sealed away because of their power?"

"One of the reasons, yes, but we don't know the others. The Norse Gods feared their power so much that they locked them away behind the Ice Wall using the power of Thor within Mjolnir. All to prevent Fimbulvetr (Great Winter) that envelops the world now."

"But that is not the worst part of this, is it?" Arthur asked, interrupting.

"Ya, we don't know what the Winter Wraiths' intentions are. But as you saw before, even individually, the Winter Wraiths are far more powerful than even we could ever imagine and fear.

"Then what do you want to do?"

Chase slowly placed his hand on his holster. "Simple, we kill it before it kills us."

The Winter Wraith, seeing him reach for the revolver, grasped its ice spear tightly.

"Our weapons are the only tools in the world that can destroy them, but we will have to end this fight because we are at an extreme disadvantage right now."

Placing his hand on his katana, James was confused. "How so?"

"With the sub-zero gear we're wearing, and with our legs in a couple of feet of snow, our mobility is extremely limited. And with the winter weather and this ice field terrain, they have the advantage."

James remained deathly silent.

"We cannot make a single mistake. If we do, it could be our last," Chase cautioned.

After a few more tense moments, Chase grew more and more anxious. *It knows it has the advantage against us. But why doesn't it move?*

The Winter Wraith, not fearing them, slowly gazed at all three of them before turning its back to Chase.

"I believe it is trying to gauge us," said Arthur.

"Gauge us, on what?"

"To see if we are a threat or not. Or it could be to see the depth of our characters."

"Why would it care about our behavior if we are a threat to it?"

Arthur put up one finger. "Language of the body can speak just as well if not more so than what is spoken. In times of peace or in war, the slightest nod can set forth a chain of events that cannot be stopped. Take this from an old king who has seen and fought many battles."

Seeing that Arthur had a point, Chase took his hand off his holster. *From what I have seen so far, it only reacts when we act—like a predator stalking its prey.*

"Given the terrain we are in, Chase, I do think you're right to believe we are at a disadvantage. And it being still like stone means it knows it as well?"

Even with this amount of distance between us, with our mobility limited in the snow, it can attack in a mere second with that ice spear.

Looking down further toward the Winter Wraith's feet, Chase was shocked. *It's standing on the snow.*

The Winter Wraith glanced down and then back at Chase. It took a few steps forward, stepping on top of the snow.

"How is that possible? It walked on the snow, and its standing on top of it," said James.

This really bad with it being able to walk on the snow, it has more advantage than it did before. There is no choice, Chase thought, approaching the Winter Wraith slowly.

"Chase, what are you doing?" James asked.

Arthur pulled James back. "He is doing what only he can do. You must not intervene. You saw what that creature just did. It knows it has all the advantage, and it just showed it to us to prove it."

James knocked away Arthur's hand. "I know that. I saw it too. But him trying to talk with it, that is insane."

"Maybe not as you make out to be, but right now, we have hope to defeat it in battle."

Chase stopped just a few feet from the Winter Wraith. Arthur watched them carefully. *It has the traits of a predator, and now it's luring in its prey. Chase my friend, what are you going to do?*

"I don't know what your purpose is, but if you would, I would like to speak with you if you're willing," said Chase, trying to reason with the Winter Wraith.

The Winter Wraith nodded in agreement.

"Forgive us if we threatened you. I'm well aware you can kill us at any moment, and I'm sure you aware of that fact because of this ice terrain."

The ice entity did not speak. Chase became careful. "I guess your kind is one of very few words. But in light that you were sealed away for centuries, I can't say that I blame you. Let me just ask this, why are you casting this endless winter over the northern hemisphere of the Earth?"

Slowing lifting its finger, the Winter Wraith pointed at Chase. "*Me.*"

"Chase, why him? He didn't do anything to them."

"No, I don't believe it is just referring to just him."

Chase's eyes turned lightning blue for a moment. "I see, humanity."

The Winter Wraith nodded its head.

"Survival of the fittest. But I know that there is more. You can't forgive the evils of humanity for its centuries of war and destruction that it has caused to nature, the very cycle of the world. I know there is nothing I can say that could please you, but I'm asking you to stop the great winter."

Before Chase could finish, the Winter Wraith pierced its ice spear into the snow.

"Then are you saying that you won't stop?" Chase asked.

Giving a silent response, the Winter Wraith closed its eyes briefly before opening them again.

"Answer me."

The clouds above became darker as the blizzard resumed. Struggling to see, Chase watched the Winter Wraith walk away. "Wait. Are you going to run away? Are you saying we're not even worth the effort?"

Hearing Chase, the Winter Wraith stopped and looked back at him. Its eyes twitched, and a piece of ice flew, cutting Chase on his cheek.

Chase didn't take his eyes off the Winter Wraith as blood dripped into the snow. *It didn't even move, and I didn't see that ice shard until I felt it cut me. Could it be because of this blizzard blinding me, or is it something else entirely? An injury shouldn't be able to freeze instantly,"* Chase seeing the cut already frozen.

Fearful, Chase blankly stared at the Winter Wraith as it disappeared into the blizzard. *Just what are they?*

Seeing the Winter Wraith vanish, James and Arthur rushed to Chase.

"Chase, are you alright?" James asked.

Feeling the numbness of the scratch, Chase covered up his face. "Ya, I am fine, just a little unnerved by what just happened."

Chase walked to where the Winter Wraith stood but saw no trace of it. *So, it truly does not leave anything behind. And it seems the blizzard has calmed down some since it left too. Perhaps, because it disappeared into it and is no longer close by.*

Turning around, Chase walked past James and Arthur in the direction of the airship. "Let's head back. I have an idea of how we can track them."

A day later, Chase made a new device to help them. "Alright, I'm done."

"That's going to help us?" James asked, seeing the device's odd features.

"Ya, this device measures weather intensity, and it's synced to my scanner to help me track it anywhere in Canada. The intensity of the storms is how we will find them."

Pulling up the map of the northern hemisphere, Chase synced the device pointing west. "Here are the winter storms to the west where they are most intense."

"I see, a very intuitive idea, my genius friend," Arthur said.

"Thanks for the compliment, but if we follow the direction of where the blizzard is most intense, I'm sure we will not find just the one, but probably all of them."

With their new lead to find them, they flew more inland into Canada.

Opening the back of the airship to resume their search, Arthur placed his hand on Chase's shoulder. "If they are aware, this could all be a trap."

"I know," Chase whispered, walking into the blizzard.

Walking west through the blizzard, James stopped, feeling something was off. "Hey, Chase."

James took the covering off Chase's face, exposing the frozen cut on his cheek. "Why did you do that?

"Why were you trying to hide it?"

"I wasn't trying to hide it; I just didn't want to worry you," Chase said.

"It marked you," James noted as he looked more closely at the cut.

"What do you mean, James?"

"Think about it Chase, why would it show itself to us at all? Because it wanted to show us that there wasn't anything we could do to stop it."

"No, it wanted you, and that cut is proof of it," James argued.

"You said it yourself, the Winter Wraiths were predatory in nature."

"The Winter Wraith choose not to hunt us," said Chase seeing James's valid points.

James nodded his head yes. "Because it already is."

"And when you provoked it, the Winter Wraith gave you that frozen cut in retaliation."

"To mark me as its prey and for the hunt to begin. You're absolutely sure about all of this, James?"

"Hey, it's just like you said, I may not be the smartest person, but even I can have my moments," said James, feeling somewhat insulted.

"Ya, that is true. You do have moments of brilliance from time to time. It's just even after all this time we have been together, it still surprises me."

James smiled. "Well, continue to be surprised. But if all of what I told you is true, do you still want to track them?"

"Yes, even if they are hunting us now, it doesn't change anything. We'll track west for a few more hours. If we don't find anything, then we'll head back to the airship and try again."

Pressing forward through the blizzard, Chase looked back at James and Arthur. "Alright, be sure to stick together, the blizzard is only going to get worse from here."

Over the coming hours, they struggled, tracking through the snow the more they went west.

"I think we should start heading back now," Chase yelled not seeing anything.

James and Arthur nodding their heads in agreement, started to trek back. Taking one last glance, Chase saw numerous pale blue eyes move in the whiteness of the blizzard.

"James, Arthur, come back," said Chase telepathically.

"What is it?"

Chase put his finger over his lips. "Shh, quiet. They are just in front of us."

"They're moving around us," said Arthur, watching the eyes closely.

Confused by them, Chase had a weird feeling. *For some reason, when I stare at them, I get a weird feeling. Like it is something that is mindless.*

The eyes moved closer as the figures started to appear.

"Wait, I thought the Winter Wraiths were like over seven feet," said James. "These guys barely look over six feet."

"They are. All Winter Wraiths are over seven feet. Whatever these things are, they are not Winter Wraiths.

James pointed out their pale blue eyes. "If they aren't, then why are their eyes the same as the Winter Wraiths?"

Seeing their features steadily appear, everyone stood in shock by their decomposing appearance.

Those are," Chase thought as his eyes turned lighting blue.

"What are those things?" James asked, creeped out by their decayed appearance.

Arthur drew his sword. "They look like humans but it appears they are dead."

Chase grabbed his head slightly in pain. "They're Wights, dead that are reanimated by the Winter Wraiths."

James, drawing one of his katanas, looked at Chase. "How do you know that?"

"Because Thor showed me."

Screeching loudly, the Wights charged at James, Chase, and Arthur.

"He fought the undead once before during the age of Vikings," said Chase, pulling out Mjolnir.

"Our sveiða weapons can kill them like the Winter Wraiths, so use them."

"I already know that."

Struggling to track through the snow to fight, suddenly, one of the Wights scratched violently at

James. Missing with his sword, the Wight tackled James into the snow.

"James."

James held back the Wight, but it started pushing down, trying to kill him. "James, hold on."

Chase and Arthur tried to reach James but were blocked by the other Wights. "These undead, they are in the way."

"Then we will just have to cut them down," said Arthur leading a few away.

Struggling to hold back the Wight, James tried to burn it with his crimson flames but could not call upon them. *What is going on? Why can't I charge my flames?*

"James, what are you doing? Kill it already," Chase yelled.

The Wight, hissing at him, reached down and started to scratch James on his neck. James seeing his Sapphire Shard katana close by, struggled to reach for it. He grabbed it and stabbed the Wight through its stomach, killing it. The blue color of its eyes disappeared as its body fell on top of James.

"Ahh, and it would fall on top of me," said James, pushing the dead body off him.

Touching the scratches on his neck, James felt them freeze. *The scratches... they feel so cold.*

James dismissed his concern and rushed over to help Chase deal with the remaining undead.

"James, stay back."

Swinging Mjolnir, Chase smashed one of the Wights down into the snow. The Wight screeched. With its jaw dislocated, it tried to stand, but Chase pinned it down with Mjolnir.

"These things don't die easy. I haven't fought zombies this hard since the Revenants in Romania."

Chase pulled out a sveiða knife, and slashed off the pinned Wight's lower body to prevent from thrashing any further. Suddenly, the other Wight jumped on Chase's back, knocking him into the snow. Rushing over, James stabbed the Wight in the back, killing it.

"Thanks," said Chase as James helped him to his feet.

"Don't mention it."

Calling back Mjolnir, Chase stared at the severed Wight, crawling toward them, hissing. Chase walked over to it, stomped his feet on. "I don't think so."

Chase smashed the head of the Wight, killing it. "Alright, that's most of them."

"Wait, where is Arthur?" James asked, looking around.

"You called," said Arthur, appearing behind them.

"Hey, don't just appear like that. If you were a Wight, I could have stabbed you."

Arthur chuckled. "Very well, my friend, but I'm sure the situation will never come to that.

"Were those the Wights that were after you?"

Arthur sheathed his sword. "I already vanquished both of them."

"How did you kill them so fast?"

"Well, to explain it simply, they ran at me from different directions, and they ran into each other. Afterward, I let them taste my sword, and after that, they did not move."

He had it easier than we did, Chase thought a little annoyed.

"Well, the reason for that is Wights are reanimated dead brought back by magic. They may be able to move and fight, but that doesn't mean they have the brains for it. But everyone came out fine, that is all that matters. "I would normally agree with you, but this time I cannot. "For I have been marked," Arthur said, rolling up his coat sleeve, showing a frozen scratch on his arm.

"Not just him," James said, partially pulling down his coat showing Chase the frozen scratches on his neck.

"You've both been mark," said Chase. "Then that means we are all being hunted by them."

Arthur, rolling down his sleeve, stood over one of the Wights. "Yes, which makes the battle to come even more difficult. Given that, what would you have us do now?" Arthur asked, staring back at Chase. "Keep moving forward or not? Because if we go from now, it will only become more dangerous."

Chase thought seriously about Arthur's suggestion as he knew more Wights laid in their path to the frozen entities.

"If we encounter Wights here, then there are bound to be more ahead. For now, let's head back to the airship and recover first," said Chase, pulling out a mystica jewel.

James and Arthur stood close to Chase. The mystic jewel glowed brightly. "Teleport."

Enveloped by the blue vortex, they all teleported back to the airship.

Chapter 28: Jǫtunheimr

A few days passed, and James, Chase, and Arthur recovered from their encounters with the manifestations of winter.

"Alright, let's go over what has happened so far," said Chase, noting the storm was not letting up. The Winter Wraiths have marked us all as prey to hunt. Second, due to the warning I received from Thor, they can reanimate powerful dead called Wights." Chase pointed to the blizzard bearing down upon them. "And finally, we know the Winter Wraiths are still near due to the intensity of the blizzard."

"It is as you said, but where we go from here is the question that needs an answer," said Arthur, thinking.

Yes, how do we narrow them down? That really is the question, Chase thought.

James paced back and forth across the airship. "I think I have an idea, so just hear me out."

James went to the holographer and brought up the map of the world. "Let's see what is to the west of us.

I think if we did, we might get a better location on the Winter Wraiths."

"That is twice you have come up with a good idea. Have you been reading a lot or something?" Chase asked, poking fun at James.

"No, I have been paying attention to what's going on all around," said James, poking back. "It's just like you said, there are still too many unknowns."

"Perhaps this one time, I will call you a genius," Chase said.

Wanting to pursue James's idea, Chase zoomed in on the dimensional map to the territory of Nunavut. "This is our current location right here—about three hundred miles away from the Arctic Ocean."

Tracking the map to the west of them, Chase found many mountains. Chase's eyes suddenly turned lightning blue when he recognized the mountains. "Tuqea Mountain, Mount Odin, Mount Asgard, and Thor's Peak, one of the battlegrounds of the gods."

"That's it, they have to be at Thor's Peak," said James, agreeing, not noticing Chase's eyes.

Chase knew instinctively from his past life what those mountains hid. *Jǫtunheimr. That means this land was once their domain.*

"That place is sacred in Norse myth, and Thor's Peak is directly in the middle of those mountains. It must be right."

"Well, the blizzard is only going to get worse from here, so what do you want to do?" James asked.

"It's worth a look at least, plus it gives me the opportunity to do something just in case," Chase said, turning off the map.

"Excellent, then let us be off before Merlin has another chance to cast another spell upon us," said Arthur, clapping his hands.

James tried to calm the enthusiasm of the king. "Before that, I think we should talk about what we've been avoiding."

Chase and Arthur knowing what James wanted to discuss, looked at him silently.

"I'm sure you have noticed the same as me since we've been marked by the Winter Wraiths, none of us can use our elements. When I was pinned down by the Wight and tried to incinerate it, I couldn't."

"You too, huh? I can't say I'm surprised," said Chase, sighing. "And you, Arthur, do you have access to your element?"

"With all honesty, I never once possessed what you call a mystical element. The only power, if you will, I ever had was Excalibur's holy light from the time I pulled it from the Stone of Scone."

"You mean the light that Merlin called Holy?" Chase asked.

"Yes, even though Merlin tried with all his knowledge in magic, he could not stop the terrible price that cost me my life. With each use of Excalibur's ultimate technique, the wielder's life is steadily drained until the bearer dies. But as you saw before from your previous journey against the gods, my soul ended up bound to my sword."

"And that sword in your sheath, I know it is forged of sveiða steel, but is it still Excalibur?" Chase asked, glancing down at the sword.

"Only in name, but nothing more," said Arthur, wielding the sword.

Looking at its golden light, Chase was amazed by the detailed runes forged into the blade. "As I mentioned to you once before, Excalibur has been reforged not just by Master Shinko's hands but also my own. The price for life it takes no longer applies, and the sword itself is more than it ever was before. My last use of Excalibur was when we encountered those creatures from the Norse."

"Then what happened to Excalibur," James asked.

"It was remade again. During my alchemy forge for what you have called sveiða steel, I searched through my soul and mind to find the mystical element I thought I had, and bound it to the sword."

"Were you able to find it?" Chase asked.

"Yes, with Master Timber's guidance and much meditation, I found and channeled it during the forge into the sveiða steel with the metal of Excalibur to make the new blade you see before you. My element is light."

Pointing the sword up, the golden runes within the blade glowed brighter as Arthur called its name. "The sword you now see is named Avalon. The light channeled into the sword is all my power and courage of my kingmanship, Goleuni Brenin (Light of the King.)"

Amazed and impressed by the sword, Chase and James could feel its sheer luster. *Avalon, the sacred isle of the fairies where Oberon, Titania, and a secret race reside. And Goleuni Brenin—a Welsh term for the King's light, Chase thought.*

The light of the sword dimmed, and Arthur placed it back in its sheath. "But like you, I am incapable of using my element besides the one that already resides within the sword."

None of us can use our elements, Chase thought, unsettled.

"It's the frozen marks without a doubt. Somehow they seal away not just our elemental magic but also our mystic energy," Chase said, examining the mark on his face. "We know that each mark is from a different Winter Wraith. Not just to take away one of our most powerful means of fighting, but also to mark us as their prey."

Coming to a frightening conclusion, Chase realized their battle against the frozen entities had become more dire. *But why seal away our magic? Whatever the reason, there is more we don't know or what we are not seeing.*

Chase set the course toward Thor's Peak. "We don't have the answers we want, so we have to put them aside for now. I set a course for the mountains, and as long as we have our sveiða steel weapons, then we'll still have means to kill them. We will end this ice age once and for all. We cannot fail. Remember, try not to be significantly injured. The healing stones are useless against them," Chase warned, flying toward the frozen mountains of Jǫtunheimr.

After an hour, they landed not too far away from the mountains. Walking into the blizzard with the others, James stared off at the mountains. "Why couldn't you fly any closer?"

"Because the airship is getting too much interference, so it's not safe to fly any closer. And because I wanted to try something."

"Bifrost Opið (Bifrost Open)," said Chase as Mjolnir sparked.

Suddenly, the aurora of the northern lights appeared in the sky, scattering the clouds above. The rainbow portal from the Bifrost descended from the Northern Lights enveloping the heroes as it sent them.

In a snowy valley between the mountains, James, Chase, and Arthur emerged from the Bifrost.

"Is this the place, Chase?" James asked, seeing the northern lights fade away.

"Ya, right now we are on the valley floor, close by the lake." Chase was puzzled as he looked up at the dark clouds forming above. "There is no blizzard." Chase walked toward a pebble shore of a lake. "But everything else is still frozen."

I may not be able to see them in this vast snow, but I feel there are eyes everywhere, Arthur thought, feeling unease.

James looked into the distance and saw the blizzard rage on. "Chase, do you…"

Before James could finish, Chase interrupted. "Yes, I know. There is no wind or blizzard, but off in the distance, there are still storms."

Chase displayed a dimensional map from his watch of the mountains and valley and saw they were clear all around. "But this doesn't make sense. Or maybe it does," Chase said, remembering the Wraiths had stopped the blizzard before.

"What did you see?"

"Well, it's the same as when we encountered the first Winter Wraith. The blizzards are several kilometers away but not here in these mountains or valley." Chase pointed James's attention to the frozen lake. "And if you look here, the lake is still frozen, so the storms had to have been down here at some point."

"What are you saying is the Winter Wraiths stopped the blizzard here but not elsewhere?"

"It's a possibility, and there's no better way to explain it since we have seen one Winter Wraith stop it with our own eyes."

Sensing the ominous presence even more, Arthur rushed to James and Chase. "You both are letting down your guards too much, stay vigilant."

"We know, but aren't you being a little paranoid?" James chuckled.

"I have never been as such and because they know we're here," Arthur lectured James for his carelessness.

Hearing the cracking of ice, Chase readied himself. "You're right, Arthur, there is no mistake about it. They know."

Suddenly, James heard splashes of water beneath the ice and looked down into it. "What? Strange I thought I saw something move down there," said James, placing his hand on the ice.

"James, what are you doing? Get away from the ice before you break it and fall in."

"Relax, I'm not going to fall in. I'm not that dumb."

A decayed hand broke through the ice. Looking again into the ice, James saw the reanimated Wight. The Wight screeched and started to drag James into the water, but Chase pulled him back, and Arthur stabbed it in the head.

"As I said, stay vigilant," said Arthur, glancing at James as the dead Wight sunk beneath the water.

"Right," said James nervously.

Concerned from the unwanted noise they just made, Arthur looked at the frozen surface of the lake. "How did that creature end up under this ice?"

"I don't know," Chase said, helping James up. "But from what we have seen of these Wights, they are not that smart, so maybe it fell in and became trapped when the lake froze back over."

Off in the distance across the lake, the ice began to break. Hearing the crackle of the ice, James, Chase, and Arthur could only look on as multiple Wights broke through the ice screeching.

"There are more of them," James said.

The Wights reached for the shore closer to James and others.

"They must have heard that Wight thrashing in the water, and now they're coming for us," Chase said.

The Wights tried to get out of the water, but James and Arthur fought them, killing many as more kept coming.

"I thought that was the only one under the ice," James said.

"Ya, you may not have fallen in the freezing water, but you are still dumb for making all that noise," said Chase bluntly. "That is why we are seeing so many right now."

"Well, I didn't think there would be more," said James.

"Ya, that's the point, you don't think," Chase said.

After a few moments, the Wights stopped coming. Fatigued from the onslaught of the dead, the trio looked off and saw the water began to erupt.

"Run," Arthur said.

"The lake is freezing over again," Chase said, looking over his shoulder.

The few remaining Wights in the snow began to stir despite their decomposed flesh and broken bones sticking out of their bodies.

"Well, that's not good," James said.

"What was your first clue, them coming out of the water or exploding from it? But Ya, this is very bad," Chase said.

"I hate to bring your moods down any further, my friends, but it just now became worse," said Arthur, gesturing toward the other side of the lake.

"What do you mean? How could it get much worse?" Chase asked.

James and Chase looked in the direction Arthur pointed and saw a Winter Wraith standing on the ice staring menacingly at them.

"It can and it just did my friends, for the worst kind has come," Arthur said.

"Why aren't the Wights coming at us?" James asked, noticing they had stopped moving.

Feeling the cold presence of the Winter Wraith, Arthur gripped Avalon tightly. "I do not know, but be that as it may, with that cold creature now here, be on your guard."

"Is that the same Winter Wraith as before?" Chase asked.

"No, it is not," said Arthur, feeling the frozen mark on his arm ache. "The one from before did not have long white hair, but this one does."

The Winter Wraith locked eyes with Arthur as it walked toward them. The valley froze more and more with each step it took.

Cytokinesis, it's freezing everything around it the closer it comes. And it's focused on Arthur, Chase thought. *Could it be the one?*

"Chase, you might need to pull your revolver for this one because it's getting closer," said James, nudging him.

Chase moved his hand toward his holster but stopped. "No, I don't think that will be a good idea, not with the remaining Wights around us. If I fired at it, the others could ambush us."

Arthur felt the aching mark become more painful as they glowed in response to the Winter Wraith getting close. *This pain it is almost unbearable.*

"Arthur, are you alright?" James said, noticing the pained expression on Arthur's face.

"I will not lie, I do feel a tremendous ache, but this icy creature is for me."

That mark belongs to this one, Chase thought, seeing the blue glow through Arthur's coat.

The Wights moved slowly to the frozen shore, standing in front of their master.

"Those Wights must have been risen by that Winter Wraith and the mark on your arm. Arthur must belong to it," Chase said.

"If that's true, if we kill this one, won't the remaining Wights and the mark disappear?" James asked.

"I can't say for sure, but it is the best shot we have."

James and Chase prepared to fight; Arthur held out his hand, stopping them. "That precisely why I must see to this task alone."

"Are you crazy? You've seen the magic those things have. There's no way I would fight alone against something like that," said James.

"That Winter Wraith is the origin of this mark, so please, my friend, let me do what I must," Arthur asked, maintaining his resolve to fight alone.

"But..."

Arthur stopped James from speaking anymore. "Have faith in me as I do you. I promise you, James Akatsuki, I will not fall on this day."

Distressed that Arthur chose to fight alone, James tried to move forward, but Chase held him back. "James, let him go."

"But..."

"Even if we were to stay and help, even if we managed to kill it together, there are more of them after that. This is the best we have right now, James, and I'm sorry. You know it, I know it, and nobody understands more than Arthur. So, do as he asks and have faith in him."

James fell deathly silent.

"Like a predator to its prey and the prey to its predator, only Arthur has the mark and right to kill this. And like all predators, it doesn't let anything stand its way," Chase explained.

"Fine," James exclaimed, pushing past Chase in frustration. James looked back at Arthur. "We'll go on ahead, but if I sense you're in danger, I will come back to help."

"I would have no other way," Arthur said, smiling.

"Just don't again," said James, moving past Chase tracking toward Thor's Peak.

"I don't foresee that will come to pass," Arthur whispered.

As James and Chase left, Arthur pointed Avalon toward the icy specter. "Now, shall we begin this battle, thou creature?"

The Winter Wraith pierced its ice spear into the snow, accepting his challenge. The ground shook violently as large glaciers enveloped the whole lake from the cold magic of the Winter Wraith.

Not intimidated by its display, Arthur stood unafraid in the face of the immortal manifestation. "From me, the prey, to you, the predator. Only one of us will claim victory today."

Chapter 29: Ice of Snow

Arthur studied the Wraith for a moment and noted that it showed no weakness in its guard. He knew this meant the Wraith would be a worthy opponent. He also knew the battle would be far more complicated because of the presence of the Wights.

The Wraith noted Arthur assess the Wights and closed its eyes. When it opened its eyes again, the Wights fell dead into the snow.

"It killed all the Wights without even moving," Arthur thought, perturbed. *"No, that's not right, it dispelled the necro magic it occulted over the dead."*

Free of the hindrance, the Winter Wraith slowly approached Arthur.

"Now then, frozen creature, shall we begin?"

Keeping his distance, Arthur ran up the gorge between the snowy mountains along the stream. The Winter Wraith waited a few moments then firmly gripped its ice spear, watching Arthur running into the frozen couloir.

A ways ahead, Arthur glanced back and saw the Winter Wraith gaining on him. *It certainly is fast, and with the stride it possesses, I will tire, but it has a chance to be. I have to stop it somehow,* Arthur thought, stopping looking up the frozen gorge. Seeing a large split within the rock wall up the gorge, Arthur smirked. *And it seems it just appeared.*

"You shall not have me today, creature," Arthur said as the Wraith approached.

The Winter Wraith charged at Arthur, but Arthur stabbed his sword into the crack of the ice gorge.

"Avalon." The light of the sword shined through the cracks as it shook violently. "Now it's your turn to run," said Arthur, seeing an avalanche come down.

Running to escape the avalanche, the Winter Wraith ran after him. The Winter Wraith lunged at Arthur with its ice spear, but Arthur repelled it with Avalon. Staring at the sword, the Winter Wraith was surprised.

"You do show surprise. The sword I wield before you is one that you fear most. One of sveiða steel, the one weapon that will not fall apart and the only one that will kill you."

Arthur knocked the Winter Wraith back. Feeling the pain of the frozen mark intensify, Arthur tried to run, but the Winter Wraith grabbed him by his foot, freezing it from its touch. The avalanche enveloped them, burying them in the snow as it raged on, stopping against the glaciers at the lake.

Hearing the sound of the avalanche, James and Chase stopped.

"Let's keep moving," said Chase, continuing to hike.

"He will come back alive He did once many lifetimes ago, the sword that brought him victory in many battles, the sword of promised victory."

Promised victory, James thought, looking back down at the valley below. "*I know that you will come back. You are, after all, the wisest king I know who was one of many who helped guide me. And more than anything else, my friend.*

Waking up beneath the snow, Arthur struggled to dig himself out of the snow. Gasped and hurt, Arthur tried to compose himself. "It is like Merlin always said, I never do well in snow."

Arthur heard the crackle of ice and looked back to see the Winter Wraith buried deep in the snow. Limping to the Wraith, it opened its icy blue eyes, staring up at Arthur.

"Perhaps it seems destiny reversed our roles," said Arthur, picking Avalon up from the snow. "The predator now becomes the prey, and prey becomes the predator."

The Winter Wraith remained silent and did not move. "Farewell ancient one of winter, may you now peace."

As Arthur was about to kill the Winter Wraith, it pulled its spear from the snow, piercing Arthur through his chest. Arthur, coughing up blood, dropped to his knees and felt his body begin to freeze from the spear.

Standing over Arthur, the Winter Wraith reached for its spear, but Arthur grabbed its wrist. Surprised Arthur was still alive the Winter Wraith tried to free itself to no avail. With the last bit of his strength, Arthur lifted Avalon and pierced the Winter Wraith through its stomach. The Winter Wraith looked down at the sword as its body began to break apart.

"You may seal away my mystic energy, but as the light running through this sword burns, you will always fall," said Arthur, looking at the Winter Wraith in defiance.

"Þrek (Strength)," said the Winter Wraith, smirking, conceding to its fate.

"Avalon."

The light surged through its body, shattering the Winter Wraith to pieces.

"I will be there soon, my friends," said Arthur, watching its icy remains blow away in the wind. The ice spear crumbled away in his chest, and Arthur fell forward in the snow. "Though it might take me some time."

Unconscious, the frozen mark on his arm disappeared, but another Winter Wraith appeared staring down at Arthur.

"Þrek (Strength)," said the Winter Wraith satisfied by the battle it witnessed.

Near Thor's Peak, Chase stopped for a moment to rest.

"Why did you stop?" James asked.

Because the oxygen at this elevation is getting thin. The higher you go, the less air there will be," said Chase breathing slowly.

That's not it, James thought, seeing Chase's expression.

"You sense it too?" Chase asked.

"Ya."

Making its cold presence felt, James and Chase stared at a Winter Wraith standing on a rock.

"Which one of us are you here for?" Chase asked, his voice echoed through the mountain.

Turning its gaze toward them, the Winter Wraith pointed toward James.

Chase glanced at James and saw his pained expression. *His frozen mark must be acting up. Then this Winter Wraith is the one that marked James.*

With its eyes still trained on James, the Winter Wraith conjured two ice swords in his hands.

It's completely focused on James, but it is wary of me, Chase thought, seeing the glow from the frozen marks on James.

"You're the one behind this mark, huh?" James asked, touching his neck.

The Winter Wraith turned its expressionless gaze toward Thor's Peak then to Chase.

It wants me gone. Chase did not move as the Wraith lifted its ice sword toward Thor's Peak. Glancing over at James, James nodded his head for him to move ahead.

"Go, I'll finish up here," James said. He noted the concern on Chase's face. "Have faith in me," James assured.

"Just don't die, and remember, don't use the Solideth katana unless you have no other choice."

The Winter Wraith wielded its two ice swords, challenging James.

"Your swords versus mine. Only one is better," James said, answering the Wraith's challenge.

James slowly walked around, gauging the Winter Wraith. The Wraith gripped its ice swords tightly, waiting for his attack.

"Well, if you won't attack, then I will," James said, clashing swords with the Winter Wraith.

The clash echoed, shifting the snow around them. The Winter Wraith, seeing James's katana, recognized their magical properties.

Seeing the Winter Wraith's blank expression, James showed its burnt blade. "That's right, these katanas are the very weapons you fear most."

Off balance, the Winter Wraith jumped back to a safe distance.

James pointed his Sapphire Shard katana at the Winter Wraith. "One forged of sveiða steel."

The Winter Wraith remained expressionless as a swirl of icy wind formed around it. Suddenly, an ice shard flew past James and cut the side of his cheek.

I didn't see it at all, James thought, seeing blood drip into the snow.

More ice shards flew at James as he tried to retreat but was continually cut by them.

Watching, the Winter Wraith formed more ice shards. James was bleeding heavily now. *Its strong if not even stronger than me. And on top of that, it can form ice shards out of thin cold air. If I approach it carelessly, I will be torn apart by those ice shards,* James, thought feeling the freezing wind around the Winter Wraith.

"Ignis (Fire)," said James, igniting the elemental flames in both katanas.

I can't close it normally, then I'll turn them to ash.

The Winter Wraith tapped its foot, curious about James's flames.

Feeling a pulse ripple through the ground, James stood in confusion. *What was that vibration just now?*

Before James could react, he felt a sharp pain through his leg. Dropping to his knees, James looked down saw a deep gash. *What just happened? I know for a fact it wasn't those ice shards. Could it be an invisible attack?*

The Winter Wraith stabbed its ice swords into the snow as the wind around began dying down. Feeling the ground become colder, James looked down and saw an ice spike pierced through his foot.

That's what cut me, James thought, painfully pulling his foot out of the ice spike.

More ice spikes sprung up from the snow, coming at James.

Moving fast, avoiding the ice, James stopped as he almost fell off the mountain side. *Damn it, I'm cornered.*

In an act of desperation, James charged at the coming ice spikes. He cut through them with his katanas, but some of the spikes still pierced through him. The Winter Wraith, impressed by James's bravery, ceased its attack.

"I will not fall," said James, bleeding, slowly walking toward the Winter Wraith.

Seeing all of James's wounds and the blood that dripped from them, the Winter Wraith picked up his ice swords from the snow. Respecting his endurance, the Winter Wraith slowly walked at James. Suddenly, both charged at each other, clashing swords shaking the whole mountainside.

Moments later, James dropped to knees, exhausted as his pain started to take its toll. "I am not... don't..."

Struggling to stand, James unsheathed Solideth katana. "I have no choice. Ignis et cinis (Ashes of Fire)," said James as the flames of life and death came to life and the katana blazed.

James charged at the Winter Wraith. "I'm not going to lose, not here." James struck his katana against that of the ice sword of the Winter Wraith. "Not after all the promises I made."

The Winter Wraith being pushed back hard by James's power, noticed cracks form in the sword from the strain.

"Just a little more."

The Winter Wraith, widening its eyes, and a blizzard formed around it and James. The ice sword snapped in half as the flames of the Solideth katana died out. The blizzard began to subside when the Winter Wraith saw its arm had been severed. Within moments, the Wraith crumbled to pieces.

James, staggering, looked down and saw the broken ice sword stabbed through his chest. "I'm sorry, Chase," said James, falling back as the ice sword disintegrated.

Moments later, another Winter Wraith emerged and approached the unconscious James. Attempting to thrust its ice spear to kill James, another Winter Wraith grabbed his arm, stopping him. The Winter Wraith nodded its head no.

Understanding what had transpired, the Winter Wraith ceased its attempt as they stared down at James. "Eljun (Endurance.)"

"Nú fyrir lastrinn. Nú þat er tími fyrir thunderinn goð til ráða. (Now for the last. Now it is time for the thunder god to decide," said the Winter Wraith picking up James, following the other into the blizzard.

Chapter 30: Aurora of The Bifröst

Not knowing the fate of his best friend, further up the mountainside, close to the Thor's Peak, Chase continued his climb.

"James, Arthur, please be safe," Chase whispered, looking back down the mountain as he had a dreadful feeling.

He finally reached Thor's Peak and looked down over the edge of the mountain. The wind howled in rage, and a blizzard appeared, blinding him. "What now?"

Chase tried to look around, but the blizzard became more violent, pushing him back. Struggling to stand, Chase saw the chieftain Winter Wraith standing at the edge of Thor's Peak. Chase felt the aching cold chill of the frozen mark on its cheek as it began to glow.

"It's you," said Chase, staring into its cold eyes.

With the full force of cold magic bearing down upon him, Chase aimed his revolver at the Winter Wraith. "This time, I will finish you, then all of this will end."

The Winter Wraith did not react to Chase's threat. Its cold gaze glaring even more menacingly at the hunter as it simply pointed to the ground before it. Chase looked down and was horrified seeing the unconscious James and Arthur lying deep in the snow.

There's no way. There is no way this can be real, Chase thought in disbelief, rushing to them.

Frantic, he broke his pinkie to compose himself. Focusing on his pain, Chase took a deep breath. *Calm yourself, do not let your fear control. My life is bound to James, the fact that I'm alive means he's alive. Their breathing is slow, but their pulses are weak from the cold.*

Looking over the rest of their bodies, Chase noticed their wounds had frozen shut. "What have you done to them?"

Knowing nothing could be done for now, Chase stood up, confronting the Winter Wraith. "Answer me."

The Winter Wraith remained silent as it tapped its ice spear into the snow. Responding to it, the blizzard off in the long distance became more malevolent. Noticing the light flicker from his of weather radar, Chase displayed the map of the world from his watch.

"How is this happening?" Chase asked, witnessing winter storms slowly blanket the whole planet. "What have you done?"

"Hvat eigmunur (What must be.)," the Winter Wraith spoke in Norse, raising its ice spear.

Other Winter Wraiths appeared from the blizzard. Chase was absolutely stunned by what he was witnessing, and tried to fire his revolver but shivered from the brutal cold. *It's too cold.*

Reaching for Mjolnir, one of the Winter Wraith's appeared before him, grabbing his wrist, freezing it with its cold touch. Chase tried to free himself from its grasp to no avail.

The frozen entity, tired of Chase's meaningless struggle, broke his wrist. "Œrinn (Enough.)"

Chase yelled in pain, and the Winter Wraith released its grip. Chase dropped to his knees and looked in horror at his hand, completely frozen. Not able to feel anything, seeing his revolver in the snow beside him, Chase grabbed and fired several shots at the Wraith. Remaining completely still where it stood, an ice barrier formed, stopping the shots.

With its bare hand, the Winter Wraith shattered the bullets as they fell into its hand. It crunched the bullets and handed them to Chase as the particles scattered in the wind. Chase, aghast at their strength and power, dropped his revolver into the snow. "No way."

"We speak your language, human," said the Winter Wraith. "Know this for your foolishness for standing against the seasons. We will wait no more for the time of the great winter has come."

Impossible. How is any of this possible? Chase thought.

Chase gazed at the Wraiths James and Arthur had killed, then back toward the one in front of him. *Our weapons are made of one of the strongest metals in the world and are meant to kill them, but they are all standing here. Is that why the Norse gods didn't...*

Before Chase could finish his thoughts, he felt his whole body go numb.

"Is there nothing I can do to save them?" Chase whispered, looking at James and Arthur.

Chase crawled and reached for them. The Winter Wraiths looked on emotionlessly. Placing his hand over James, Chase begged. "Please, is there anything I can do? Just give me an answer."

The leader of the Winter Wraiths, seeing the kindness and hearing the plea in Chase's heart, spoke silently in Old Norse. "Hjarta (Heart.)"

Chase cried over James. The Wraith who'd marked him walked over. Each step it took, the crackling of ice sounded.

The Winter Wraith looked down upon Chase. "There is, but it comes with a price." Chase, remaining silent, lifted his head and stared into the Winter Wraith's cold eyes. "I ask but one question descendant of Thor. Will you accept it?"

Lowering its ice spear toward Chase, the Winter Wraith wanted to hear his answer.

"If it means saving them both, I will pay any price," said Chase.

Intrigued by his response, the Winter Wraith lifted him. "Even if it means to condemn the world to its fate?"

"Even if the world is doomed to darkness, I don't care. If it's going to end, then so be it, I will accept that."

Despite his numb body, the hunter grabbed the Winter Wraith by its arm. "But as long as my body can move, I will still protect them."

The Winter Wraith, seeing the genuineness of Chase's heart, prepared to kill him but stopped as it noticed the Life-Lock mark on his chest through the tear.

The Order.

Releasing Chase, the Winter Wraith understood. "Neither you nor he are meant to die here."

The Winter Wraith flicked its finger, and the frozen wounds on James, Chase, and Arthur disappeared. "Not until your destiny is fulfilled."

My mystic energy, I can feel it again, Chase thought, sitting up, noticing the frozen mark on his face disappeared.

"The marks, they're gone," Chase said, examining James and Arthur. "Why?"

Stopping in its frozen tracks, the entity of the frost gazed back at him. "For you to prepare for what's to come. You and your friends have shown us the righteousness of your hearts. By our decree, the great winter shall be postponed for now, but only for a time," said the Winter Wraith as all of them tapped their ice spears in the snow.

"This very earth will one day have to endure the frost."

Surrounded by a blizzard, the Winter Wraiths disappeared into it. "For that is our responsibility charged to us to protect the Order."

The clouds above broke apart. The aurora of the Bifrost shined through. Staring at it, Chase turned lightning blue. "I never thought I would see the Bifrost again."

Hours later, James now awake, started to move. "What?" Sitting up, he saw Chase sitting at the ledge. "Chase?"

You truly do have great friends, my descendant. Cherish them always," Thor thought smiling, giving control back to Chase.

"You're finally awake," Chase said, looking at James.

"Ya, it's good to be," said James, smiling back, sitting next to Chase.

"It truly is over," Chase said as he looked at the dimensional map and watched the storms disappear around the globe.

"Why did they spare us?" Arthur asked, standing behind them.

Chase turned off the map. "I'm not too sure myself actually. All the Winter Wraith said was to prepare for what was to come. What that is, I don't know."

"A vague answer, if there was any," Arthur commented.

James pointed out the change in the aurora. "Look, look, the Northern Lights are changing colors."

Chase, James, and Arthur joyously watched the lights change colors as it danced into the sky.

"Probably the best light show I have ever seen," Chase said.

Standing up, wielding Mjolnir, Chase called upon the Bifrost. With the rainbow portal summoned from the Northern Lights before him, Chase looked back at James and Arthur. "Shall we?"

Walking into the Bifrost together, they were enveloped by its rainbow of light and into the sky as their journey to stop the age of the winter came to an end.